Jim Barnes, MD

GRAVE
CONCERN

Erica House

BALTIMORE   AMSTERDAM   SALAMANCA

Copyright 1997 by Jim Barnes, MD

First printing

.

ISBN: 1-893162-21-4

PUBLISHED BY AMERICA HOUSE BOOK PUBLISHERS
www.ericahouse.com
Baltimore

Printed in the United States of America

*This book is dedicated to my son Blake,
who inspires me on a daily basis.*

PROLOGUE

Rick had seen Charlie Ellis in the Emergency Room on three previous occasions, but tonight he had the look of death in his eyes. He had walked into the waiting room under his own power, but was quickly placed in a wheelchair and rushed back into Room 5, bypassing the normal two to three hour wait. His eyes were retracted and underlined with dark circles. His glazed-over look showed little sign of conscious thought. Charlie Ellis was in trouble.

Rick watched as the nurses went to work, hastily writing down vital signs, then ordering an EKG, chest xray, and blood work before the doctor had even seen the patient. There was a sense of urgency that permeated the air. Rick positioned himself in the corner of the bustling room, out of the way, but still in plain view of everything taking place. He wanted to try and speak with Charlie, but knew the time was not right. He looked anxiously towards the door, hoping to see one of the on-call residents make a quick appearance. When no help seemed forthcoming, he decided to take matters into his own hands and drag someone into the room.

He spotted Susan Bennett out in the hallway with a chart in her hand, about to enter one of the cubicles at the far end. Susan (she insisted he call her that) was one of the second year residents, and had been especially friendly to Rick. He strode over towards her, and she looked up as he approached.

"Rick, I was just about to send someone to find you. We may have an acute appendicitis in here and I thought you might like to examine him."

"Thanks Susan, but I was actually wondering if you could see a patient over in Room 5 first. He looks kinda bad."

"Well, I've already started with this one here. I'm sure somebody will pick him up in a few minutes."

"I'm not sure that he should really wait a few minutes, from the looks of him. Remember Charlie Ellis, that homeless guy we saw together in here last weekend?"

She thought for a second. "That guy with the pancreatitis? I thought we admitted him to surgery the other day."

"He checked himself out a few days ago, but he's back now and looks really bad. Would you please come see him?"

She glanced down at the chart in her hand, then reluctantly followed him towards the front of the department. The work load was busy enough without looking for extra things to do. Rick led the way, glancing back twice to hurry her along. He sensed that his friend had little time.

Rick Stanley was a freshman medical student. At least that's what he told anyone who asked. Technically med school didn't start for another four weeks, but he had finally been accepted, and that was all that mattered. At first glance he looked more like a blue collar worker than a neophyte physician. Athletics had always been his forte, usually taking precedence over schoolwork. His work ethic at the gym had continued long past the glory days of high school football. His six foot two frame carried over two hundred pounds, but not an ounce of it was fat. Glasses and short brown hair made him appear almost scholarly from the neck up, but the rest of his body was all muscle. A full time summer job in construction helped him maintain his physique, as well as providing a much-needed income, which he knew would be his last for the next four years. He went out with friends on occasion, but most of his spare time was now spent in the Emergency Room....watching, helping, learning. It was a great way to get fired up about his new career, and it took little convincing on his part to get approval from the chief resident.

It was on a night like this that Rick first met Charlie. He was a homeless man in his sixties who had hit a bad stretch of luck starting about two years ago. He was an educated man, a former humorist who once wrote a column for the city paper. He had fallen on harder times recently, and spent most of his days roaming the streets, observing people. A skirmish with a couple of these people resulted in a long knife gash across his chest, and Rick had kept him company while the intern sutured for hours. They had never met outside of the hospital, but he had seen him twice more in the Emergency Room, once with a gallstone and again two weeks later with a rip-roaring case of pancreatitis. Both times they talked for over an hour, and seemed to have formed a friendship of sorts. Rick had even visited him in the hospital twice, until he left against medical advice two days ago. Now he was back.

Dr. Bennett followed him into the room, and was immediately glad that she did. This man was sick. At first glance his face stood out the most. The eyes were a dull shade of yellow, while his lips were deep blue. He was breathing hard, too hard, and was unable to control the secretions from his mouth. Saliva rolled out onto his long unkempt beard.

"Why the hell isn't there a doctor in here yet?" she asked to no one in particular.

One of the nurses had followed her in the door. "I was about to page overhead for help when I saw you come in. He's only been here a couple of minutes."

"What have you got on him so far?"

"We've called for Respiratory to come draw some blood gases. Xray's supposed to be on they're way too." She picked up his heart tracing from the machine next to the bed. "Here's his EKG. Sinus tach was all I saw."

Dr. Bennett took the paper from her and scanned it quickly. "Let's get some oxygen on him, draw some more blood for the lab, and find out where the hell Respiratory is!"

Rick resumed his position in the corner of the room. He wanted to talk to the old man, but knew he would only be in the way. He thought it best to stay where he was, realizing there was little he could do to help. Susan seemed in control of the situation, and everyone in the room responded well to her direction. Charlie did seem to be pinking up a bit with the oxygen, and his eyes were slowly clearing.

"What kind of IV access do we have?"

"Nothing yet Dr. Bennett. We've tried in both arms, but he's a tough stick."

She looked over at the tech standing behind her, not remembering his name. "Get me a central line kit and open it up on the table over there."

He moved quickly, and within thirty seconds she had on a pair of sterile gloves and was prepping his chest with iodine. "Mr. Ellis, I'm Dr. Bennett. How are you feeling?" It was her first attempt to talk with the man, and he did not respond. She raised her voice slightly. "We've got to put a large IV in your chest right here under your collar bone. It may hurt a little, but it's very important that you hold still." Still no response. "Do you understand me?"

There was a short pause, but then he did look up and appeared to nod his head slightly. This was taken as verbal consent, and she reached for the 3 inch long needle. Her hand was steady as the razor-sharp tip pierced the skin. Susan had put in over a hundred central lines in the last year, and they had become somewhat routine. She noticed Rick in the corner, and motioned him over with her head.

"You've seen one of these go in before, haven't you Rick?"

"Yes ma'am, I watched you do one on that gunshot victim last week."

"That's right. Just remember, the key is to keep the needle parallel to the floor, and aspirate as you go in." She advanced the needle deeper, almost to the hub, when there was a sudden rush of blood back into the syringe. A guide wire passed easily through the needle, and the catheter was then slid in over the wire and into the first chamber of the heart.

"Give me a line before this clots off." Another nurse handed her the primed IV tubing, and she attached it to the catheter. The fluid ran in quickly.

She looked back up at Rick. "You said he left the hospital early?"

"Yes ma'am. They were talking about an operation to take out his gall bladder as soon as his pancreas settled down. He said they were gonna use those lasers on him. I think it kinda scared him off."

"Run in two liters of Ringers as fast as they'll go, then back him off to a maintenance rate." She stepped back and almost ran in to the large portable xray machine being wheeled into the room by a tech half its size. They helped position the plate behind his back, then sat him straight upright. Everyone cleared the room as the xray was shot, and returned just as quickly when it was done. Dr. Bennett returned to the head of the table to try and speak with her new patient once again.

"Mr. Ellis." She shook his shoulder firmly. Getting no response, she then rubbed the knuckles of her fist up and down on his sternum. He winced slightly, but still would not make a sound. "Mr. Ellis!" she yelled even more loudly. "Mr. Ellis, open your eyes!" His lids fluttered, but remained closed.

"I've got a pressure of sixty!" shouted the nurse by his left arm. "Heart rate's shooting up, too."

"Let's lie him back flat. He's not ready to sit upright just yet." She glanced up at the empty IV bag atop the pole. "Is that his first or second liter?"

"That's number two since he got here. You want another?"

"Give him two more, but use the pressure bag to force 'em in faster. He's dry as a chip." She looked back at the blood pressure machine. "Cycle the machine again and see what his pressure's doing."

Everyone stood quietly for a few brief seconds as the cuff inflated briskly, then slowly emptied down again. Rick was enthralled from his corner of the room. His emotions were mixed with concern for his friend and excitement of the whole scene unfolding. This was what he loved about medicine. He longed for the day when he would be the one up there barking out orders, leading the team, running the show. It was fascinating.

Everyone saw the red digital numbers together. 52 over 24. Now dropping dangerously low. Not looking good for the home team.

"Check it manually and see if it correlates. That can't be right."

It was right.

Their patient was looking much worse again. Lips were blue, respirations were shallow and labored, neck veins were bulging.

Suddenly a light went on inside Susan's brain. "That's it. Look at his neck. He's got a tension pneumothorax." She looked back at one of the nurses. "Get me a 14 gauge needle and some alcohol, and find out where the hell that chest xray is!"

Almost on cue, the diminutive tech slipped back into the room with the film in her hand. Susan held it up to the light with both hands and immediately recognized the problem. The left lung, the side of her central line, had completely collapsed, and the heart was shifted over noticeably, occupying most of the right chest. She had nicked the tip of his lung with the needle, causing it to drop and allow pressure to build up inside the left chest.

Susan took the large needle from the nurse, wiped off his anterior chest with the alcohol, and pressed it in to the hilt just above the left nipple. There was an audible rush of air as the pressure was allowed to escape. At the very same instant, his heart stopped beating, entering a very lethal rhythm known as ventricular fibrillation.

"Dammit, get the crash cart in here."

It had already been positioned just outside the door in anticipation of things turning bad. The defibrillator was on and ready as Susan reached for the paddles.

"Charge to 200." A conductive jelly was squirted onto one side, and she rubbed the two together to assure a good conductive pathway from the machine to the heart. "Everyone clear!" she shouted above the noise. Rick's hand remained resting at the head of the bed. "Rick. Clear the bed," she said, looking him directly in the eyes. He pulled his hand away and she depressed the red buttons with each of her thumbs.

Charlie's chest lurched forward as 200 Joules of electricity shot through his body. Everyone turned to the monitor, hoping for a heartbeat, but again saw the fine fluttering of v tach. "Resume CPR and charge to 300."

Another shock. Another lurch. Same result.

"Charge to 360."

Rick felt his mind began to stray. He looked slowly around the room at the many varied faces. He watched as Susan continued her valiant effort, trying to bring back Charlie from the grave. He had little experience with situations such as this, but could sense they were fighting a losing battle. He began to think of Charlie, a man he had known for less than a month, spoken to only a handful of times, yet he still called him a friend. He thought of the man's family, a group of people he knew little about. Divorced for years, he had spoken little of his ex-wife. He had a son and a daughter, both long since moved away, and a brother he hadn't spoken to in twenty years. Both of his parents were dead. He knew that his son shared his name, and realized he would have to be the one to attempt to notify him. If there were a funeral, Rick decided he would attend.

"That's it. I'm calling it. Time of death is 2115."

The words brought Rick's wandering mind back to the present. Time of death. It sounded so final. So definite. He looked over at Susan, who had now moved off to the side to tackle a mountain of paperwork. One thing Rick had learned during his time here was that nobody was dead until the paperwork was complete. This usually took longer than the act of dying itself.

Within a few short moments, the trauma room was transformed from controlled chaos to surreal desolation. A nurse and a housekeeper were all that remained as they began the task of clearing the room. He looked down at Charlie, wondering if he should touch the unshaven face. He felt saddened by his loss, yet somehow detached from the whole situation. The last thirty minutes had taken on a dreamlike slant in his mind, brought on by the conflict of yet another code in the Emergency Room with the loss of a real person. Not just another body rushed in by the ambulance, but a living, breathing, talking human being. Someone he had once known.

Rick took one final look at Charlie Ellis. He saw his crooked nose, his scarred right shoulder and chest, the giant falcon tattooed across left forearm. He turned and walked out of the room, down a long back hallway into the parking deck, and straight to his car. He drove straight home in the pouring rain, then sprinted up the stairs and into his empty apartment. He knew a cold fifth of vodka was waiting for him in the freezer.

CHAPTER 1

FOUR WEEKS LATER

"The men and women you are about to see have presented you with the ultimate gift. I want each and every one of you to think about what it means to donate one's body to science. It is something that few of us will ever consider doing, yet without those that do, your medical education would be horribly incomplete. For without knowing and understanding every aspect of the human body, one cannot possibly treat that body and make it well. These individuals are allowing you to learn what must be learned in order for you to become a physician."

Dr. Shires paused and scanned the room. He knew that this was the one moment out of every year when he would capture the attention of every single person in the room. Nobody was looking around, nobody was talking in the back, and nobody's mind was wandering where it shouldn't be. He knew for certain that all eyes and thoughts were focused on him. He was right.

"Before we remove the covers on your table, I want you to think about that for a moment. I want you to remember that the body under that lid was once a walking, talking, breathing human being. Someone who thought so highly of the medical field, that they were willing to donate their body so that you could become a better doctor."

He paused once again as he made his way up to the front of the laboratory. The room remained drenched in total deafening silence. Every head turned as they watched him make his way down the narrow aisle. They knew the moment was very near.

Rick Stanley could not remember any moment in his life as intense as what he was experiencing right now. Even the late nights in the Emergency Room watching a code blue or a major trauma did not compare. For then he was simply an observer. The proverbial fly on the wall. But today was different. This was it. The big time. The moment when he realized he was no longer in college anymore. This was the first day of medical school, and he was about to begin dissecting a cadaver.

"Some of you may feel faint, others queasy. If you feel as if you may pass out, sit down on the floor as quickly as you can. I promise you that by the end of the week you will all be fine." He reached for the dissecting manual on the counter, a red spiral bound paperback that would serve as the owner's manual for the next three and a half months. The room remained silent.

"We will actually be starting on page 52. The back. A region with large muscles, which makes it very difficult to make any significant error. Dr. Schwartz, Dr. Little, Dr. Saunders, and myself will be circulating throughout the lab this afternoon to answer any questions you may have. Unfortunately we are three cadavers short at present, and have had to double up on some of the tables. For those of you with five at your station, I apologize for the inconvenience. We hope to have this corrected by your next session on Wednesday afternoon." He set down the book and looked out across the room. "I wish you all well in your first step to becoming a physician."

With that the lecture was over. Dr. Shires raised both his arms upwards, signaling the class to begin. After a few anxious looks, the lids were lifted slowly, and the exercise commenced. Nobody fell to the floor. Nobody threw up. There were a few quiet moans and a couple of gasps, but everyone soon relaxed and eagerly began their work.

Rick Stanley was the first to reach for the table cover in his group. He was assigned to Table 21, along with three other classmates. Cameron Sharp was an acquaintance from college. Not really someone he would call a friend, because they just didn't know each other all that well. They had shared a couple of pre med classes together two years ago, and were actually lab partners in Organic Chemistry for one semester. They hadn't seen much of each other over the last year and a half, but Rick was still glad to see a familiar face.

Monika Reese was blonde and thirty and gorgeous. Rick had noticed her earlier in the day, during one of their lectures. She had already become a topic of conversation among the single men in the class, most of whom were several years her junior. It was rumored that she had graduated from a small private college somewhere up north, and nobody in the class seemed to know anything about her. Rick was fortunate to share a similar last name, since table assignments were made in alphabetical order. He was anxious to learn more about her.

Evan Sanders completed the new team. He was rumored to be the youngest person in the class, and had already picked up the nickname

12

'Doogie'. He appeared nervous and quiet, and Rick was sure he would be the one to hit the floor. So far he was holding his own.

"Give me a hand with this lid, will you Cameron?"

"Sure thing Rick," he replied, reaching for the handle.

The cover flipped over and hinged back under the table. Beneath it lay an elderly appearing man with a beard. They all stared in silence for a few moments, then looked up at one another and smiled.

Cameron was the first to speak. "So this is a cadaver?" They all nodded in agreement. "Sure as hell smells like one."

Formaldehyde was no longer used, due to its potential to cause cancer with prolonged contact, but whatever the preservative was, it was certainly strong. A box of rubber gloves sat at the head of the table, and they each slipped on a pair. Rick was the first to actually touch the body, but Cameron and Monika quickly followed suit. Doogie was content to sit back and watch.

"So what do we do now?" asked Monica.

"I guess we gotta flip him over if we're gonna start cuttin' on the back."

Rick lifted the arm on his side, and found the whole body came along with it. Rigor mortis had set in weeks ago, and the entire body moved as a single unit. Cameron pushed the right arm under the body as Rick swung the left over the top. He rolled with surprising ease, and landed back on the table face first with a loud thump. The same sound echoed throughout the room as each cadaver was rolled into position. Fortunately, not one of them hit the floor.

By this time Evan was looking a little green. He had found a seat on a tall stool, but a sprint to the bathroom seemed imminent. The other three read over the instructions in the manual and prepared to begin. The room was strangely quiet as everyone spoke in hushed tones.

They had each purchased a set of instruments for this lab, part of the package of material that every student was required to buy. It contained a scalpel with several extra blades, scissors, tissue forceps, and a hemostat. They took out their equipment, and reread the first page of instructions. Cameron was the first to finally speak.

"All right guys, we gotta start sometime. Who wants to make the first cut?"

Everyone looked around at each other. "It's all yours, my friend," Rick finally said to Cameron. "You know where to start?"

He looked at the diagram once more, carefully picked his spot, and made a long, bold stroke with the knife. They halfway expected to see blood erupt from the wound, but of course there was none.

Cameron looked up at Rick and smiled. "Just like skinning a deer, isn't it chief?".

Rick didn't quite know how to respond, so he said nothing.

"Did you two guys know each other before this week?" asked Monika.

"We had a few of the same pre med classes in college," answered Cameron.

"Haven't really seen much of each other the last year and a half, though," added Rick.

Soon Rick and Monika joined in and helped. They made the cuts according to the diagram in the book, and before long had exposed all of the major muscles in the back. It was actually much easier than they had anticipated. Evan's contribution to the afternoon had been three trips to the bathroom, each time returning a little worse for the wear. He had shown little interest in participating in today's lesson. His three lab partners were more than happy to do the dissection themselves. They worked well together, and were already forming quite a team.

"You gonna be all right, Evan?" asked Rick, feeling a little guilty that they had already begun to exclude him.

"I'll be fine. Don't worry about me." He wasn't too convincing. "It's just going to take me a moment to acclimate to this new environment."

"Hell Evan, the way you look, it's gonna take more than a moment for you to acclimate," said Cameron, emphasizing the last word.

"I assure you I will be just fine. I had the same response when we were forced to dissect a cat in Zoology lab two years ago. You three seem to be managing just fine without my assistance."

And that they were. The three of them felt as if they had been at this for weeks. They were amazed at how quickly their apprehensions vanished once they had begun their work. Their minds had managed to separate the latissimus and deltoid muscles from an actual human being. They were merely observing a set of muscles, and no longer thought of it as cutting apart a real person. Some sort of built in defense mechanism that had served them well today.

"You never told us where you were from," said Cameron, looking up at Monika.

"You're right, I didn't."

They waited for her to finish, and when she did not, Cameron shot back. "And that would be?"

She paused again, but this time answered the question. "I actually lived around here when I was a kid. But I've been up north for the last fifteen years or so."

"Up north? Like Canada or something?"

"Not quite that far north."

"So how did you get in to a state school in the south if you're from somewhere up north? I didn't think they took out of state residents."

"They don't. My dad lives here and I was able to establish residency through him."

Rick finally spoke up. "Come on guys, let's get this finished so we can get out of here. I already feel like I'm behind, and it's just the first day."

"Sounds like we better get used to that feeling," said Monika.

"Why don't we finish this up and all go out to eat somewhere?"

"I don't know Cameron. I kinda want to get back and hit the books."

"Shit Rick, you gotta eat. Let's just get a quick pizza and a beer, then I promise it's straight back to the dorm to start cramming."

"He's right, Rick. It'll give us all a chance to get to know each other a little bit," said Monika. "You've got the next four years to study."

Rick hesitated for a second. "All right, what the hell. I'm in."

"There ya go," answered Cameron. "What about you Evan? You wanna join us?"

"You guys go ahead. I don't really feel much like a meal right now, and I need to get ready for tomorrow's lecture."

"OK chief, your choice," said Cameron. He was only inviting him out of courtesy anyway, so he didn't push it. "Let's get this finished up."

They spent the next hour completing their dissection, then reviewing the major muscles and nerves which they had rather skillfully exposed. Dr. Shires had come by once and spent a few minutes observing their work. He quizzed them about the origins and insertions of various muscles, and they actually did quite well. The hour flew by quickly, and soon it was 4 o'clock and time to call it a day.

"OK Cameron, this was your idea. Where to?" They were all in the dressing room changing back into their real clothes. They had been cautioned to bring some old clothes to wear during the lab, and they now knew why. The preservative smell permeated the room, their clothes, and their skin. The large sink was elbow to elbow people, as everyone tried in futility to scrub off the aroma. Most eventually gave up, dressed quickly, and left. Rick and Cameron were still trying.

"Did you see that place called Beck's across the street? I wonder what's in there."

"Kinda looked like a dive, but it is close by," replied Rick. "You think Monika would go for it?"

"I bet she's been in worse places before. Let's check it out. It might be fun."

They finally gave up washing and started to change back into their clothes.

"What do you think her story is, anyway?" asked Cameron.

"Hard to tell. She seems nice enough."

"You think anyone's doin' her?"

"Hell Cameron, how would I know? Why don't you ask her when we get out there?"

"You're a real funny guy, Rick. Real funny. Maybe I will ask her."

"You realize you look like some stupid kid to her. She's probably close to thirty years old."

"I'll be twenty-three in two weeks. That's only seven years. That's nothing," said Cameron.

"Nothing to you maybe. I'll bet she sees it a little different."

"I'm older than you are, chief."

"True, but I'm not chasing after some thirty year old, either."

"Just watch me work the charm tonight. We'll see who's too young for who."

"You're the man, Cameron. You're the man."

Rick and Cameron dressed and headed outside to wait on Monika. When they stepped out of the dressing room, she was standing there fully dressed and ready to go.

"What took you girls so long?"

"Trying to wash this smell off our hands, but it didn't work too well."

"I guess I just gave up quicker than you did." They began walking out of the lab towards the elevator. "So where are we going, anyway?"

"Have you heard anything about this Beck's place across the street?"

"I saw it over the weekend, but haven't ventured in there yet."

"It looks like it'd be close and quick. You feeling brave enough to give it a try?"

"Sure, why not," said Monika. "I'm game."

"Are you guys really hungry yet?" asked Rick, as they stepped into the elevator. "It's only 4:30 and we had that late lunch today."

"You're the one who was in a hurry to eat and get back to the books," replied Cameron.

"What if we meet out there a little later?" suggested Rick. "Around seven or so."

"What do you think, Monika?"

"That's fine with me. I've got a few errands I need to run anyway."

The elevator stopped on one and they all got out. They stepped out into the breezeway that connected the anatomy building with the main hospital.

"All right, we'll meet you out there at seven."

"I'll see you then." Monika turned and walked towards the parking deck. It was a rule that all freshmen lived in the dorm, but somehow they both knew that she had some nice apartment somewhere off campus. They watched her walk away, both enjoying the view, then turned the opposite direction and headed back for the dorm.

"What are you gonna do?" asked Rick.

"I don't know. I've still got a little unpacking to do. I may try and get the last of the cardboard boxes out of my room." They stepped up the curb and into the dorm building. "What about you?"

"I told you what I'm doing tonight. And probably every night for the next four years."

"Can't study all the time, chief."

"Just watch me," Rick laughed.

They parted at the elevators, Cameron walking up the one flight of stairs to his room, and Rick riding up to the eighth floor to the place he now called home.

CHAPTER 2

The medical university dormitory was an interesting piece of architecture. Built shortly after World War II, it had become dreadfully outdated. Numerous renovations had been attempted, but they did little to improve the aging structure. It was no surprise that filling the rooms was becoming an ever-worsening problem for the administration. It was for that reason that the Dean's office sent out a letter every year requiring all freshmen to live on campus. This was undoubtedly just a bluff to keep up occupancy, but incoming freshmen are easily fooled. Most of the sophomores had already moved out at the end of their first year, finding apartment living a small escape from the daily grind. Living in the dorm essentially meant never leaving the campus, and all but a few grew tired of the monotony rather quickly. What they saved in gas money, they gave up in freedom. Rick knew the walls would soon be closing in, and the semester had barely started.

The dorm rooms were small and drab. Each man had a bed and a desk, but there was little room for much else. Rick had brought along an old recliner, but there wasn't room to recline it. It mainly just took up space in the corner. He had brought along a tiny refrigerator that he had used in college, which he sat next to a small kitchen sink. There was no stove. The bathrooms were community, with one located on each floor. There were no coed floors of course, although the idea had been suggested by more than a few as a means of recruiting more residents. The dean was not receptive to this particular suggestion. Each room had a window, which actually opened, and a balcony that they were forbidden to use due to the age of the structure. A rule that was largely ignored by most of the residents.

Rick walked into his room and tossed his backpack onto the recliner. The place seemed empty and bare, as Rick had not yet taken the time to hang up some of the pictures and posters he had brought with him from college. He had spent the summer staying with the parents of a friend, who was away at law school. It had met his needs at the time, most importantly being rent free, but he could never get over the feeling that he was intruding on their lives. That perception was the worst in the evenings, especially at suppertime, and Rick tried to schedule either work or his ER shifts to avoid that time of the day at the house. It was probably a sentiment shared only by himself, but he couldn't shake it nonetheless. He had always preferred living alone. It was why he was willing to pay an extra seventy five dollars a month in rent not to share this small cubicle they called a room.

Other than the ten year old microwave by the bathrooms, there were no kitchen facilities available. Rick had already grown tired of fast food and the hospital cafeteria, and the thought of another year of this depressed him to no end. He looked up at the clock and saw it was quarter till five. Two hours before he left for supper, and he was already starving. Certainly too hungry to get any significant studying accomplished. There had been no time to shop, and the only food in the room was a half eaten bag of Baked Lays and a six pack of warm Coke. Not exactly what he had in mind. He thought of the vending machines in the basement, gathered up a handful of change, and headed out the door.

The elevator had never left his floor, and he rode it quickly down the nine flights. The hallways and elevators somehow managed to avoid the cool breeze of the air conditioner, and the ride down was a hot one. The basement was empty except for a couple of strangers doing laundry. He spotted a favorite candy bar and a cold Dr. Pepper, dropped in his money, then made his way back upstairs with his late afternoon snack. He would have to start eating better than this.

Rick spread out on the twin bed with two full notebooks and three or four texts, all neatly arranged in a half circle around him. He rarely studied at his desk, finding the bed somehow more conducive to learning. Some nights in college it would become a little too comfortable as he would fight off sleep, but he did not see that as a problem now. He spent the next hour and a half reviewing his notes from the day, then began reading over tomorrow's lectures. The time passed quickly, and soon he was changing clothes and heading out the door for tonight's dinner rendezvous.

He rode the elevator down to the second floor, where he exited into Cameron's hallway. He'd told him his was the first room on the right and Rick found it easily. He knocked firmly on the door, but there was no reply. He yelled out Cameron's name, but again no answer. He considered trying the doorknob, but instead decided to turn and walk away. He headed out the building, across the parking lot, and down the street.

To use the term 'restaurant'to describe Beck's was somewhat of an overstatement. The phrase 'greasy spoon' came to mind as Rick pushed through the half open door and sampled the ambience. He squinted through the dim light and rising smoke, but saw no sign of Monika or Cameron. It was only quarter till seven, and Rick was his usual early self. He took a seat at the bar to wait for his companions, and ordered a Miller Lite when the bartender came around. George Strait was playing softly in the background, and he hummed along to himself. Maybe this place wasn't all that bad.

Two shuffleboard tables lined the back wall, with a couple of dart boards down at one end. There was also a pool table in the far corner by the back door. The clientele was varied, but looked to be mostly good folks. He saw a few faces he had recognized from class earlier today, but decided not to approach them right now. Many people were finishing off a meal, which seemed to consist of a burger and fries out of a red plastic basket at almost every table. The ketchup was flowing freely.

Rick was hungry, and debating whether or not to order without them, when Monika walked in the door. She turned heads there tonight the same way she had turned heads in the classroom this morning. Rick felt his pulse quicken slightly as they made eye contact across the room.

"Where's your buddy?" she asked.

"I was about to ask you the same thing. I haven't seen him since this afternoon."

He pulled out the stool next to his and she sat down with grace. "Interesting place you've found here."

"If you remember correctly, it was Cameron who selected our dinner accommodations."

"So where is our distinguished host? I figured you two would come over together."

"Beats me? I knocked on his door before I walked over and nobody answered. I was expecting to find him already here, working on his second beer."

"I see you decided to start without us," she said, looking down at his empty longneck. Rick was genuinely surprised to see it was gone. "Let me get this round," added Monika, signaling the bar keep. He brought two more of the same, and she paid him with a five and a one out of her purse. "Shall we find a table?"

There were only about a dozen or so tables in the place to begin with, and most of those were taken. They did manage to snatch up one of the booths just as a young couple was getting up. They sat in silence for a moment as the waitress quickly cleared the table between them.

"Can I get y'all anything right now?" she asked, eyeing their fresh beers.

"Check back in a few minutes," answered Rick. "We're waiting on one more person."

"Sure thing honey," she replied, flashing him a smile. "My name's Ginger."

Rick watched her leave, then turned back to Monika. "So what the hell are you doing in medical school, anyway?"

She did not seem startled by his abruptness. "I was about to ask you the same question."

"You first."

"That's not an easy question to answer just like that," she said.

"Sure it is. Aren't you here to make a difference, save lives, help others, and all that other crap?"

"Is that why you're here, Rick?"

"I asked first, remember?"

Monika appeared to be really pondering her answer. "I think those answers are partially right for everyone here. They have to be, or we shouldn't be here." She had started peeling the label on her beer. "I guess I needed a fresh start too."

"Fresh start from what?" Rick asked, genuinely interested.

"From just about everything, to be honest. An ex-husband for one thing"

"How long were you married?"

"Almost seven years. And dated for three before that. We split up for the last time about two years ago. I haven't seen him since the divorce was final."

"Any children?"

She looked up at him for the first time since this discussion had started. She appeared as if she were about to say something, then changed her mind. "You've used up your twenty questions, Dr. Stanley. Now it's my turn."

Rick sat back into the booth. "Fair enough. Shoot."

"Ok Mister Man With The Questions. Why did you decide to go to medical school?"

Rick answered without hesitation. "That's easy. To get chicks."

She laughed and Rick couldn't help but notice her radiance. Her hair was blonde and fell gracefully just over her shoulders. Her deep hazel eyes were captivating as well, yet seemed to reflect a hint of harder times. The faint lines fanning out from the corners of her mouth and eyes only added to her beauty. He fought not to stare, but was losing the battle.

"Be serious," she finally said, still smiling.

"I am being serious. I'm in it for the chicks. And don't forget the sports cars. Another fringe benefit."

They shared another laugh. Rick already felt very comfortable with her, despite being a day removed from complete strangers.

"I'm glad to see you two waited for me before you got started." They both looked up at Cameron, who was already sliding in next to Monika.

"Where the hell have you been?" asked Rick. "I knocked on your door before I came over here."

"I told you I was unpacking. I was back and forth to that damn dumpster about ten times. You must have caught me when I was out."

"The waitress has been through once, but all we've ordered so far is the beer," said Monika.

Cameron placed his right arm on top of the booth, gently brushing Monika's shoulder. "So what have I missed?"

"I was just telling Monika why I went to medical school, but she thinks I'm holding back on her."

"I know you're holding back on me." She looked to her left. "What about you, Cameron? What brings you here?"

"That's easy. To get chicks."

They all laughed. "You guys rehearsed this, didn't you?"

"We're just trying to be honest with you, that's all," said Rick.

"You two are a real piece of work."

Ginger made her second appearance of the evening, walking up and standing behind Cameron's left shoulder. "Are y'all ready to order, or ya need a few minutes yet?"

"Could you bring us some menus," asked Rick.

Ginger smiled. "Honey, you don't need no menus here. We got hamburgers, cheeseburgers, and French fries. And pretty much anything you want to drink."

Rick looked across the table. "Three burgers and fries?"

They nodded in agreement.

"And three more beers," added Cameron.

"Make that two and a glass of water," said Rick.

"Sure thing darlin'." She headed back to the grill.

Cameron stared across at Rick. "A glass of water?"

"I told you I'm studying tonight."

"You better loosen a button, chief. You gotta relax and have a little fun along the way, or life's gonna fly right by you."

22

"Cameron, the great philosopher," Rick smiled. "You sound like the Ferris Bueller of medical school."

"All right you two," Monika finally interrupted. "I thought we came here to have a nice leisurely dinner on our first night of school. Let's save the heavy stuff for another time."

Rick and Cameron looked at each other.

"She's right, you know," said Rick. "And she is our elder, so I guess we better listen to her."

Rick smiled as she threw a handful of sugar packets in his direction.

"Very funny," she smirked back, not truly offended.

The next twenty minutes were spent joking about nothing in particular. Just blowing off a little steam after a very stressful day. They ordered another round of beer for the table, and despite Rick's half-hearted protests, he started his third bottle. When the food finally came, he ordered a fourth.

"Cameron, I think we've created a monster."

"Don't think this is gonna become a habit," Rick replied. "I'm gonna write tonight off, but tomorrow you'll see the new and serious Rick Stanley." The truth was, Rick was having a great time. He had spent the summer in a sort of social isolation, dividing his time between work and the Emergency Room. It felt good to relax, have a few beers, and enjoy the company of a beautiful woman and a new friend.

The conversation lagged over the next several minutes, as all three devoured the food set before them. The burgers were perfect, the kind where the juice drips off your elbows. The fries were crisp and salted just right. The beer was ice cold. Hard to imagine a more perfect meal for their first night of school.

As their plates emptied, their conversation resumed. "Where are you from anyway, Cameron?" asked Monika.

"No place you've ever heard of, I'm sure."

"I guess I don't know where you're from either, come to think of it."

"You ever heard of Woodbury, Mississippi?" he asked, looking at Rick.

"I've been to Woodbury. Actually grew up not too far from there."

Cameron took a drink and continued.

"That's the place. Dad was a cotton farmer there for years and years. I grew up helping out around the farm."

"Is he still farming?" asked Rick.

"He died about five years ago." Cameron looked down at his beer. "Shot to death by one of his workers arguing over a paycheck."

"Oh Cameron, I'm sorry," said Monika. "That's just awful."

"Well, that was a long time ago," he finally responded.

"What about your mother?"

"I don't remember much about her, really. She died during childbirth when I was four. It was always just me and dad."

"What happened to the farm?" asked Rick.

"I got rid of the damn thing. I was up at college by that time. Thought about coming back down to run it, but after that my heart just wasn't in it."

"I'm sorry man," said Rick. "I sure didn't mean to stir all that up tonight."

Cameron shook it off quickly. "Don't worry about it. It's old news." He finished off the last of his beer. "I vote we change the subject. How bout you, Monika? Care to share your life story with the group tonight?"

"What did you say your dad did, Rick?" she answered back. They decided to let her get away with the not-so-subtle segue.

"He's the sheriff over in Corman County."

"No kidding?" said Cameron. "That's just one county over from where I grew up. You're dad's a cop there, huh? For some reason I never pictured that."

"He's been sheriff for almost twenty years now. He'll probably retire before long. He and mom want to do some traveling while they're still young enough to enjoy it."

Cameron had been thinking. "So that means if I get pulled over in Corman county I can just tell 'em I know your old man and walk free?"

"Good luck with that plan. They've got speed traps every two blocks down there. Even I stay under the speed limit when I go home."

Time passed quickly as they finished their fries and drank one final beer. They weren't sure what time the place closed, but it was close to ten o'clock and the crowd had thinned considerably. They had all enjoyed themselves immensely, but they knew the night had to come to an end. Rick was the first to suggest it.

"It's getting kinda late for a school night, guys."

They all looked at their watches and agreed it was time to call it a night.

"This is a great trend we've started here," said Rick. "The first day of med school and we all go out drinking. My folks would be so proud."

"Don't worry about it, Rick. Besides, you've always got that truck driving school to fall back on."

"You're a great comfort, Cameron. I feel so much better about myself now."

They walked outside and were enveloped in the humid night air. They followed Monika out to her car, staying with her while she rummaged through her purse.

"You gonna be ok to drive?" asked Rick.

"Yeah, I'm fine. Besides, I just live up the street a ways. I'll be in bed asleep in five minutes."

"Why don't you let me drive you home?" asked Cameron.

"And then how would you get back to the dorm?"

"I could walk back. You said you just lived down the street."

"I think I can manage just fine."

"I'd just hate for something to happen to you. You know, beautiful girl, all alone."

"And I need a big strong man to protect me, is that it?"

"I'm just lookin' out for you, that's all."

"Save it for some poor nursing student, Romeo. You two get home and get some sleep. Class starts at eight sharp. I hear Robbins locks the door at 7:59. No one gets in or out till his lecture's over."

Rick was tired and had to pee. "You comin' or not, Cameron. I'm walking."

"Pretty sad when you're my best offer for the night, Stanley."

"You guys be careful. I had fun tonight."

Monika got into her car, fastened her seat belt, and drove off, turning on her lights as she pulled out of the parking lot. They watched her cruise up the hill, then turn off on one of the side streets. They turned and walked back to the dorm, parting ways at the elevator as they headed to their respective rooms.

* * * *

The phone was finally answered on the tenth ring. "Where the hell have you been?"

"Who is this?"

"You know damn well who this is. Dammit Harper, I've been trying to reach you for three days. Why don't you return your calls?"

"I've been away at a meeting, not that it's any of your business. I just walked in the door and the phone was ringing."

"Well you should have told me you were gonna be gone."

"Screw you, Shires. I don't have to clear my calendar with you or anyone. What's so damn important, anyway?"

"I'm short three, and I need 'em tomorrow."

"Tomorrow!" he yelled. "Are you nuts?"

"We were promised twenty-five, but they delivered Saturday and were three short."

"Well talk to them. That's not my problem."

"I tried, but that's all they've got. I've called every other source I have and I'm coming up blank. The accreditation committee's breathing down my throat, and I'm hearing rumors of inspectors coming through this week."

"Just tell them you're a few short. Double up a couple of students and who'll know the difference?"

"They'll know the difference. That's exactly the kind of thing they're looking for, and don't think they won't be counting."

"How am I gonna come up with three bodies with a twelve hour notice?"

"I don't know, don't you have any in stock?"

"Christ Shires, this isn't fucking Wal Mart."

"Look Harper, can you help me or not?"

"Let me check into a couple of leads. Call me back in the morning and I'll see what I can do. *Late* morning."

"I'm counting on you, Harper."

"Call me tomorrow. I've got to get some sleep."

CHAPTER 3

The big news the following morning was an unsubstantiated report that two students had dropped out. Rick did not know either of them except by name. Nobody knew any real details, but most assumed the anatomy lab had pushed them over the edge. Their suspicions were confirmed shortly after the beginning of class.

"Ladies and gentlemen, welcome to Behavioral Sciences. I'd like to take this opportunity to congratulate you on a new beginning. I look forward to spending the next four months educating you about the human mind."

Rick looked up at the door and noticed it had been closed. He was sure that it was locked as well.

"As you have all certainly heard by now, you are now ninety eight in number. Two of your fellow classmates have opted for a career other than medicine. There will be others of you departing by the end of the semester as well. Some voluntarily. Others not. The first year serves as somewhat of a weed out process, if you will. Those who are not meant to be here in the first place will most likely not be by year's end. Those who persevere will be rewarded with a fascinating and fulfilling career in the field of medicine."

Rick's mind began to wander. He scanned the room once more for Cameron, but he was nowhere to be seen. He had hoped to sit by Monika this morning, but the seats on either side of her were already occupied. He smiled and waved to her across the room, and she returned the greeting. Rick found a seat where he could still see her easily, which was primarily the reason for his wandering mind. She looked incredible, even more so than last night. Her hair was pulled back into a pony tail, she wore little make-up, and was clad in worn out blue jeans, a sweat shirt, and a baseball cap. Yet still she was ravishing. A true beauty.

Rick forced himself back to reality. Here it was, the second day of med school, and he was sitting in class, hung over, and not paying any attention to the professor at the front of the room. Not exactly what he had in mind, and he was furious at himself because of it. He tried to concentrate on Dr. Robbins'lecture, and managed to do so for most of the remainder of the class. He finished up right at 9:30, ten minutes longer than scheduled. Rick looked down proudly at the four pages of notes he had taken. He filed them away carefully in their assigned slot where they would be ready for review later tonight.

There was an hour long break before the next class, which was not a lecture, but micro anatomy lab. Rick had some papers to sign to finalize one of his student loans, and decided to use the break to visit the financial aid office. He spoke briefly with Mr. Harvey, the financial officer for the medical school. A good ally to have, since he controlled everyone's access to the loan money necessary for most to get through school. Even though this was a state sponsored school, tuition still ran over $6000 a year. Add food, rent, and books and the total quickly topped ten grand. With numbers like that going out and no money coming in, student loans became the only means of support.

He signed the final copy of his loan agreement and was told the first check would be in by the end of the week. The numbers were somewhat intimidating to someone who had never earned more than 6 dollars an hour.

Rick swung by the cafeteria, familiar territory after his days and nights in the emergency room, to pick up a cup of coffee. He had befriended one of the cashiers there, a rather obese black lady in her early sixties named Jessie, who seemed to always be at work. She would only ring up about half the items on his tray when he came through, and coffee was usually free unless there was a crowd. Today he had to wait in a short line, and one of the managers was circulating nearby.

"Morning Miss Jessie. How are you feeling today?"

"I can't complain Dr. Stanley. The good Lord keeps me blessed."

She had called him Dr. Stanley from the beginning. Rick had corrected her the first few times, but finally just gave in. Besides, it felt pretty good to hear, even though they both knew it wasn't true. Yet.

"Second day of med school. They haven't run me off yet."

"I know you'll be at the top of your class." She rang up the coffee. "You still working down in that emergency room?"

"Not any more, Miss Jessie. I got no time now that school's started up."

"That'll be fifty cents today." She looked at him and winked.

"Here you go," he said, handing over the two quarters. "I'll see ya later."

"You take care Dr. Stanley."

Rick glanced at his watch as he walked out into the hallway. Ten minutes until the lab was scheduled to begin. He decided to show up a few minutes early, and made his way to the elevators down the hall.

There were three main buildings in this part of the campus. The hospital was a seven story structure. The ground floor contained both the cafeteria and the emergency room, and was really the only part that Rick was at all familiar with. The other two buildings housed the medical, pharmacy, and nursing schools. They had the innovative names Education 1 and Education 2. Most of the laboratories were inside Ed 1, while Ed 2 contained assorted lecture halls and smaller study rooms. All three buildings shared a ground floor, making it simple to walk from one to the other without exposure to the elements.

Rick walked back into the Ed 1 building with his coffee, and rode the elevator up to the sixth floor. He had run into several other classmates on the way up, and they joked about the locked door at their lecture this morning.

Rick and the others walked into the lab about five minutes early, but at least half the class had already arrived and found their seats. As in the gross anatomy lab, seating was pre-assigned and again alphabetical. He walked towards the back of the room and saw the familiar faces of Cameron, Monika, and of course, Evan.

"You're gonna be late for your own funeral, Stanley."

"I'm five minutes early, thank you very much, and look who the hell's talking. Where were you this morning?"

"I haven't unpacked my alarm clock yet," answered Cameron. "Guess I overslept a bit. I hope you took good notes for me."

"Fat chance you'll ever see 'em."

"Am I gonna have to separate you two?" asked Monika.

"A distinct possibility," answered Cameron, smiling.

"How are you doing this morning, Monika?" asked Rick.

"I'm great, thanks for asking. I looked for you after class this morning."

Rick tossed his backpack onto the table and sat down next to her.

"I had some financial aid stuff I had to take care of. And a caffeine fix." Rick looked across the table at Evan, who looked even smaller and younger today for some reason. "Hey Evan, what's going on?"

"Oh, nothing I guess. Did you all go out to eat last night?"

"Yeah, we tried out Beck's across the street. Kind of a dive, but we had a good time. You should've come along."

"Maybe next time. I stayed in and got caught up on some reading."

"Shit Evan, it's the second day of school," said Cameron. "How could you possibly have to catch up already?"

"I like to stay a week ahead on my assignments whenever I can. I'm up to Thursday so far, but should be able to finish up the week by tonight."

"How old are you, anyway?" asked Cameron. Something they had all wanted to know.

"I'll be twenty next month," answered Evan.

"How the hell did you get to med school when you're still a teenager?"

"I was promoted ahead two grades in elementary school, and I finished college in three years by going to summer school."

"Where'd you go to college?" asked Monika.

"Princeton."

"Hey, great basketball team there," said Cameron.

"I didn't really follow the sporting events too closely. I got my degree in Zoology, with a minor in German."

"Why German?"

"My grandfather emigrated from Germany when he was younger. I have some relatives over there that I've visited a few times."

"I think we're about to start," said Rick, looking up at the front of the room.

Dr. Williams was the chairman of the Micro Anatomy Department. He had a rather large microphone in hand, and when he flipped the switch on, the feedback immediately drowned out every other sound in the room. He quickly turned it off again, laid it on the table, and spoke loudly.

"Good morning everyone. I am Dr. Williams and this is the micro anatomy lab. I see a few empty chairs out there. Hopefully the stragglers will join us shortly."

He walked towards the center of the room. "Can everyone hear me all right?" Nobody answered, a few nodded. "The seating in this lab is pre-assigned, so everyone please check now to be certain they are in their proper seat."

Everyone looked around, but nobody moved.

"We will be coming around momentarily bringing each of you your box of assigned slides. These are all sections of normal anatomy which we will be going through part by part as the semester progresses. By mid December I will expect each of you to know every cell of every part of every slide. If you do that, I promise that each and every one of you will pass my course."

"Is that all we have to do?" whispered Cameron.

"We will cover the first ten pages in the manual today. I expect each table to work as a group to complete your assignment. There will be several of us circulating around if you have any questions. You may begin."

The next hour and a half was spent reading the manual and studying the first eight slides under the microscope. Several graduate assistants were available for assistance, as well as two of the professors. Rick and his table completed their assignment rather easily. They had all had a similar course in college, and most of the initial part of this class would be a review. By 11:30 they felt comfortable with the new material and were ready for lunch.

"Who's starving besides me?" asked Monika.

"I could sure eat," answered Rick.

"Me too," said Evan. "I never ate breakfast this morning."

"What about you, Cameron?"

"You guys go ahead. I've got some things I need to take care of before class this afternoon."

"You mean you're actually gonna go to a lecture?" asked Rick.

"All right, smart ass. You worry about your grade point, I'll worry about mine."

They all loaded their things into their new lockers which lined the hallway on the sixth floor. Hospital food had little appeal for some strange reason, and they decided to walk the half block down the street to the Burger King on the corner. Rick and Evan ordered burgers and fries. Monika got a salad with low fat dressing on the side. They found a clean table by a window and began to eat.

"So what do you think so far, Evan?" asked Rick.

"About what?"

"About med school, what else?"

He took a long drink from his soda. "I think it will be intellectually stimulating. I'm looking forward to a new set of challenges."

"Princeton wasn't challenging enough?"

"Not particularly. I mean I had to study a little bit, but really no more that I did in high school."

"So are you like some kind of genius or something?" asked Monika.

"My IQ says that I am, if you put much stock into tests such as those."

"Do you have one of those photographic memories?"

"Pretty much so. If I read something through slowly and carefully, I will usually retain over 95%. Even better if I read it twice."

"How do you do that anyway?" asked Rick. "Is it something you learned how to do, or just some natural kind of talent?"

"I think it's something I've just always had. Like I told you earlier, I was moved up twice in grade school, so I was no dummy back then either."

"Must be nice," said Monika.

"Well you guys are no slouches either. There were close to 700 applicants for the 100 positions this year, so you two can't tell me you weren't at the top of your classes as well."

"I did all right," said Rick. "Certainly no genius, though. I'm the type who has to really push hard to stay ahead. Things don't come very natural to me, but if I read something six or eight times I can usually remember it for the test. Just don't ask me about it a week later, cause by then it's gone."

"I'm the same way," said Monika. "I can do the work, but I've got to put in the time or you might as well hang it up."

"Are your brothers and sisters the same as you, Evan?" asked Monika.

"I'm an only child."

"Maybe that's my problem," said Rick. "My two sisters have diluted our gene pool. I could be a rocket scientist if it hadn't been for them."

"You're dreamin' Rick Stanley."

"Maybe if I bumped them off, I could shoot up to the top of the class with ol' Evan here."

"Till the first test comes out, we're all at the top of the class," said Monika.

"Or the bottom, depending on how you look at it," added Evan.

They all took a bite at once, and the table was silent while they chewed.

"Are you living in the dorm, Evan?" asked Rick

"Yes, I am. I thought all freshmen were required to live there." Rick did not respond, so he continued. "My folks wanted me to move back home with them, but I couldn't see doing that after living out of state for the last three years."

Rick looked over at Monika. "You never told me how you managed to avoid dorm life, by the way."

"You're right, I didn't."

"What, are you sleeping with the dean or something," Rick smiled.

"I get free parking that way too," she fired back.

"Seriously, how'd you get out of that?"

"I just wrote him a letter saying I had an attention deficit problem and that I wouldn't be able to study in a dormitory atmosphere."

"And that load of crap worked?"

"Like a charm."

"I wish I would have thought of that. I've been there four days and I already hate the place."

"It's not that bad," said Evan. "You should have seen the dorms at Princeton. This place is a palace in comparison."

"I thought all that Ivy League shit was full of gorgeous antiques and oriental rugs."

"Only in the brochures."

"I was gonna move out of there in May when school let out, but I may try and break my lease at semester. Worth a shot."

"You guys about ready to go? I've got to run by the bank before class at one."

"I need to swing back by the dorm too. I'm done. Anyone want the rest of these fries?"

"A gram of fat in every bite," said Monika.

"And worth every artery clogging bit of it."

They emptied their trays in the trash can and headed out the door. Evan asked the other two to wait while he made a quick stop in the restroom. He and Rick then walked together back to the dorm, while Monika split off towards the parking deck.

"I'll see you guys at one."

"We'll be there with bells on."

CHAPTER 4

Rick was almost ten minutes late to class the next morning, but fortunately this was not one of those door locking lectures. He came in through the back door and slipped into the first available seat in the rear of the classroom. The lights were dimmed to help see the slides on the screen, and a couple of people were already nodding off. He sat next to one of his old buddies from college, someone he hadn't really had much time to talk with during the last few days.

"Did I miss anything good?" he whispered.

"So far he's just reading straight from the syllabus, same as Monday."

"I hit snooze about five times this morning. Couldn't seem to roll out of bed."

"Well, you ain't missin' much. I'm gonna start sleepin' in on purpose if he's just gonna read to us straight out of this thing," he said, pointing to the spiral bound book of notes.

Rick looked around the room at the backs of everyone's heads. He spotted Monika in her usual seat across the room. He was going to have to start getting there much sooner if he were ever going to sit with her. People had already begun to settle into 'their seat', and the class looked about the same today as it had the last two. Including the fact that Cameron was nowhere to be seen.

Rick forced himself to focus in on Dr. Shires. He followed along in the book, underlining pertinent facts and adding a few comments out to the side. But for the most part, he was reading verbatim from the syllabus. The occasional slide added little to the talk.

It wasn't long before he began to wander again. He studied Dr. Shires himself, a rather strange sort of man. He was tall, at least six feet, but not an athletic tall. He probably weighed no more than 150 or 160, and even at that had a small noticeable bulge protruding over his belt. He had a thick graying moustache, too thick to be stylish, and was beginning to lose a significant amount of hair up top. He never really seemed to look at ease when speaking to the class, not exactly nervous, but never quite in control. He spoke with monotony, and as class went on, Rick noticed more and more heads beginning to sway. Including his own.

The morning passed quite slowly. After Shires' lecture, most everyone headed to the cafeteria for a quick cup of coffee, hoping to clear the cobwebs. Rick ran into Monika, and they talked briefly. She seemed somewhat preoccupied, and excused herself after a couple of minutes. He thought about calling up to Cameron's room, realized he didn't know the number, then decided he didn't really want to call anyway. If he wanted to skip class that was his business.

The second lecture of the morning was only slightly less sleep provoking. Rick managed to stay awake throughout, no small accomplishment, and took a reasonable amount of notes. He spent lunch with a group of people he knew from college. His last two years had been spent working construction and retaking the MCAT three times. This meant that most of the people he knew in his class now were actually two years behind him in college. Most of his friends who went to medical school had either left the state, or were here but in their third year. The junior year was purely clinical, twelve long months spent in the hospital, and he knew they would rarely cross paths.

Rick spent the lunch break back in his dorm room alone. He realized that eating out every day just wasn't possible on his meager budget, and opted instead for peanut butter and jelly on white, some chips, and a Dr. Pepper. He had nearly two hours before anatomy lab, and spent most of that time spread out on his bed studying. He resisted the urge to flip on the television, relying on a strong willpower that had gotten him through college. He made good use of his time, both reviewing this morning's assignments and reading in the dissector manual for the afternoon ahead. Today they would finish up the muscles of the back, then flip over their bodies and begin work on the chest. This was definitely the most weirdly fascinating thing he had ever done.

Soon it was ten till one, and Rick gathered up his things and headed off for the lab. He ran into several of his classmates on the way, and they rode back up to the eighth floor together. They all quickly changed into their dissecting clothes, which for Rick was an old fraternity t-shirt and a pair of torn jeans. He had also dug up a wornout pair of Reeboks, and slipped into them as well. The other three were at the table about to get started when he walked up.

"Hey Stanley, 'bout to send out a search party looking for you."

"You know, it's funny," answered Rick, "how you never seem to see some people until it's time to start cutting on the bodies. Then they're the first ones here."

"I'll have you know I had some very important business to attend to this morning, but tomorrow I'll be the first one in class," said Cameron.

"Anyone else buying a word of this?"

"We'll all be sure and save you a seat," said Monika.

"You want to sit up front with me?" asked Evan, joining in on the laugh.

Cameron looked over at Evan. "Awfully hard to sleep on the front row, isn't it?"

"I wouldn't know. I've never tried it," said Evan truthfully.

Rick looked around the room for Dr. Shires. "You think he lectures to us each time first, or can we just dive right in?"

They noticed several other tables had already started the day's assignment, and decided to move along. Evan seemed a little more at ease today, and actually put on a pair of gloves for the first time.

"You gonna join us today, Sanders?" asked Cameron.

"I told you it would just take me a little while to get accustomed to this. I think I'm ready to give it a try today." He still looked a little green.

"Good for you," said Monika. "That's the only way you're ever going to do this. Just jump right in there."

"I don't know if I'll be doing much jumping, but I am ready to help out a little bit."

"Hey look over there," said Cameron. "Looks like they dug up a few more bodies."

The three tables along the far wall, all empty on Monday, now each supported a new cadaver. The covers had been removed, and three new bodies laid atop the metal surface. Everybody assumed they were for the students who had been forced to double up, but no one was sure if they should move over there and begin to work. For now they were left alone, and everyone began the day's dissection on their bodies from yesterday.

At 1:15, Dr. Shires entered the room, slightly out of breath. He went quickly to the front of the laboratory, and everyone quieted as he did.

"Good afternoon class," he said, setting several books down on the table beside him. "I apologize for my tardiness. I'm glad to see you have all begun your work. You may have noticed the arrival of three more cadavers at the far end of the room. There was an unfortunate delay in their arrival, but we now have enough specimens that there should be no more than four of you per table. For those of you that are five in number, I will be coming around momentarily and making some reassignments."

There were some grumblings around the room as several students anticipated what was coming next.

"Unfortunately those that are to be moved will need to repeat Monday's dissection in order to catch up with the rest of the class. I apologize for the inconvenience, but it was something beyond our control. I have arranged for two graduate assistants to stay late today and help you with your work. I will, however, expect you to be completely caught up by the start of the next lab on Friday afternoon."

"Today we will be finishing our work on the back as you complete the exposure of the serratus anterior and teres major muscles. We will then begin our work on the chest, exposing the pectoralis major and minor muscles. Those of you with female cadavers will also begin dissecting the breast today as well. There will be many instances where the anatomy will be gender specific, necessitating cooperation between tables to assure everyone adequate exposure to both sexes. Today will be the first such instance." He paused and looked around the room.

"Are there any questions before you begin?"

There were none.

"Very well then. You may proceed."

The background noise slowly escalated as both work and conversation resumed. Everyone watched as all of the fifth men out (or women) were uprooted from their table and forced to start over from the beginning. Rick felt very fortunate that none of them would have to be moved, both for the obvious reason of the extra work, but also because he was looking forward to working with the others for the semester. Even with Evan.

"That's just awful for those guys," said Monika.

"Better them than us," replied Cameron.

"You're just bubbling over with sympathy, aren't you?" said Rick.

"Not exactly my style, I guess. When I see something bad happen to someone, I think 'thank God it wasn't me', not 'poor old Joe'."

"I guess I'm more the 'poor old Joe' type myself," said Monika.

"Well if you feel so bad for them, you can stay after class and help them out."

"I just may do that."

"Come on guys, let's get started with this, or we're gonna be here as late as they are anyway."

Evan had the manual in his hands, and was already looking over the next section. "Let's get this back part finished up so we can flip him and start on the chest."

"Look at Evan go," said Cameron. "Last time we were here you were puking your guts up every five minutes."

"I threw up one time, and that was from some bad Mexican food the night before."

"Whatever you say there, chief. Whatever you say."

"Lay off him, Cameron," said Rick. "He can't help it if he puked."

"One time," Evan added.

"I thought we were gonna get started, but if you guys would rather bicker all afternoon, I can sure find better use of my time than watching you all go at it."

"OK Monika," said Rick. "I'm willing to call a truce if these two boneheads are."

"I'm the one trying to get started on the assignment," said Evan.

"Fine by me," said Cameron. "You wanna kiss or hug or something, Evan?"

"How 'bout a handshake and we drop the whole matter?"

They looked each other in the eye for a moment, then Cameron extended his hand. "Deal."

"We'll save the kiss for later tonight," joked Evan, and everyone laughed.

The next two and a half hours simply flew by. They had all gotten over the cadaver jitters (including Evan), and they worked with surprising efficiency for only their second time here. In fact, theirs was the first thump heard in the lab as they flipped their body over to begin work on the chest. They took turns reading from the manual as the other three would cut. Dr. Shires even praised them during one of his passes through, commenting on their meticulous dissection. They all beamed with self-esteem, but Monika seemed especially proud of their work.

"How bout a name for the old son of a bitch?" asked Cameron out of the blue.

"A what?" said Rick.

"A name. Everyone deserves a name."

"I'm quite sure he already has a name," said Evan. "I'm not sure it's fair to him to give him another."

"Shit Sanders, he's dead. It's gonna be kinda hard to offend him there, chief."

"I wonder if they have his real name on record somewhere?" asked Rick.

"Who cares what his real name is. "Let's give him one that we like."

"I'm with Cameron," said Monika. "I don't really care what his real name is. Let's give him one of our own. It'll be fun."

"Any brilliant ideas?"

"Not off the top of my head," she said. "Why don't we all think of one tonight, and we'll pick out one of the four when we're back here on Friday."

"Sounds fair enough," said Cameron. "But I already have the perfect name."

"Save it for Friday," said Rick.

By four o'clock, they had completed the day's assignment, and actually looked ahead a little at Friday's work. Once they got going, it was a little hard to stop. This was still by far the coolest thing any of them had ever done. The work was fascinating, and seemed much more fun than they had thought it would be. Of course it was still only the first week of school. Rick realized the newness would have to wear off at some point. He hoped that point was a long ways away.

Cameron set down the manual and stretched. "You guys about ready to wrap this up for the night? I'm beat."

"Worn out from those grueling lectures this morning?" asked Rick, smiling back at him.

"My body just happens to need a little more sleep than most, that's all."

"Well, I'm with Cameron," said Monika. "I'm ready to call it a day."

"I thought you were gonna be the good Samaritan and help out those poor souls in the corner over there." Cameron looked over to see how they were coming. "Looks like they just got started with today's dissection."

"Maybe we should at least go over there and offer a hand."

"Let's get our guy wrapped up and go over there for a sec," said Rick.

"You see what I mean," said Cameron. "He needs a name. Then we won't have to call him 'our guy'."

"We'll see what we can come up with tonight."

Rick tucked the clear plastic wrap around the body, then reached for the cover. "You wanna give me a hand here, Evan?"

"Sure thing." Evan and Rick reached under the table, removed the heavy lid, and replaced it on top of the man without a name. They all walked over to the new tables together to see if they could lend a quick hand.

"You guys really got screwed," said Cameron.

"Thanks, we hadn't noticed."

"We thought we'd see if any of y'all needed a hand," said Rick.

"Appreciate the offer, but I think we're moving along pretty well. Not much to do to speed it up, really. We've just gotta make the cuts."

Rick heard the familiar thump from the next table over. He looked over and saw they had finished the back and were moving over to the chest. Cameron was over there talking with one of the women assigned to that table. Always scheming. Rick and Monika stayed with the other group for a while, showing them a couple of quick shortcuts they had discovered throughout the afternoon. Evan had gone over to the third table for a few minutes, but then quickly made his exit, no doubt off to go study somewhere. Rick was becoming bored and hungry.

"You about ready to get out of here," he said to Monika.

"Yeah, I need to get going."

"Back to the books tonight?"

"Actually I've got some dinner plans in a little while."

"A date?" Rick asked, caught off guard by the sudden rush of jealousy that came out of nowhere.

"Not really a date. Just dinner with a friend."

"A male friend or a female friend?" he asked, joking, but not really.

Monika smiled back at him. "What's it to you, Mr. Twenty Questions. It's just a friend, that's all."

"Fine by me," he replied, realizing he was overstepping his boundaries. "I hope you have a great time."

"You going to Robbins' lecture in the morning?" They were walking towards the changing rooms now.

"As far as I know. I don't plan on skipping too many lectures," he said. "I may not stay awake through all of them, but I'll at least be there in body."

Monika laughed. "Why don't you save me a seat, and I'll see you in the morning."

"Sure thing," he replied, trying to sound as casual as he could with his heart in his throat. He felt his face flush slightly, and hoped she wouldn't notice.

"I'll see you then." She turned and headed in to change.

Cameron shouted from across the room. "You guys come here and look at this."

Monika continued through the door without turning her head. Rick decided to take a quick look before he changed. He walked back to the table where Cameron and four others were standing. The lab was now nearly empty except for the unfortunate three tables.

"Come here and look at this guy."

Rick looked down at the body. "What ya got, Cam?"

"Check out the scar on this guy. Looks like somebody tried to dissect him while he was still alive."

Rick noticed the long jagged scar that extended from his right shoulder all the way across his chest. Probably somebody on the losing end of a bad fight. A long beard covered the end of the scar. A red flag went up in his mind, but he did not know the reason why.

"I bet this guy's got some stories to tell," said Cameron. "Check out this tattoo on his arm over here."

Rick looked down at the man's left forearm being held up by Cameron. His eyes widened as they focused in on the large eagle with its wings spread wide. He put one hand down on the table to steady himself, then looked up at the bearded face. The silent eyes of Charlie Ellis stared up blankly at the ceiling.

CHAPTER 5

Monika changed quickly and left out the back door of the dressing room. She wore a white cotton blouse, khaki shorts and a pair of brown sandals. Nobody was really sure if there was any sort of dress code to adhere to, but with the thermometer pushing a hundred on a regular basis, over half the class was wearing shorts and nobody seemed to notice.

She made her way down to the parking garage and climbed into her red Z28. The top was already down from her ride in this morning. She turned over the engine, flipped on the air conditioning, and decided to leave the top down for the ride home. It was a little warmer that way, but so much more fun. She pulled out of the deck and headed towards home.

The Briarwood area was one of the oldest parts of the city. The homes there had been built in the thirties and forties, and most of them had now been restored to their original splendor. They had all been bought up years ago by the doctors and the lawyers, which had inflated their value tremendously. One of these doctors was an old college buddy of her father's, a general surgeon in his late fifties who had known Monika when she was growing up. His wife had passed away last year, and his three children were all married and moved off. He had just left for a year long sabbatical in South America, and had graciously offered the use of his house to Monika rent free in exchange for keeping up with a few things there.

The house was not even a half mile from the medical center. She had brought her bicycle down with her, and planned to pedal to class this fall if it would ever cool off. She pulled into the drive and parked under a giant oak tree which shaded most of the yard. The mailbox contained a stack of catalogs and a couple bills. She laid these on the back of her car, bent over to pick up the newspaper, then decided to sit right there on the grass and browse over the half day old news.

The heat and the flies quickly chased her inside. The cool dry air felt wonderful on her moist body, and she fanned her shirt to create a nice breeze. It was already after 5:30 and she had less than an hour to shower, dress, and get to Bella's across town. She took a beer out of the fridge and buried it in the ice cubes in the freezer. There were no messages on the machine, which she always found disappointing. Everything she needed was there on the first floor, and she rarely ventured upstairs. The master bedroom had its own bath, and she turned on the separate hot and cold faucets to fill the tub. After stripping down naked, she walked into the kitchen to retrieve her beer, then settled into the tub for a few moments of peace.

Monika could have lain there soaking all night, but knew she was on a rather tight schedule. By 6:00 she had finished her beer and managed to pull herself out of the warm soapy water. She dressed quickly, looking casual yet somehow still very elegant. She wore very little makeup, and had the kind of face that could get away with it.

The shadows outside were growing long, but if anything it felt even hotter than it had an hour ago. She put the top back up on the car, deciding not to do battle with the heat and the breeze. The air conditioner blew with all its might as she made her way across town to the old favorite restaurant. It had been there for over twenty years, and Monika had many fond memories of their family nights out. Clint Black filled the speakers, and she sang along with the parts she knew. Monika was one of those closet country music fans. She would deny it till the end, but anyone checking her car would find four of the five buttons on the console preset to country stations.

The crowd was thin on a weekday, and she pulled into a spot near the front door. Walking into the lobby, she spotted him almost right away. He was speaking with one of the waitresses, no doubt lining up their table for the night. Monika walked up quietly and grabbed him from behind. He jumped as if startled, which she knew was an act, then turned and gave her a long hug.

"There you are, sweetheart. Right on time."

"I wasn't sure I was gonna make it. We ran a little late in the lab this afternoon."

"Well I'm glad you're here." He looked around for the waitress, who had disappeared somewhere into the back. "Are you hungry?"

"Starving. I never really ate lunch today. I had some errands to run between classes and had to grab lunch out of one of those machines."

The waitress finally made it back out front, and he signaled to her that they were ready to be seated. She led them towards the back corner to a quiet table for two in the middle of the smoking section. He helped

Monika with her chair, then seated himself. Their server quickly went through the daily specials, both of which sounded delicious, then left them to study their menus while she retrieved a bottle of Mondavi Reserve Cabernet which he had apparently ordered earlier.

In a short time a middle-aged Italian man returned with the bottle and two glasses. He presented the label for them to approve, then skillfully removed the cork as they watched.

"Did we run off our waitress already?" asked Monika.

"She is not yet of the age to serve the alcohol," he replied with a thick accent. "She will return shortly to take your orders."

He poured a small sample into the gentleman's glass, which he then swirled, sniffed, and sipped.

"Very good," he said, pushing his glass forward to be filled. "This will be fine."

The waiter poured both glasses, set the bottle on the table, and then left them alone to enjoy their evening. They were both rather quiet as they scanned the menu, finally settling on the two pasta specials, one of each so they could try them both. The waitress came back shortly and took their orders. They both lit up a cigarette, then sank back into their chairs to relax and wait for their food.

"You know those things will kill you," said Monika.

"I'll put 'em down tonight if you promise to do the same," he replied without even thinking.

"But I'm much younger than you are. I've got years to smoke before I catch up with you," she said smiling.

"I can see we're going to get nowhere with this discussion."

"You're probably right. How bout we call a truce and both put 'em down for the night after this one."

"Not even one more after dessert?"

"That's right."

"All right then, you've got a deal." They shook hands in agreement, both already planning to light one up as soon as they got to their cars.

"So tell me about the first week of school so far. We've hardly had a chance to talk. I can't believe the only woman I love is about to become a doctor."

"Who's about to become a doctor?" she replied. "I can hardly think past this weekend. Graduation's still four years away."

"It will fly by, I know. It seems like an eternity, but it will...."

"Ray, I thought that was you. How the hell are you?"

They both turned and saw a rather large man approaching.

"David Mattox? I haven't seen you in years. What are you doing back in town?"

"I'm just down visiting dad for a few days. He's in the hospital with pneumonia, so Ellen and I flew down to keep him company for a little while."

"I hope he's doing ok."

"Oh he'll be fine. He's too damn mean to die yet."

"Well it's good to see you, anyway. How long will you be in town?"

"Probably through the weekend. We've got a flight out Sunday morning if everything's still going ok by then."

"Well if you have a chance why don't you give me a call and we can go have a cup of coffee or something. Talk about old times and catch up a little."

"That sounds great Ray. I haven't seen you in years. Who's this beautiful lady you're out with tonight?"

"You don't recognize her?"

He looked more closely this time. "Well I'll be damned, is that you, Monika? I haven't seen you since you was maybe fifteen years old."

"She started medical school this week," Ray said proudly.

"Who'd have ever thought any kin of Ray's here would ever turn out something like a doctor?"

"It's good to see you again Mr. Mattox."

"Well you too, darling. So you're gonna make a doctor, huh? That's just great."

He looked over at his table, and then his watch. "I guess I better have a seat before the misses thinks I've left or something. It's great to see you both. Call me Ray."

"Sure thing, David. Good to see you."

Their salads arrived as he was leaving the table. Monika and her father were both starving, and the bowls were quickly emptied. They talked quietly as they waited for their dinner to arrive.

"So how's school going, really?"

"I think I'm really going to like it. Definitely will be a challenge, but I think I'm up to it."

"You'll do just great. You've always been a great student."

"I know, but everybody in the class has always been a great student. I'm going up against the best of the best."

"And I'm sure you'll come out on top, just like you've always done."

"I hope you're right. I really am looking forward to it."

45

"Have you met many folks yet?"

"I'm getting to know a few of the guys in the class," she answered. "Three of us actually went out to dinner together the other night, after that first anatomy lab."

"Any romantic prospects yet?"

"Dad!" she replied, blushing. "That's the last thing I'm looking for right now."

"I'm not saying you have to go out looking. Just keep an open mind, that's all."

"I've got way too much to worry about to be thinking about dating right now."

"That's what you've been saying for the last two and a half years, Monika. You've got to start dating again sometime."

"I've had some dates. Just nobody steady, that's all."

"When's the last time you had a real date?"

"I've had plenty of real dates. It's just not something I'm interested in right now, that's all."

"Well it's something you should be interested in. You're a beautiful, smart, interesting young woman. It's not normal for you to isolate yourself like this."

"So now I'm not normal, is that it?" she asked, beginning to get a little upset.

"Monika, I didn't say that. I'm just concerned, that's all. Ever since the accident, you've been a different person. You're going to have to put that behind you and get on with your life."

"I just started medical school this week. Don't you consider that getting on with my life?"

"You know what I mean. Socially you've completely shut yourself off from the rest of the world. You've got to let go of Tom and Will and start thinking about yourself again."

"Dammit Dad, it's not that easy. I've got to do this my own way, in my own time."

The waitress arrived with their dinners, two steaming plates of pasta, and placed them on the table. She refilled their water, asked if they needed anything else, then headed back towards the kitchen. They ate in silence for a few minutes.

"I think you should talk to someone about this."

"I'm talking to you tonight, aren't I?" she replied, knowing full well where he was headed.

"I'm talking about a counselor of some type. Somebody who can help you with some of these issues that you need to resolve."

"Is that what I have? Issues?"

"Yes Monika, you do. And I think you need professional help to get you through this."

"I'm not seeing a shrink."

"I'm sure the school has a system set up to help students with emotional type problems. I want you to look into it tomorrow."

"I told you dad, I'm not seeing a shrink."

"Nobody's saying you're crazy. You just need a little help right now, that's all. There's no crime in admitting a need for help. You're not quite as tough as you think you are."

Monika didn't answer right away, instead taking a bite of her meal and a sip of wine. "If I agree to talk with someone one time, will you get off my case?"

"That's fair enough."

"I'll think about it this weekend. Maybe Monday I'll look into it."

"No maybe. I want a definite yes out of you, or I'm going to keep harping."

"All right, fine. I'll check on it Monday morning," she lied. "Now can we change the subject?"

"Sure, that's fair enough. Tell me who you had dinner with the other night."

"I thought we were changing the subject?"

"This is a different subject. I'm asking about your new friends."

"You're asking if I had a date."

"Well did you?"

"It was just three med students spending their first night of school getting to know some of their classmates. Nothing more."

"I'm just asking a question, that's all. Did you have a good time?"

"Yeah, as a matter of fact, we did."

"I'm glad, sweetheart." He finished the last of his wine, then poured another glass for himself and filled Monika's back up to the top. "I really am just concerned about you. I just want you to be happy."

"I know, daddy. And I really think I am. More so than in the last three years, anyway."

They eventually did change the subject, and the rest of the dinner, including dessert, was spent talking about everything and nothing. Monika began to loosen up and was surprised at how much she enjoyed the evening. The subject of her social life did not come up again, for which she was delighted. After a cup and a half of coffee, they finally decided to call it a night. They argued briefly over the check before he handed the waitress his credit card. They both knew who would pay, but Monika would always make an attempt.

They hugged briefly in the parking lot, then got into their cars and drove away. Monika's father went home, reviewed a few things for work in the morning, then went to bed. He slept well knowing he had helped his only daughter tonight.

Monika drove home slowly with the top down. The air was still warm, but not as stifling now that the sun had dropped below the horizon. She thought about their conversation at dinner tonight, and begrudgingly admitted to herself that her father had a few valid points. The neighborhood was quiet as she pulled into the driveway, and Monika sat alone under the large oak for a while, listening to the local jazz station playing softly on the car's stereo and thinking about the direction her life was taking. Only yesterday she had been living the fairy tale life. A loving husband. A beautiful son. The house on the hill. Every girl's dream. How abruptly the rug had been pulled out from underneath her, and she had yet to land on her feet. There were days when she could almost forget, but then some subtle reminder would bring it all crashing back.

A passing car interrupted her reflection, and she was startled back to reality. She realized she had been crying, and was embarrassed even though no one was there to see her. She quickly composed herself as she walked back into the house. There were no messages on the machine, and tonight she was glad. Plans for studying went quickly by the wayside as she settled in on the couch with a large bowl of microwave popcorn. By nine-thirty she was safely tucked in bed. She fell asleep just after midnight.

CHAPTER 6

As fitful a night of sleep that Monika had, Rick Stanley's was ten times worse. He felt as if he had seen a ghost, and was unable to shake that feeling ever since. Charlie Ellis, a man he knew, a man whose funeral he had attended, a man whom he had watched placed into the ground, was now lying atop a dissecting table with the muscles in his back splayed out for all to see. This simply could not be. The entire night Rick had tried to come up with a simple logical explanation to account for what he had seen. He could think of none.

Although his actions probably gave him away, Rick told no one about his visitor from the grave. Once he had steadied his wobbly knees, he told Cameron he was feeling a little sick and made a quick exit out the building. He wanted to be alone for a moment to gather his thoughts, which were myriad. There was simply no plausible way in which that body could be where it was this afternoon. Yet there had to be a reasonable, sane explanation for what had occurred.

Rick went by the cafeteria, bought a large Dr. Pepper, then went outside to a concrete table by the dorm building to think this through. He reviewed in his mind everything he could recall about the events surrounding the death, going over what he considered the facts. He knew Charlie Ellis had died that night in the emergency room. He was there when they pronounced him. The funeral was five days later, on a muggy Thursday morning. Rick had been the one to notify the family. He had managed to track down the man's son the following morning with some difficulty. He was living outside of Dallas where he taught English at a small junior college. He hadn't spoken with his father in over two years, but did seem somewhat concerned and took over the necessary arrangements.

The funeral was small, no more than twenty-five people, and was held in a nearby church. The minister did a commendable job, considering he had never even met the deceased. Charlie's daughter was in attendance. His ex wife was not. There were a few friends, mostly those who had known him five or ten years ago. The casket was closed.

After the brief ceremony, they had driven out to the cemetery for a short grave side service. Rick watched as the old man was lowered into the ground. A prayer was said and a few tears fell. Everyone walked by and tossed a flower on top of the casket, and then it was over. Rick had even gone by a week later to pay his personal respects in private. He was saddened by the loss, but Charlie soon began to fade from his memory as Rick transitioned into the first year of medical school. Now he was back.

The temperature was still well over ninety degrees, probably hotter than that in the direct sunlight, but Rick didn't notice. He was deep in thought. He realized this was not something he could simply let go. He would have to know what had happened, both for his own peace of mind and for poor Charlie. This just didn't make sense.

He had to decide how best to approach the situation. There had to be records kept somewhere about the cadavers. Where they came from, cause of death, and probably some type of consent form granting the school permission to use their bodies. This would be the best place to start. Somehow he would uncover a very logical explanation for the whole incident, but Rick could not begin to imagine what it would be.

Rick looked down at his watch and saw it was nearly six o'clock. His drink was gone now, along with all of the ice. He became suddenly aware of just how hot he was, and decided it was time to get inside. The death of Charlie Ellis had completely taken over his conscious thoughts, and he knew he would have to find some answers. He decided to go straight to the top, and headed back inside towards Dr. Shires' office in the Education One Building. He would certainly know where his cadavers had come from. He would have to. This would be the man with the answers. This is where Rick would start.

The offices were located on the fifth floor of the building, three stories below the cadaver lab. Rick stepped out of the elevator and looked both ways down the deserted hallway. He had forgotten how late it was, and quickly realized that the offices would probably all be vacant. A black felt sign on the wall listed everyone's name in alphabetical order, followed by their office number. Rick found Dr. Shires' listing and headed down the hallway to 513. It was about halfway down on the left, and he walked in through the open door into a small suite of offices.

There was a main desk in front of him, probably for a secretary or something, and four separate offices fanning out in all directions. The doors were all closed and there was no one in sight.

"Hello," Rick called out, softly at first but then again a little louder. "Hello!"

There was no answer. He stuck his head back out into the hallway and again saw no one. Dr. Shires' name and title, Chairman Department of Anatomy, were posted to the side of one of the doors. Rick walked up and knocked firmly. No answer. "Dr. Shires?" he called out. Again silence. He contemplated briefly what to do next, and before really thinking tried the handle on the door. It was unlocked.

"Dr. Shires?" he tried again, but knew there would be no response. He looked back over his shoulder one final time, then opened the door a little further and stepped inside. His heart was racing. He knew he shouldn't be here. He knew he should turn and walk away, but something was drawing him inside. He had to have some answers.

The man's desk was a whirlwind of papers, textbooks, and assorted other objects of clutter. There were three large filing cabinets off to one side, and a massive bookshelf directly behind his chair. The desk itself also had three drawers down each side, all of which were closed and probably locked. An enormous mountain of paperwork, and Rick was not even sure what he was looking for. He stood there and stared, not knowing what he should do next. He considered going through some of the drawers, looking for something about the cadavers, but then realized just what would happen if somebody would walk in on him with his hand in the cookie jar. Almost on cue, Rick heard footsteps out in the hall, the kind of sound made by hard soled dress shoes on a hard floor.

He panicked. His mind was racing. Should he hide in the office? What if it was Shires? What if he were coming back to the office? How could he possible explain his presence there? He knew that he couldn't.

He stepped quickly into the outer office. The footsteps were growing louder. He heard a man clear his throat. Then he began to whistle. There was really no place to hide where he was standing. Then he thought maybe he didn't have to hide. What was he doing wrong? He had simply come by to speak with one of professors after hours. Nothing wrong with that.

Rick stood perfectly still, listening as the footsteps grew louder. He felt his knees weaken, and he knew he was starting to perspire. He had to calm himself down, or he would look guilty as hell standing there in the vacant outer office. He decided to position himself in front of Dr. Shires' door, raising his arm up as if he were about to knock on the door. The footsteps were almost here.

The next five seconds lasted about three hours. Rick heard the footsteps slow, and he knew it was Dr. Shires coming back into his office. He thought about what he would say to him...what he would ask. As the man took his first step in from the hallway, Rick knocked on the office door and called out.

"Dr. Shires?" He waited for him to answer over his shoulder.

"He's already left for the day."

Rick turned quickly, startled both by the voice, and the fact that it didn't belong to Shires. He looked up and saw Dr. Williams standing before him.

"Oh hello sir," he said, trying to look as casual as he could. "You said he's left for the day?"

"Yeah, he took off about 4:30 or so. He's gone for the day." Neither of them spoke for a long second. "Anything I can help you with?"

"No sir. I just had a few questions about a cadaver in there. I'll just come by tomorrow." Rick had never wanted out of a room as badly as he did right now.

"You're Rick Stanley, right?"

"Yes sir," he replied, surprised that he knew his name. "One of the new freshmen."

"All right Rick. I'll see you in micro lab in the morning."

"Thank you sir. I'm looking forward to it."

He immediately realized how stupid that last sentence sounded, but it was too late to get it back. He walked quickly into the hallway, hearing Williams enter his own office as he left. The elevator was still on the floor, and it opened right away as he pressed the down button. He stepped inside and rode down to the ground without stopping. The butterflies were beginning to leave his stomach, and he decided to stop by the cafeteria for a quick bite before heading up to his room to study. It was already getting late, and he didn't feel like wasting any more time by heating up a frozen TV dinner in the ancient community microwave at the end of the hall.

There were perhaps twenty people total in the entire cafeteria, almost deserted when compared with the bustling lunch crowd. Rick walked through the line, getting a baked chicken breast and two vegetables. He grabbed two cartons of milk, and was proud of himself for eating right tonight. Jessie was the only cashier working and Rick stopped there to pay.

"Hi Jessie. How ya doin' tonight?"

"I can't complain, Dr. Stanley. How are you tonight?"

"I've been better," he said, but did not elaborate.

"Such a serious face tonight. Is all that studying already getting you down?"

"I'm fine, Jessie. It's just been a rather trying day."

"Anything I can help you with?" she asked.

"I wish you could. It's something I'm gonna have to work out for myself."

"Well I trust you'll let me know if there's anything I can do for you."

"You'll be the first Jessie. I promise."

She rang up his tray, then looked up at him and smiled. "That'll be forty two cents."

Rick had long since given up arguing with her, and handed over two quarters.

"We're not gonna get you in trouble, are we Miss Jessie?" he asked. "Cause I could pay for this right if I had to."

"You are payin' right," she said. "We just havin' a special tonight, that's all."

"Well, I honestly do appreciate it. Every penny helps right now."

"Besides, I'm gonna be hittin' you up for free medical advice every chance I get. You're gonna wish I were overcharging you here before long."

They both laughed. Rick spent another minute or two discussing the weather and other mundane topics. He finally excused himself and headed for the back of the dining area to be alone with his thoughts. He saw Evan sitting alone in a corner booth, reviewing what appeared to be his notes from today's lecture. He tried to turn and head off to another section, but Evan looked up and saw him.

"Rick, over here."

Rick acted as if he hadn't noticed him and headed in his direction. "Hey Evan, didn't see you there. What are you up to tonight?"

"Same as every night, I guess. Just studying."

"Can I join you here?"

"Sure, have a seat," he said, motioning to the empty booth across from him. Evan gathered up his notes from across that side of the table to make room for Rick.

"What are you studying?" asked Rick.

"Just looking over a few things for tomorrow's lecture. Trying to stay ahead."

"Do you just study all the time?"

Evan smiled. "Not in the past, but I seem to be here. To be honest, I really didn't have to study all that much in high school or college. I seem to pick things up pretty quickly. I'm just being extra cautious since I got here."

"Were you valedictorian in high school?"

"Actually co-valedictorian. I shared it with my brother."

"You're kidding? You mean you have a twin brother?"

"No, he's two years older than I am. I think I told you, they moved me up two years in grade school. They didn't do that with him, so we were together in school ever since fifth grade."

"So you're saying he was the dumb one in the family."

"Yeah, something like that," replied Evan.

"That's pretty weird, you know that."

"I guess it is, but we were accustomed to it." He took a drink of his Coke. "What about you, Rick? What were you like in high school?"

"Well, I was no valedictorian, I can assure you of that. I was more into playing football and chasing women I guess."

"I could see that," said Evan. They both laughed.

"I'm more of the blue collar med student, I guess," said Rick. "I pretty much have to study my ass off to get by. I won't be setting any curves here, I can promise you that."

"Well, you can't be as dumb as you pretend to be, or you wouldn't be here."

"Who said anything about being dumb?" he asked, shoving him playfully from across the table. "I just said I had to study a lot, that's all."

"You're a dumb jock and you know it, Rick."

"Better than being some pocket-protector-wearing teenage nerd."

"All right, let's call a truce," said Evan. "You're a jock and I'm a nerd."

"Fair enough. How about you help me with the hard classes and I'll explain baseball to you."

"Sounds like a fair trade," laughed Evan.

They sat in silence for a minute. Rick started in on his supper, but his mind quickly drifted back to Charlie. It was all he could think about, and it was making studying impossible. How in the hell did Charlie's body end up in the anatomy lab? There was just no reasonable explanation for it. He had played it over and over again in his mind, and he was beginning to realize that there was no legitimate way that this could have occurred. Somebody had to have intentionally taken his body out of the casket and gotten it to the lab. But why?

"You're in a deep trance over there," said Evan, startling Rick.

"Just doing a little thinking, that's all."

"Anything you want to think out loud?"

"Not really. At least not right now anyway. It's nothing important."

"Ok, suit yourself. I think I'm going to head to the library for a while. I've got some things I need to look up tonight."

"I may be joining you there in a bit. I'm gonna finish this delightful supper and head back to the dorm for a while."

"Are you coming to class in the morning?"

"Oh I'll be there, don't worry. It's Cameron who likes to pull that disappearing act, remember?"

"I don't even expect him there anymore." Evan gathered up the rest of his notes, put them neatly into his backpack, and stood. "I guess I'll see you in the morning then."

"All right, Evan. Don't stay up all night."

"I'll try not to. See you in the morning."

Rick sat there alone and finished his supper in silence. In his mind he was replaying the whole scenario over and over again, hoping to find an answer to a question that did not have one. He was beginning to realize this himself, and turned his thoughts towards the steps it would take to solve this morbid mystery. It had to center around Dr. Shires. It was his department, his lab, and his cadavers. If anyone would be able to help it would be him. And if he didn't know, he would surely know someone who would. Rick cursed himself for not going to Shire's office directly from the lab, when he would most certainly still have been around. But now he would have to wait. Another sleuthing trip up to the fifth floor was most certainly out of the question. Rick would no doubt perforate an ulcer if he tried a repeat of that performance. It would simply have to wait until later.

Rick carried his tray back up to the front and set it down on the empty conveyer belt. He thought about heading straight to the library, but there were a couple of books in his room he had wanted to look over tonight. He took the tunnel back to the basement of the dorm building, a rather eerie trek after hours. Perhaps it was that strange darkened solitude, almost a sense of danger, that got him thinking the implausible. He started in with the what-ifs.

What if Dr. Shires knew about Charlie's body from the start? What if he was somehow involved in something unethical, or worse yet, illegal? How could he have innocently obtained a body that was supposedly buried in the ground over three weeks ago? Maybe he was robbing graves to get his bodies. Maybe he was involved in some secret plot. What if the mafia was at work? Did they have a mafia in the south?

Rick reached the elevators and shook his head. Was this just the crazy imagination of a stressed-out medical student, or was he on to something here. Maybe Shires was legit, and had no knowledge of the source of his bodies. But what if there were more? What if he knew more? Then he would be walking into God knows what, and any chance of finding out the truth would most certainly be lost.

He decided to put the cloak and dagger stuff out of his mind for the rest of the evening. He settled in on the bed in his room, choosing to camp out and study there rather then another trek over to the library. He was tired, and the long walk back across campus had little appeal. He spent the next two hours looking over a variety of topics, including reading ahead for tomorrow's lectures. By ten o'clock, he was exhausted, more mentally than physically. He stacked everything back up and decided to call it a night.

He thought once more of the Charlie enigma, but his mind was spent. A good night's sleep would hopefully shed some new light on the matter, and he deferred any decisions until in the morning.

He crawled into bed after his usual nightly routine. Feeling a little lost and alone, he picked up the phone and tried to call his parents. There was no answer, and he wondered what the hell his mom and dad would possibly be doing at 10:30 on a week night. Probably out somewhere having more fun than he was.

Sleep did not come easily that night for Rick as his mind jumped from one topic to the next. He finally made himself relax and slow down by forcing his mind to concentrate on relaxing his body, one part at a time. It did the trick, and he fell into a restless sleep around midnight.

CHAPTER 7

Despite all of the recent chaos in his life, Rick had not forgotten Monika's parting words yesterday. He did not sleep well, and was wide awake when his alarm went off at 6:30. Class didn't start until 8:00, but he was accustomed to hitting the snooze button three or four times, and set the alarm early enough to compensate. This morning he got up with the first alarm, and ate a leisurely breakfast while watching the sun rise and fill his room. His thoughts alternated between sitting next to Monika in class today and solving the Charlie mystery. Both subjects were equally captivating.

By 7:30 the walls were closing in. Rick gathered his things and headed out the door. The hallways were beginning to come alive as everyone prepared to start their day. He took a detour through the cafeteria and bought a large cup of coffee. He looked around briefly for Jessie, but she was nowhere to be seen. He arrived at the lecture hall twenty minutes early, but decided to go on inside and claim his spot. Much to his delight, a familiar face was there to greet him.

"I see I'm not the only early bird around here," said Monika. She was sitting on the opposite side of the room from her usual locale, and was actually in the exact same seat that Rick had used yesterday. Rick smiled widely with genuine enthusiasm.

"Good morning," he answered, wishing he had something more clever to say.

"I hope I didn't get your seat," she said.

"Actually, I'm afraid I'm going to have to ask you to move. I've got some gum stuck under the desk right there that I was saving for this morning."

They both smiled and laughed. "I'll tell you what," said Monika. "I'll give you a brand new piece of gum if you don't make me move. I've got it in my purse right here."

"I don't know," he said, sitting down to her left. "That was a real special piece."

"Well, you're just gonna have to get over it, cause I'm not moving."

"I'd fight you for it, but it's too early in the morning and I don't want to spill my coffee."

Rick set his backpack on the desk in front of him and began pulling out his text and notebooks. A few others had begun to arrive, but the room was still mostly empty. Monika had only a loose leaf notebook and a pen, both of which sat in front of her on the desk.

"So what are you doing here so early?" asked Rick.

"I don't know. Couldn't sleep this morning, I guess. Thought I'd just come on and wait up here instead of pacing at home."

"Sounds like my morning. I didn't sleep too good either."

"The pressures of med school getting to you already?" she asked.

"Something like that," he replied, not really sure just what he should tell her about last night. It was something he hadn't really thought about, but was wishing now that he had. "Just got a lot of things on my mind."

"Don't we all."

"So what do you have on your mind, Dr. Reese?" he asked. The title sounded odd to them both.

"Nothing in particular really. Just a bunch of little things catching up with me."

"Anything I can help out with?" he asked, happy to shift the line of questioning from him to her.

"No, it's nothing. I just had dinner with my father last night, and he stirred up a bunch of things that I don't really want stirred up right now."

"I think that's what families are for, isn't it?"

"My father certainly is, anyway," she replied, staring down at her blank paper.

Rick could sense her uneasiness with the conversation, and decided to let her off the hook. Making her uncomfortable was the last thing he wanted to do right now.

"I'm hoping this large cup of coffee will get me through this lecture today, but give me a shove if I start snoring too loudly."

"Only if you promise to do the same."

By five till eight, most of the class had arrived. Dr. Robbins' policy of locking the doors at eight was very effective, and the few that had tried unsuccessfully to sneak in late on Tuesday were already in their seats and ready to begin. Cameron was of course nowhere to be seen. Evan had just arrived and took the empty seat on the other side of Rick.

"Mind if I join you two?" he asked.

"Not at all. Pull up a chair."

"Hi Evan," said Monika, leaning forward to see around Rick.

"Hi Monika. How are you this morning?"

"I've been worse. You doing ok?"

"I'm fine, thanks. Ready to get through another day."

As Evan got settled in, Dr. Robbins walked up to the podium from out of nowhere and tapped his finger on the microphone. There was no sound heard over the speakers, which he signaled to the technician in the control booth by cupping his right hand behind his ear. A few seconds later he tried again and this time the mic seemed to be working fine.

"Good morning class. Let's all take our seats and prepare to begin."

Rick leaned over to Evan and whispered. "Kinda sounds like Mr. Rogers, doesn't he."

"A little bit," he answered back. "Think he's going to change into tennis shoes and a sweater before he starts talking?"

"I wouldn't be surprised."

"Ladies and gentlemen, if you will please open your syllabus to page 8 and follow along with me."

Rick leaned over to Monika. "Wake me when it's over."

"You think we can make a break for it before they lock the door?"

"It's probably already too late," he replied, not sure if she was serious or not.

The next fifty minutes was mostly spent fighting off sleep. Somehow Dr. Robbins could take a subject like psychology and the human mind, something Rick found fascinating, and turn it into drudgery. He decided Cameron might just be on to something, and thought seriously about sleeping in on Tuesday and Thursday mornings from now on. His mind wandered aimlessly, thinking mostly about Charlie Ellis once again. He and Monika would whisper a few comments back and forth, and Evan actually made them laugh once or twice with the occasional smart remark. He finished at ten till nine, right on time, and everyone quickly exited the lecture hall.

The class moved as one large flock up to the fifth floor Microanatomy lab. Cameron was there waiting when the other three arrived at their table. He had a bagel in one hand and a large cup of coffee in the other.

"You didn't have to bring us breakfast, Cameron," said Evan. "What a nice gesture."

"Not a chance, chief. Get your own damn food."

"I already had my Cocoa Puffs this morning. I'll just wait till lunch."

"Did I miss anything this morning?" asked Cameron.

"I wouldn't know. I slept through most of it," said Monika.

"Just read your syllabus and you'll find it all there," said Evan.

"If you would just spend that extra hour sleeping in your bed, and not in that uncomfortable chair, you wouldn't be getting those dark circles under your eyes."

"Who's got dark circles?" she replied, wiping with her fingers as if to rub them away.

"How would you know the seats were uncomfortable anyway?" asked Evan, smiling. "You ever sit in one?"

"Everyone's a smart ass."

"Are we gonna get started, or just jack around all day?" asked Rick, seeming somewhat annoyed.

"No one's stopping you, chief. You just have at it."

"Rick's right. We better get to work or we're gonna be spending lunch up here."

"Williams hasn't even given us his spiel for the day. We've got plenty of time."

"I don't think he does that every day," said Evan. "I think we're just supposed to dive right in."

"Speaking of diving," said Cameron, "I thought ol' Rick here was gonna take a dive at the end of that lab yesterday. What the hell was that all about?"

Rick looked up from his microscope, where he was already looking at the first slide. "I just felt a little sick, that's all." He quickly looked back down.

"You sound like Evan over here. Why the hell would you be feeling sick?"

This time he didn't even bother looking up. "I don't know, maybe just a stomach bug or something."

"Stomach bug hell. You looked like you saw a ghost or something."

Rick wasn't sure if he was ready to talk about all of this just yet. He still had no real idea what was going on, and had hoped to look into it all a bit more before discussing it with anyone.

"I just thought that cadaver looked familiar, that's all."

Evan and Monika were listening with interest. This was the first they had heard of any of this.

"Oh Rick, tell me it wasn't somebody you knew," said Monika.

Rick thought for a second. Maybe it wasn't such a bad idea to talk about this a little bit. Maybe someone would be able to figure out what had happened to Charlie. He had turned it over in his own mind so many times, that it made less sense now than it had from the beginning.

"Remember that ER rotation I did right before school started up?" Everyone nodded.

"I kind of got to know one of the patients that had come through there several times. I was also there the night he died."

"And that's who's body you saw in the lab yesterday?" asked Evan.

"Yeah. Charlie Ellis. Back from the grave."

"You sure it was him?" asked Cameron.

"Positive. I watched an intern sew up that scar across his chest. It was him."

Monika finally jumped in. "So you think he donated his body to the lab?"

"That's just it. I know he didn't. I even went to his funeral and watched them drop him into the ground. He's supposed to be out in Lawson's cemetery feeding the earthworms."

"Then how the hell could he be lying up there in that lab?" said Cameron.

"That's the million dollar question."

"That's pretty damn strange," said Evan. "Like something straight out of a horror movie or something."

"Except this time it's real."

"So what are you gonna do about it?" asked Evan.

"I don't know. Thought about talking to Shires today, but now I'm not so sure."

"What do you mean?" said Monika.

"What if this isn't all on the up and up? What if something illegal's going on here and Shires is behind it. I'm not sure approaching him is the best idea."

Cameron started laughing. "You have been watching too many late night movies, chief."

"Have I, Cameron? Then tell me how somebody I saw buried three weeks ago is now lying up there on a dissecting table."

He thought for a moment. "Maybe that's what he wanted to do. Maybe he just did the funeral thing for his family, but really wanted his body donated to science."

"I don't think so. This guy wasn't all that close to his family. He hadn't seen any of them in years. Why would he go to all that trouble for some people he didn't really care all that much about?"

"People do strange things when they're dying."

"If he did want his body up there," said Evan, "there would be record of a consent form giving the school permission."

"That's what made me think of Shires. If this is legit, then he'll have some kind of paperwork showing that it is."

Evan was really getting into this now. "But if this is some sort of scam, there won't be any paperwork to find."

"Unless the CIA helped him obtain some forgeries that they got from the mob in exchange for a cut of some confiscated drug money, as long as they promised not to tell who shot JFK."

"I'm being serious, Cameron. I want to know what the hell's going on."

"It does sound very unusual," added Evan.

"You two are a couple of fruitcakes. Some old homeless guy dies and gives up his body to science, and you two are trying to make some big conspiracy out of the whole thing."

"You've been awfully quiet Monika. What do you think?"

"I'm afraid I'm with Cameron on this one. Anything besides what he just said sounds awfully far-fetched."

"Far-fetched maybe, but I know what I saw. I'm willing to bet that Charlie Ellis and his family had no intentions other than him pushing up daisies in Lawson's cemetery."

"I think you're losing it, chief. Pressures of school and all that."

"I'm done talking about it. I know what I saw."

"So what are you gonna do about it?" asked Monika.

"I don't know yet. I'm not sure what I can do, but I'm not ready to let it go yet."

Cameron was growing impatient with the whole discussion. "Are we gonna do any real work today, or are you guys gonna keep talking about dead bodies all morning?"

"Cameron's right," said Rick, ready to change the subject. "We've got to get through the next twenty slides before lunch, and I sure don't need to get behind this early in the year."

As if on cue, Dr. Williams came out of nowhere and stood in front of their table. He looked down at the unopened slide boxes and empty microscopes, then spoke to Rick.

"So tell me, Mr. Stanley, how are we coming along today?"

Rick looked up sheepishly. "We're actually just getting started here, sir."

How much of their conversation had he just heard?

"I can see that. The laboratory started over twenty minutes ago, and I see that you and your partners have yet to view your first slide."

It was not really a question, but nevertheless Rick had no answer.

"I suggest you all get on with your work. The first week of medical school is no time to get behind. It will become progressively more difficult from this point forward."

"Yes sir," they all mumbled together.

"Very well then. If you should require any assistance, I shall be available the remainder of the morning."

"Thank you Dr. Williams," said Monika. "We'll get right to work."

He walked away deliberately, stopping two tables down to terrorize the next batch of victims. They all took a deep breath.

"Nice work there, guys," said Cameron. "Way to start off the new class."

"You think he picked up on much of that?" asked Rick.

"Much of what, your little fairy tale over there?" replied Cameron.

"I don't think he heard anything," said Evan. "He just walked up right there at the end.

"I hope you're right," said Rick. He looked around and saw Williams still two tables down. "Let's get started before he comes back around again."

Everyone plugged in their microscopes and began working through the morning's assignment. Rick looked down at the first slide, but found it difficult to concentrate. His mind began to wander, and his eyes soon followed suit. He realized how close together the lab tables were, and hoped no one else had been listening to their conversation this morning. It was bad enough that Williams might have been eavesdropping. This was not something he was prepared to discuss with anyone else right now. He cursed himself for bringing it up at all, wishing he had kept it to himself until he decided on a course of action.

The lab seemed to drag on forever. The images on the slides began blurring together, and Rick knew halfway through that he would have to review them all again. They made idle small talk at the table, but things were uncharacteristically subdued. Monika seemed especially withdrawn, and spent most of the morning looking quietly through her scope. Evan was his usual intense self, no doubt memorizing every microscopic detail of every slide. Cameron was working quickly, making only a cursory glance at each piece of tissue. By 11:30 he had finished his assignment and was out the door with little more than a goodbye.

Most people in the room finished up around noon, including Rick and his remaining two partners. Thursday would become the favorite day for most of the class, as there were no activities scheduled on that afternoon. Their only half day off, unless you took Cameron's attitude, and then every day was a half day. Most would spend the time studying, and the library would no doubt be full after lunch today.

Rick did not feel like making conversation, about Charlie or anything else for that matter. He made his quick goodbyes and headed back to the dorm by himself. He ate lunch, but wasn't hungry. Studying would be difficult, but he knew that he must.

He surprised himself over the next two hours. He had been able to clear his mind with relative ease, and actually accomplished a good bit of work. The anatomy slides from this morning crossed his mind, and he knew they would require much more intense examination before they would be mastered. He was mostly caught up with the lecture material, and had even read ahead some for tomorrow. The micro lab was definitely where he needed to spend the rest of his time this afternoon.

It was 3 o'clock now, and a slow afternoon drizzle fell outside his window. Great sleeping weather, he thought, if only he had the time to enjoy the luxury of an afternoon nap. His stomach was reminding him that he had little appetite at lunch time, and he decided it was time for a quick snack.

Rick had bought a few essentials at the grocery store last weekend, but the cupboards were still mostly empty. He rummaged through them briefly, but no matter how hard he looked, there was just nothing there. A little fresh air might do him good anyway, so he opted for a quick trip to the cafeteria on his way to the micro lab.

The underground tunnel was meant for days like this. Rick rode down to the basement and headed across to the main hospital complex. The rain was falling harder now, and he watched it slam into the small skylights in the ceiling as he walked along. Definitely a day for playing inside.

The cafeteria was almost deserted. He walked through the line and poured himself a large cup of coffee. The large cookies they sold were homemade and delicious, and Rick gathered up three of them to go along with the coffee. He smiled when he noticed Jessie manning the cash register.

"Hello Dr. Stanley, why aren't you in class?"

Rick set his backpack down and reached for his wallet. "You checkin' up on me or something, Miss Jessie?"

"I don't want nothin' to do with your business. I'm just makin' talk, that's all."

"We don't have any classes on Thursday afternoons, if you must know," he said smiling. "And I'm heading over to the lab to do some studying."

"Not that lab with all those dead bodies? I don't know how y'all do all that."

"It's not that bad once you get used to it, but today I'm going to the lab with all the microscopes. I've had enough of dead bodies for right now." He had almost managed to forget about Charlie for a few minutes, but there he was right back again.

"I heard there was a girl in there a few years ago who saw her own daddy on one of them tables. I swear I would've had a heart attack and died right there."

"Now Jessie, you know that's probably just some story that's been spread around that never really happened."

"I don't know, Dr. Stanley. There ain't no tellin' where they get them bodies."

Rick was amazed at how her last sentence had summarized his thoughts over the last couple of days. He found himself wondering if she knew something more than she was telling, but realized it was simply idle small talk.

"I'm sure that's just some wild story that's gotten blown out of proportion over the years."

"I just don't trust that man up there," she offered.

"What man?"

"You know, that man. Dr. Shires. I just don't trust him, that's all."

She had piqued his interest. "What do you mean, you don't trust him?"

"I just don't trust him."

"You've got to have a reason. Why do you say that?"

"It's just a feeling, that's all. I don't have to explain it. It's just a feeling."

Several junior students had entered the cafeteria, all clad in their short white coats, and were making their way to the register. Rick glanced at his watch and knew he had to get back to work. He wanted to pin Jessie down more on her story, but this wasn't the time.

"How much do I owe you, Miss Jessie?"

"Let's see," she said, pretending to add in her head. "Three cookies and one large coffee. That comes to thirty two cents with tax."

"One of these days you're gonna have to teach me this new math of yours," he said, handing her two quarters.

She gave him back his change and he walked away just as the small group of students approached. He decided to head straight for the lab, starting in on one of the cookies as he walked. He was already working on the third one by the time he got to his table. He was not really surprised to find Evan sitting there.

"Hey Evan, what's going on?"

He looked up from his microscope. "Hey Rick. Just looking over these slides from this morning. What are you doing here?"

"Same thing, I guess. Gotta keep up with you, ya know."

"I don't know about that. I'm just trying to keep up myself."

Rick set his backpack down on the table, took a drink of his coffee, and finished the last of the cookies. He looked around and saw twenty five or thirty people scattered across the room. Evidently they were not the only ones just trying to keep up. He walked out to his locker in the hallway and retrieved his scope and slides, stopping along the way to speak with a few friends.

Back at the table, he plugged in the scope and opened the box of slides. The first one was a section of skeletal muscle, which he locked into place and began to review under low power. Evan seemed deep in thought, alternating between an intense stare into the scope and writing down careful notes.

"You seen Cameron or Monika this afternoon?" asked Rick.

"Not since lunchtime. I'm not sure what they're doing this afternoon."

Rick flipped over to high power. "I felt like I rushed through all these this morning. I probably don't remember a thing."

"Have you thought any more about what we talked about this morning?" asked Evan.

"About the cadavers? I've thought about it plenty. Just haven't come up with anything yet."

Evan looked up and turned off the light on his scope. "Well I've been thinking about it lately myself."

"Oh you have?"

"Yeah. And I think you've got a point. It doesn't make any sense, does it?"

"I sure can't put it together."

"You're one hundred percent certain that the body in the lab is the person you say it is?"

"No doubt in my mind."

"Well then there can't be any legitimate explanation for him being there. Not if you saw him buried at his funeral. There's got to be a scam working somehow."

"That's about what I've decided myself."

"It has to be one of two things, really. Either this man wanted his body donated to the school and didn't tell his family, or somebody took it illegally without his consent."

"Well, he was a little quirky. I guess it's possible that he put on the funeral just for show and really wanted us to use his body."

"That's certainly a possibility."

"It just doesn't sound like him, that's all. I didn't know him all that well, but he hadn't spoken with his family in years. I can't imagine him going through all that trouble and expense just for them. If he wanted to donate his body, he would have just done it."

"So what are you gonna do about it?" asked Evan.

"I don't know. I should just drop it and forget the whole thing, but I'm not sure that I can."

"I'm not sure that you should, either."

"What do you mean?"

"What if they did obtain his body illegally? If that's what happened, you really think this is the first and only person it's happened to? It's unlikely that this is an isolated incident."

"Why would they do something like this in the first place? There's obviously a legitimate place to get cadavers. You wouldn't think they'd have to resort to stealing bodies."

"You said he was one of those last three they brought in?"

"Yeah, he wasn't there at Monday's lab. At least he wasn't out on one of the tables anyway."

"I think we're going to have to figure out what's happened here."

"What are you thinking, Evan? I think I hate it already."

"I think we need to do a little detective work and sort this out."

"You mean like checking with Dr. Shires?"

"Well not exactly," he smiled.

"What does that mean?"

"You said it yourself earlier. What if Shires is involved in this somehow? It's hard to imagine that he's not. Unless your buddy wanted to be up there in that lab, which seems unlikely, then Shires has got to be tied into this somehow."

"I don't know, Evan. He's the fucking chairman for Christ's sake. He might not even be involved in obtaining the cadavers. There's probably someone else in the department who oversees all of that."

"He may be totally innocent, I agree. But what if he's not? We certainly can't just walk right up to him and ask."

"I almost did last night."

"It's probably best that you didn't find him."

"All right, Columbo, what do you think we should do next then?"

Evan paused for a second. "We need to have a look in his office."

"There is no fucking way I'm going back into that office after hours again. I nearly had a heart attack last night when Dr. Williams walked in on me."

"You didn't tell me about that."

"I was actually inside Shires' office last night. I went looking for him, and when he wasn't there I walked into his office. I was thinking about nosing around a little when I heard footsteps. Williams walked in and I made up some lame story about looking for Shires."

"You think he knew what you were up to?"

"I don't think so, but who knows."

"So you were thinking about looking around there last night then, weren't you?"

"I was then, but I'm not so sure now. You're talking about breaking into the office of the department chairman. You know what that would mean if we got caught?"

"Then we won't get caught," smiled Evan.

"Dammit Evan," he whispered loudly. "This isn't a fucking game. If they catch us snooping around in his office they'll throw us both out of med school."

"So you're gonna just let them get away with stealing bodies?"

"We don't know that's what they're doing."

"That's why we need to find out for sure. If we find something suspicious, then we can go to the cops."

"Why don't we just go to the cops right now?" asked Rick.

"And tell them what?"

"That there's a body upstairs that ain't supposed to be there."

"For all we know it is supposed to be there. If we drag the cops down here and this turn's out to be something stupid, can you imagine what that's gonna be like for us afterwards?"

"It beats getting caught breaking and entering."

"Who's breaking anything? You said yourself the door was unlocked last night. All we have to do is have one of us stand guard at the door into the hallway. If someone comes by we just act like we were up there looking for Shires to ask him a question or something."

Rick searched for another argument, but was running out of them quickly. He stared at Evan who was smiling from ear to ear. "This ain't the damn Hardy Boys, you know that."

"I never said it was. I'm right and you know it. We slip in, find what we need to find, and slip out. How could it be any easier?"

"I can't believe you're actually talking me into going back up there."

"Cause you know I'm right."

"So what's your plan, Mr. Bigshot Detective?"

"What time were you up there last night?"

"I don't know. Around six thirty or seven."

"Then let's make it seven thirty. Hopefully everyone will be cleared out of there by then."

"Maybe we ought to wait until after dark, like ten or eleven," said Rick.

"They might lock things up by that time. I'm surprised he doesn't lock his office when he leaves for the night. Maybe security comes through and locks everything."

"Great. There's another way for us to get busted. I hadn't even thought about security."

"Like I said, we're just two med students looking for a little after hours help from one of our professors. We'll be fine."

"You wanna meet up somewhere?" asked Rick.

"How bout I come by your room around seven o'clock tonight. We can go over this one more time and then head out from there."

"Ok, that sounds good. You know we're crazy for trying this."

"We're gonna be fine, don't worry."

Rick looked back down at his microscope. He had almost forgotten why he had come up here in the first place. "I've got to get to work on this stuff."

"I think I'm about finished here for the day," said Evan as he began to gather up his things. "I'm going to the library for a while to look over tomorrow's stuff."

"I guess I'll see you tonight then."

"I'll be there at seven sharp."

"I think I'm gonna throw up," Rick said quietly. Evan was halfway out the door and didn't hear him.

*   *   *   *

Lloyd Harper sat alone in his office, looking over last month's official financial statements. The real reports, the one's showing the true debits and credits, were carefully locked away in the office safe. Only he knew the combination, and he planned to keep it that way. He was deep in thought, pouring over the numbers to be sure they added up properly and looked appropriate. The IRS could be meticulous if they so desired, and he was extremely cognizant of that fact. Everything would be perfect.

The sound of the phone startled him. He picked it up before the second ring, annoyed by the interruption. It was his private line, not the number listed for the public.

"Yeah."

"What the hell do you think you're doing?"

"Whatever happened to hello?"

"Tell me you're not selling bodies."

"I don't know what you're talking about."

"Don't play that with me, Harper. The new bodies in the cadaver lab. Tell me you've got nothing to do with that."

"I don't know what you're talking about. Why would you think I was selling bodies?"

"Cause I know you Harper. And I know that you'll do anything for a buck. This whole thing just sounds like something you'd be involved in."

"Look dammit. The only body business that I'm in besides our work is putting them in the ground."

"You better be telling me the truth. Cause if I find out you're picking up a little extra work on the side, you'll be the next one they're cutting up into little pieces."

"Are we done talkin', or do you wanna threaten me some more?"

"I mean it Harper. Don't fuck around with me. Our work is too important to risk for a few extra bucks."

"I'm not gonna say it again. I had nothing to do with your little black market cadavers, and if you accuse me of any more bullshit, our association is finished."

The caller hung up the phone without another word.

CHAPTER 8

Even though Rick was expecting the visitor, the knock at seven o'clock made him jump. Evan was predictably punctual, and entered the room quickly.

"I half expected you to show up wearing dark clothes and a ski mask," said Rick.

"I didn't have time to pick one up, or I just might have."

"Are we really going through with this? Seems kinda crazy, doesn't it?"

"Sure it's crazy. This whole thing is crazy. But we're gonna find some answers."

"I know we're doing the right thing," said Rick. I just can't get rid of this sick feeling in my stomach."

"I'm nervous too, but like you said, it's the right thing to do."

"So how are we gonna do this?"

"Pretty much like we said this afternoon, I guess. One of us stands guard, and the other slips into the office and looks for clues."

"Now you sound like Velma from Scooby Doo."

"I'll go with you for two Scooby Snacks." Evan was enjoying this just a little too much.

"If anyone walks in, let's say we were working up in the lab, had a few questions, and stopped in to see if Shires could come up and give us a hand."

"That sounds pretty good," said Evan. "Maybe we should swing through the lab first to help back up our story. Make sure it's unlocked and everything."

"Good idea. I think you should be the one to stand guard. I started this whole mess, and if anything goes wrong, I should be the one who's hand is in the cookie jar."

"I guess I won't argue with that. What kind of things are you gonna look for?"

"I think it's something I won't know until I see it. Hopefully there'll be some kind of paperwork showing where the cadavers are from. Or maybe some type of consent form, like we said earlier."

"We're sure we want to do this?" asked Evan. It was the first hint of uncertainty he had shown since this started earlier this morning.

"I know I don't want to do this. But I can't think of any other option, can you?"

"There isn't one. Just making sure you don't want to back out."

"Let's get going before we talk each other out of this."

The two prowlers left Rick's dorm room and rode down to the basement. It was still raining, perhaps even harder now. An occasional clap of thunder could be heard, even on the underground level. It seemed to fit the aura of the night.

Once in the Education 1 Building, they rode up to the 8th floor. The evening was darker than usual with the storm clouds filling the sky. The hall lights were out as well, giving the air a surreal glow. They walked to the end of the long hallway, following the light to the anatomy lab. The door was unlocked and several students were inside looking over their dissections from the day before. Rick and Evan peered through the glass in the door, but decided not to go inside. No point in raising any more suspicion as to why they were there. They had seen enough to support their bailout story, and that was all they needed.

The stairwell opened up directly in front of the laboratory entrance, and they decided to walk down the three flights. Stepping out onto the 5th floor, they saw the lights were turned off there as well. The offices seemed miles down the hallway, but fortunately it was deserted and they passed through undisturbed. The outer door was wide open, just as it had been last night. They took a deep breath and walked in shoulder to shoulder.

"Dr. Shires?" said Rick softly.

They were answered with silence.

"There's his office right there," he whispered to Evan.

"I don't see anyone around," he replied, a look of both fear and excitement in his eyes.

"Wait here. I'm gonna try the door."

Rick walked the few steps over to the office door. He tapped lightly and called out his name once more, but Dr. Shires was not there. The knob turned easily, and Rick stepped inside, trying not to think about what he was doing. The office was dark and without windows. He flipped on the small desk lamp in front of him, leaving the overhead turned off. He glanced up at Evan, flashed him the ok sign, and got to work.

If only he knew what he were looking for. Some kind of paperwork showing receipt of the bodies was his best bet. He searched on the desktop first, which was littered with journals, textbooks, old mail, and a few note pads. He rifled through the mail but saw nothing of interest. Nothing was written on any of the note pads. None of the desk drawers were locked, but they seemed to contain little of interest.   There was a mountain of bookshelves and two large filing cabinets behind him and it was difficult to know where to even start.

He checked the large clock on the wall. It felt like he had been inside for hours, but was really less than three minutes. The rhythmic tick of the second hand was deafening, and Rick felt the walls moving in on him. He walked around the desk back to the door and saw Evan, his head stuck out in the hallway looking left and right, like he was about to cross a street. He forced himself back into the office. They had come this far. He had to find something before they left.

Both file cabinets were locked from top to bottom. The keyhole in the top right corner was depressed in the locked position, and there was no key in sight. He spent the next couple of minutes looking for one, but found nothing that would fit into the lock. This had to be where the papers were kept. The desk was clean, and the bookshelves were filled with texts and little else. If something was here, it was behind those locked drawers.

"How you coming?"

Rick jumped so hard he thought he would throw up.

"Shit Evan! Don't sneak up on me like that!" He took his first breath. "You're supposed to be guarding the door."

"There's nobody out there. I want to come help you look for a minute. Have you found anything in here?"

"Not a thing, and get back out at that door!" Rick was ready to leave. He just wasn't cut out for a life of crime.

"I told you there's nobody out there. What's in those file cabinets?"

"That's what we need to find out. Whatever we're looking for has got to be in there."

"Are they locked?"

"No, I just didn't want to open them until the mood was just right." Rick was really ready to leave.

"You don't have to be a smart ass. I'm just asking a question. Have you found anything at all?"

"Nothing. The desk drawers are clean. Just these note pads on top of the desk, but there's nothing written on any of them. It's got to be in the file cabinets."

"I've got an idea," said Evan.

Rick watched as he tore the front page off each of the three pads, folded them in half, and placed them inside his pocket.

"What are you doing?"

"I'll show you later. Let's look for the key for this thing," he said, looking back at the cabinets.

"That's what I was doing before you scared the hell out of me. One of us should really be watching the door."

Evan continued on as if he hadn't heard a word out of Rick's mouth. "Where have you looked so far?"

"Well, everywhere in the desk." He looked around the room. "And in Shires' coat pockets. That's about it I guess."

"Feel around underneath all these surfaces. He may have it taped or nailed underneath here somewhere."

They had just begun their search when Rick heard the noise. Evan was intense and focused, but soon heard it too. Footsteps. Coming down the hallway. Towards them.

"Somebody's coming!" whispered Rick loudly.

Both men panicked. All contingency plans were immediately forgotten. The scene unfolded in slow motion as their minds raced. Evan fell to the floor behind the large oak desk. Rick stood in the middle of the room helpless. Then his head began to clear.

"Out here Evan, let's go!" he cried, motioning to the outer office.

"Not a chance. It's too late. Find some cover."

Rick's supper was in his throat as his head whirled left, then right, looking for a place to hide. There were none. He started to go back out of the office, but the visitor was now much to close. Another couple of seconds and he would be there. He knew there was no way he could step out of the office and compose himself without appearing guilty as hell, especially with Evan hiding underneath the desk. He saw a man's hand reach in and push open the door from the hall.

*   *   *   *

It had been over an hour since the phone call, but Mr. Harper was still hot. He did not like being threatened, and the thought of it made him crazy. He paced the floor like a caged cat, feeling strangely claustrophobic in the small office. Mumbling and cursing to no one but himself, he would appear to the casual observer as delusional, perhaps almost schizophrenic. He was neither.

Lloyd Harper was a very smart man. He had two major weaknesses, however, both of which he readily acknowledged. Money and women. The money came rather easily to him, through a large number of mostly illegal activities. The women were a different story, and most of his contact with the opposite sex required cash up front, whether on the phone or live and in person. The fact that he bought all of his women did not seem to bother him in the least.

What bothered him was being threatened. It showed disrespect, something he had put up with for a good portion of his existence, but was now in a position where he would tolerate it no longer. He knew he should just let things roll off his back, but that was not easy for a man such as him.

He finally forced himself back to the task at hand. He had become quite adept at working the books, almost to the point of enjoying it. The hardest part about illegal moneys was the paper trail. Most of his endeavors had become a cash only business, which did simplify things somewhat. He would then transfer the cash to one of several offshore accounts, always using a different local bank for each transaction. He kept a careful account of every penny, as well as a separate set of books with a proper set of numbers for an occupation such as his.

Most people squirmed at the thought of working with the dead, but Lloyd Harper had an odd morbid fascination with the non living. Working with a lifeless body gave him a sort of euphoria, almost, but not quite, sexual. His favorite part was the rush of blood when he slid a large catheter into one jugular vein and bled them out from the opposite side of the neck.

He would spend hours preparing them for their departure. They would always be meticulously dressed, hair just right, a little smile formed at the edge of their mouths. Often he would talk to them, asking questions about what it was like to move on to the next level. Most undertakers had a staff that took care of these sorts of things, but Mr. Harper would never be able to hand this part of his job over to anyone. He loved it too much.

Whenever he felt himself losing control, he would go downstairs to view the bodies. He felt that need tonight, and left his office to do just that, locking the door behind him. It was already early evening, and his sparse staff had all left long ago. He walked through the empty dim hallway to the long skinny elevator on the left. Just big enough to hold two people, one lying flat and the other standing. He activated the lift with his key and rode down the one flight with a smile on his face. He felt better already.

There were only two bodies in stock tonight, a rather small inventory by his standards. His funeral home was one of the busiest in this part of the city, and his census usually ran much higher. It had been a regrettably slow week. He was fortunate that he had enough to fill the order from Dr. Shires on Monday. He hated to part with any of his collection, but for $5000 a head, it was impossible to pass it up. As much as he loved his bodies, he loved his money even more.

The only two he had left had actually both come in today. One was a nice looking older lady from one of the nursing homes just down the street. Harper had chosen the site carefully when he built this structure several years ago, and it was no coincidence that there were three nursing homes and a hospital all within a half mile radius. After all, location was everything.

The second body was a young black man who had been shot in the chest. Some sort of gang activity he had guessed, based on the appearance of the man when he was brought in. Harper hated working with the 'niggers', and would always find a way to charge those families more. That made it only slightly more bearable. He would spend little time preparing the black man for his funeral. He knew it would be an open casket, they always were, so he would have to at least dress him. That would take no longer than fifteen minutes. Sometimes he wouldn't even embalm the 'niggers', and this would probably be one of those times. He couldn't wait to get him into the ground and out of his home.

He felt very much at ease in this room. He could feel his blood pressure dropping and his tension slipping away. He was at home here. The outside world did not exist. Just himself and his bodies. A man at peace. He sat down on the floor in the corner and rested his eyes. Tomorrow would be a better day.

CHAPTER 9

"Raymond?"

Rick and Evan did not move. They did not blink. They did not breathe.

"Anyone here?"

Silence.

Glenn Williams stepped into the well lit office, the one next to his own. The door pushed open, almost back to the wall, and he stepped inside. Evan was still crouched underneath the desk, but could not be seen. Rick had sprinted back into the office just as Dr. Williams was entering from the hallway. With only a second or two to react, he slipped behind the door in Shires' office and pressed himself into the wall. Through the crack at the hinges he could see Williams standing there, less than two feet away. He could see his face clearly, which meant that if he turned to the left about ninety degrees, they would be looking eye to eye. The thought was nauseating.

Rick watched as Williams walked over to the desk, switched off the lamp, and turned to leave. Rick leaned away from the hinges and prayed he would not be seen. He watched as Williams stopped at the door, turned to face into the room, and stood for a moment in silence. He then took a few steps back into the office and paused once again. Rick could not actually see him now, but his other senses were hyperacute as he listened to his every move.

After what felt like two hours, but was probably less than thirty seconds, Dr. Williams turned to leave once again. This time he did not pause at the door. He continued walking out the office, slowing to grab the doorknob as he pulled the door to behind him. Rick remained motionless against the wall. The room was now pitch black except for a small sliver of light which crept in from under the door. They both waited in silence, neither knowing what to do next. Rick's eyes slowly grew accustomed to the darkness, and soon he could make out the outline of the desk. Within five minutes he could actually see quite well.

Rick watched as the chair pushed slowly away from the desk. Evan's head first appeared, then the rest of his body as he put an arm onto the desk and struggled to pull himself up. He stared silently at Rick, both of them afraid to speak.

"You Ok?" mouthed Rick.

Evan nodded quickly but did not speak.

Rick walked over to Evan behind the desk where they could speak without being heard. He leaned over to him, his mouth almost touching his ear.

"We've gotta get outta here."

Evan nodded once again. "Now?" he asked silently.

"Not yet. Let's give Williams a little time."

"You think he went into his office?"

"Who knows. There's no way to see out there without opening the door. We're just gonna have to wait it out for a little while."

"What if Shires comes back?"

"Then we're screwed."

They stood in dark silence for a time, then growing weary, decided to sit down on the floor. Rick thought about continuing their search, but the darkness in the room made it nearly impossible. Besides, the only thing they really needed to search was the locked file cabinet, and without a key they were simply out of luck. He realized the best thing at this point was to wait in silence, which is exactly what they did.

It was nearly eight o'clock when their search was interrupted. Together they watched each minute tick off the clock until now it was almost nine. The sheer terror they had initially felt had given way to boredom. They both wanted out of the room badly, yet were afraid to open the door. By nine o'clock Rick had had enough.

"We've got to make a break for it," he said softly to Evan.

"I'm ready whenever you are. Surely he's left by now."

"Who knows. We've got to look sometime."

They gathered themselves off the floor, both somewhat stiff from the long delay. They looked around the room one final time. Everything appeared to be in order as far as they could tell, but it was hard to see much in the limited light. They walked over towards the door, almost afraid to touch the knob. Finally Rick reached his hand forward and turned it slowly. He took a deep breath in and pulled it open about an inch. Just enough to see.

What he saw was more darkness. They listened for a full thirty seconds, but the outer room remained silent. The door opened wider and Rick slipped only his head outside. A beam of light shone out from under Dr. Williams's door, and through the crack that was open up one side.

Rick stepped through the doorway, then waved Evan out as well. He pressed a finger to his lips, then pointed at the illuminated office as Evan made his way towards freedom. They continued quickly through the office towards the outer door, which was partially open in anticipation of their retreat. Rick led the way with Evan right on his heels, and they were soon into the hallway and headed for the stairs. Free at last.

The euphoria was short-lived, for as they rounded the corner towards the stairwell Rick ran full into Dr. Shires. His heart stopped once again.

"Hello gentlemen, working late I see."

Rick struggled for words as he felt the flush play up his neck and across his face. "Yes sir Dr. Shires. Working late sir."

"Did you fellows get lost? I'm not accustomed to running into students on this floor. Especially this time of night."

Rick's mind was a total and complete blank. If Shires had asked him his name, he would have been stumped. Fortunately Evan was thinking a little more clearly.

"We were actually coming to see you, Dr. Shires. We had a few questions about our dissection for tomorrow."

"Well, I'm certain that whatever you need to ask can wait until in the morning. I've got some business to attend to in my office, then I've got to get myself home. Perhaps you could come by in the morning?"

"Yes sir, that would be fine," answered Rick. He was coming around now.

"Very well then," he said, beginning to move down the hallway. "Good night gentlemen."

"Good night sir," they replied in unison.

"Do you realize," asked Rick, "just exactly how close we were to being thrown out of medical school? Another two minutes and he would have sat at his desk and kicked you in the nuts when he stretched out his legs."

"Let's get out of here. I can't stand another thing tonight."

Both men were stressed and ready to call it a day. They opted for the stairs, taking them slowly and one at a time. No need to run now. It was over. They walked back to the dorm in silence, not speaking until they had reached the elevators.

* * * *

Glenn Williams stepped out into the hallway and watched as the two intruders walked briskly away. He had heard a noise in the outer office, prompting him to get out of his chair and have a look. By the time he opened his door they were gone, but he could see them well as they scurried down the hall. He recognized them from his class, and knew them both by name.

He stepped back inside and noticed Dr. Shires' door widely ajar. He peered into the office for the second time that night. Everything appeared to be in order, but something wasn't right. He now knew that the two young men had been inside. They were probably there when he had come in earlier. Something was definitely amiss.

He walked back into his office where he had just finished going over his lecture for the next day. He gathered his things, stacked them neatly in his briefcase, and turned to leave. He checked twice to be certain the door was locked securely. Turning left into the hallway, he just missed Raymond Shires coming from the opposite direction.

* * * *

"So what's next?" asked Rick.

"You're not gonna like it."

"You can't scare me any worse than we have been tonight."

"We've got to see what's inside that file cabinet."

"Somehow I had a feeling you were gonna say that."

"Cause you know it's true."

Rick suddenly remembered something from the office. "What was with the note pad thing? You know they were all blank."

"No, I don't know that."

"What the hell are you talking about. I saw them myself. There's nothing on them."

"Come down to the room and let's try something."

Rick followed Evan down the hallway and into his room. The dorm was relatively quiet as most of the students were either off somewhere studying or lying in bed dreaming about the next day. Evan flipped on the overhead in the room and sat down at the desk. Rick pulled the other chair over and sat beside him.

"Didn't you ever watch any cop shows growing up?"

"My dad *was* a cop. He'd never let us watch any of them. Said they were too unrealistic or something like that."

"Hand me that pencil over there."

Rick reached over to the end of the desk and suddenly realized what he was doing. Evan pulled out the three blank pages from his back pocket and flattened them out on the desk with his hands. He took the pencil from Rick, lowered it almost flat with the first page, and began rubbing the lead back and forth, working from the top of the page down to the bottom. They held it up under the light and could just make out the writing.

> *dozen eggs*
> *2% milk (big one)*
> *cereal*
> *Prep H*
> *bread*

"It's a damn shopping list."

"Looks like the wife's got ole Raymond jumping."

"I don't think he's married," said Evan. "He doesn't wear a ring."

"That doesn't mean he's not married. Maybe he leaves it at home so he can pick up chicks."

"He doesn't strike me as the chick magnet type," replied Evan.

"At least not until he gets those hemorrhoids taken care of." They both shared a laugh.

"What's on the next one?" asked Rick.

Evan laid it down on the table and began his work with the pencil.

"This really works great," he said. "I've never actually done this before."

"What's it say?" asked Rick.

"Hang on. It's almost finished."

Together they lifted the paper up and held it to the light.

> *Harper*
> *297-9789*

"Who do you suppose Harper is?"

"There's one way to find out," replied Evan, reaching for the phone.

"You're gonna call right now? What the hell are you gonna say?"

Evan was already dialing. He leaned back in his chair and listened. Rick watched as the next twenty seconds went by. Finally Evan set the phone back down on the receiver.

"What were you gonna do if they answered?"

"They just did."

"They just did? Well who was it?"

"Harper Funeral Home."

"Isn't that over there on Jackson Parkway?"

"The one just down from that Super Wal Mart? I think so."

"What did they say?"

"I told you. Harper Funeral Home. That was it. Then I hung up."

"Why didn't you talk to them?"

"And say what?"

"I don't know," thought Rick. "Ask them if they knew Shires."

"You sure you're dad was a cop?"

"Still is a cop, smart ass."

"Let's see what this last one says."

"Here, let me try it," said Rick.

Evan handed over the pencil and Rick went to work. Thirty seconds later they held up the third and final sheet of paper. Besides the coloring from the pencil, the page was blank. Not a word to be found.

"That's what I thought we'd find. One of the notebooks looked brand new. It's probably never been written on."

"Not exactly a wealth of information we've uncovered here, Evan."

"I'm curious about this number. Doesn't it seem odd that an anatomy professor would be calling a funeral home?"

"You think there's a connection to the bodies?"

"Where was that funeral you said you went to?"

"The funeral itself was in that First Baptist Church off of Markham. They also had a grave side service out at Lawson's Cemetery."

"Don't suppose you know who the funeral home was, do you?"

"Not off the top of my head. I may actually have it written down somewhere though. I sort of helped plan things a little bit."

"I'm willing to bet anything you want that they used Harper's funeral home."

"I'll check when I get back upstairs, but that sounds familiar now that I think about it."

"You know we're gonna have to check this out some more."

"What about the cops? Maybe it's time we went to them."

"We still don't have anything to show them," said Evan.

"I guess you're right. All we've got is a phone number, and we found that by breaking into an office."

"We need to check out the funeral home. Maybe this weekend sometime."

"You realize we're still gonna need to check out that file cabinet too."

"I know. I've been trying to figure out how to get into it though."

"I've got an idea, but I'll have to check it out first."

"You think you can get a key?"

"I don't know," answered Rick. "I may know somebody who can get us one, but I'm not sure. I'll check on it tomorrow."

"We better call it a night. I've still got to look over tomorrow's lecture."

"Yeah, I need to do some work myself. It's already almost ten."

"I guess I'll see you in the morning then."

"I'll be there. I think Shires is giving the first lecture."

"It starts at eight o'clock, right?"

"I think so. I'll see ya then."

"Good night Rick."

Rick walked down the empty hallway and rode the elevator up to the eighth floor. His hallway was empty as well, as it usually was this time of night. He flipped on a few lights, turned on the stereo, and changed into a pair of shorts and a t shirt. He thought about calling Monika, but decided to wait until morning and talk to her between classes. He really needed to get some studying done tonight, and he knew if he called it could wipe out the rest of the evening.

It was difficult to concentrate on school as thoughts of black market bodies continued to enter his conscious mind. He thought about the implications of what they believed was taking place. If their suspicions were correct, then the chairman of the anatomy department was into some seriously illegal shit. The repercussions would be huge once word of this escaped. It would most certainly mean his job, and possible criminal charges. He felt a chill run down his spine as the realization began to sink in. They were about to open an epic can of worms, the fallout from which would most certainly shock the medical community. For the first time in his life he was truly scared.

CHAPTER 10

Rick stayed up late, but accomplished little. He finally gave it up around midnight, and had little trouble falling asleep. He awoke with his alarm, hitting the snooze button two or three times in a futile attempt to postpone the inevitable start of the day. His clock eventually won the battle, and he reluctantly got up and headed for the shower. It was Friday and he allowed himself the luxury of not shaving. Maybe he would try and grow a beard.

The classroom was remarkably full this morning, and most of the seats were already taken when he arrived. He found an empty chair towards the back of the room, sitting down just as Dr. Shires was walking towards the front. Rick immediately thought of their conversation last night, and how close they had really come to being discovered sitting there in his dark office. Somebody must have been watching out for them, because they should have been caught.

Monika was down towards the front of the room, sitting next to Evan. An unlikely pair, but they seemed to be getting along quite well. He was even more surprised when he spotted Cameron two rows down, poised with pen and paper in hand as if he might actually take a note. He was anxious to hear what strange force had drug him out of bed and brought him here today.

Class moved along at a fairly brisk pace. Shires spoke about some of the large arteries and veins found in the chest, the same ones they would be dissecting out in the lab this afternoon. It was actually quite interesting, and Rick's attention was held for most of the ninety minutes. There was a quick break before Microanatomy, and by the time he ran to the bathroom and back, Dr. Williams was ready to begin. He had wanted to slip down and talk with Monika, but it would have to wait until the next break.

When Williams finally finished talking it was nearly eleven thirty. Rick was one of the first out of the room, and he waited in the hallway for Monika and the rest of the team. She and Evan walked out together, followed closely by Cameron. They saw Rick standing alone and walked over to speak.

"I don't know what possessed me to sit through this crap today, but don't expect it to happen again."

"Guilty conscience Cam?" asked Rick.

"Hardly. Just wanted to see what I was missing. Doesn't look like it was much."

"I saw you taking notes down there," said Monika.

"A man's gotta do something to stay awake."

"You guys wanna get some lunch?" said Evan.

In a strange sort of way, Evan had almost become the leader of their little group. He had gone from meek little freshman to brimming with confidence in just a few short days. A strange transformation no doubt, but they all found themselves enjoying his presence. Even Cameron.

"You buying, chief?"

He thought for a moment. "I'll make you a deal Cameron. You start coming to all the lectures and I'll buy you lunch every Friday. You can even choose the place."

"I'll do a lot of things for free food, but I'm afraid that ain't one of 'em."

"Well, I guess you're on your own then."

Monika finally jumped in. "Why don't we all go eat at the cafeteria. We've only got about forty five minutes anyway. Not much time for anything else."

"If we're eating here, let's get moving. The noon mob is about to descend."

They walked quickly over to the cafeteria. It was still fairly early for lunch, but there were already several lines beginning to form. The four split up and filled their trays, then slowly made their way through the line at one of the registers. They met up on the other side and found an empty booth near the back. Yesterday's rain was a distant memory, and they could see the heat rising off the asphalt as the sun beat down. Thank God for air conditioning.

"So what'd you guys do last night?" asked Monika.

"Not a damn thing," answered Cameron. "I watched the Braves beat the hell out of the Twins."

"You better start studying Cameron. Our first round of tests is just over two weeks away."

"I'll study when I have to study. It's only the first week, give me a break."

"I looked for you two in the library last night," said Monika. "Don't tell me you got sucked into some baseball game too."

Evan and Rick looked at each other, not sure how much they should repeat of their little expedition last night. Finally Rick spoke.

"We went out on a little reconnaissance last night."

"A little what?"

"You guys aren't still working on that mystery cadaver crap, are you?"

"It's not crap," Evan shot back. "We're on to something huge."

"So what did you two do exactly?" asked Monika.

"We went straight to the source. Shires' office."

"And did what?" asked Cameron.

"We just poked around a little, that's all."

"Are you fucking nuts?" asked Monika, surprising them with the emotion of her response.

"I'm telling you guys, Rick has stumbled on to some serious shit here." Evan went on to detail the events of last night. He told them everything that had happened, and Rick decided not to stop him. He actually wanted to hear their thoughts on matter, and it felt good to get everything out in the open. When Evan finished the story, they both sat back and waited for the reaction.

"So what are you gonna do now?" asked Cameron, appearing slightly interested for the first time.

Rick shrugged. "We're not exactly sure."

"We know what we need to do, Rick's just not sure he wants to do it."

"And what is that exactly?"

"Two things really," said Evan. "We've got to see what's in that file cabinet in Shires' office. It's the only thing locked in that whole room. I'll bet there's some incriminating papers in there of some kind."

"Incriminating him in what?" asked Monika.

"I'm not sure really. He's probably involved in illegally obtaining cadavers from this funeral home."

"I still don't get why he would even have to do something like that," said Cameron. "Surely he can get whatever he needs from the state."

"I would have thought so too, but apparently not."

"You said two things. What's the other?"

Evan smiled. "The funeral home."

"I suppose you're gonna break in there too?"

"Perhaps. But first I think we should just go down there and talk with them."

"Excuse me sir," said Cameron. "I'm looking to obtain a few dead bodies and I was wondering if you might have any in stock for sale today."

They all laughed. "That wouldn't be my exact approach, but I do think we should check things out down there."

"You're awful quiet over there, Rick," said Monika. "What do you think about all of this?"

"I guess we need to follow through with everything like Evan was saying."

"You don't sound very convincing," said Monika.

"And it's your dead buddy up there," added Cameron.

"I guess all this detective shit makes me kinda nervous. I can't help but think what if we get caught. We were about two minutes away from being busted in Shires' office last night. We'd have been tossed out of medical school. I've worked too damn hard getting here to be kicked out now."

"I think you guys have lost your minds for doing what you've done already," said Monika. "You can't just go around breaking into professors' offices. I think you should both just let this whole thing drop. It's not worth it."

"What about you, Cameron?" asked Rick.

Cameron appeared serious for the first time all week. "I'm afraid I'm with Monika on this one guys. You're all playing like this is some big game or something. If you get caught going through Shires' things, you'll both be gone. I heard you say it, but I'm not sure it's really sunk in. Kicked out of medical school for chasing some BS story that will probably end up with some stupid, logical explanation anyway. Why take that chance and risk your whole career?"

Rick looked over to Evan. "They've got some good points."

"And we don't?" he replied without hesitation.

"Sure we do. I'm just not sure I'm willing to risk everything to prove we're right."

"We already know something's going on. We just need a little more information to back up our story."

"What about the police?" asked Rick. "Maybe we're at the point where we could talk with the police now."

"And tell them what?" asked Cameron. "That you broke into your professor's office and found a phone number to a funeral home? Best case scenario, they'll laugh you out of the office. Or maybe they'll just decide to arrest you both for breaking and entering. Or maybe they'll decide to ask

Shires a few questions, and then you get kicked out of school by him personally for breaking into his office."

"Not exactly the top three outcomes I was hoping for," said Rick.

"Maybe not your favorite, but they're the three most likely," replied Cameron.

"So what are you gonna do?" asked Monika.

Rick and Evan were silent. They looked at each other, then across the table at the voices of reason. There wasn't an easy answer. At least not for Rick.

"I already know what I'm doing. I'm gonna see what's in that file cabinet, and I'm gonna talk with this Harper guy at the funeral home."

"Why are you so damn fired up about this?" asked Cameron. "You didn't even know the guy that started this whole thing. I don't get it."

"What about you, Rick? You're the one that got me into this whole mess. Are you still with me on this one?"

"I'm gonna have to take some time and think about this Evan. Yesterday there was no doubt in my mind. Now that I've had some time to think on it, I just don't know. I still think something bad is happening here, I'm just not sure I'm willing to risk my career to figure it out."

"At least now you're talking a little sense," said Monika.

"You ought to listen to what he's saying," Cameron said to Evan. "You're all caught up in this like you're James Bond or something. You're gonna wind up getting your ass kicked out of here."

"Not if I'm careful I won't. My mind's made up. The rest of you can do whatever you want, but if you're not gonna help, then stay out of my way."

They finished their lunch quickly, making some small talk, but saying very little. No more was mentioned about the cadavers. When they were done, Cameron and Evan had to run back to the dorm to get their books for the afternoon lab. Rick and Monika walked together slowly by themselves. It was the first time they had really been alone in quite a while.

"What are you doing this weekend?" he asked her.

"To be honest, I haven't really even thought about it. What about you?"

"Studying mostly I guess." He tried not to think about cadavers and funeral homes. "I've kind of been slacking off these last few days. I've got some catching up to do."

"Yeah, me too. I feel like I'm three weeks behind, and this is still the first week."

Rick was suddenly very nervous. He had posed the weekend question innocently, but now had an idea. An idea that made his heart race and his stomach flip.

"Maybe we could get together Saturday night sometime? Go out for dinner or something."

They continued walking. Rick stared down at his shoes, afraid to make any eye contact. She answered quickly.

"You mean like a date?"

"Yeah. I guess it would be." He was beginning to sweat now. "If you've already got plans that's fine. I know it's kinda last minute. You've probably already got something lined up. Just forget I ever mentioned it." He could feel his face starting to flush.

"Actually, I don't have any plans at all. Other than studying I guess, which I've got to start tonight."

"So is that a yes?"

"Sure. Why not? Sounds like fun." She looked over at him and smiled. He knew his face was beet red, and he was embarrassed by it. She either didn't notice, or didn't say anything about it if she did. He actually thought she looked a bit flushed herself, but maybe it was just the lighting.

Rick wasn't sure what to say next. Fortunately they ran into a small crowd as they reached the elevator and avoided the uncomfortable silence. They chatted with their other classmates as they rode up to the eighth floor. Rick and Monika split into separate dressing rooms, changed into their old rags, and headed out to their table. Rick tried not to look over at Charlie's body, but found it very difficult. He tried to force it out of his mind and focus on other things, namely his own cadaver and Monika. Evan and Cameron were late, and they decided to begin without them. No mention was made of their new date tomorrow night.

They were joined by the rest of the team within a few minutes. They worked efficiently, but rather quietly, as everyone at the table seemed somewhat preoccupied. Most of the conversation was business only as they dissected out the great vessels in the chest. Time dragged on mercilessly.

They finished their work by 3:30 and were all ready to call it a day. Rick thought about going over to look at Charlie's body, but decided it best not to. Fortunately it was over on the other side of the lab, where he could continue to avoid it if he so desired.

After changing back into their clothes, they all met briefly outside the lab.

"So what's everyone doing this weekend?" asked Cameron.

"Studying," answered Rick quickly. "Lots of studying." He decided not to say anything about the date, and hoped Monika would do the same.

"Me too," she said. "That and hopefully catch up on a little sleep."

"Sounds too exciting for me," said Cameron.

"What big plans do you have then?"

"I'm going back home for a couple of days."

"You mean back to the farm? I thought you said you got rid of it."

"Well, not exactly. I still own it, I'm just leasing the land right now. I go back to the house every now and then. I've just got someone else working the farm."

"So what are you gonna do down there?" asked Rick.

"I've just got some business to take care of with some folks. I try to get down there every few months to keep the bankers and the lawyers happy. And I've got some friends that still live in the area."

"What about you Evan?"

"You guys know what I've got planned."

Rick was afraid to ask, but did anyway. "And just what is that?"

"You're all going around pretending like last night didn't happen. I told you, I'm gonna get to the bottom of this whole thing and figure out what's going on here."

"I was afraid you were gonna say that," said Rick.

"Shit Evan, let it go," added Cameron.

"He's right Evan," said Monika. "It's not worth it. Just give it up."

"Ok, whatever." They could tell he would not be persuaded.

"I guess I'll see you guys Monday morning," said Cameron.

"Don't you mean Monday afternoon?" replied Rick.

"I guess you're right. Monday afternoon it is." With that Cameron turned to leave, apparently heading for the stairwell. They watched him leave in silence, then walked over to the elevators to make their own exit.

"Can I come by tonight?" asked Evan, looking directly at Rick.

Rick glanced at Monika before answering. She frowned back at him. "Sure, I guess so. But I'm not promising anything."

"We'll talk more tonight."

Once outside, Rick and Monika paused while Evan continued on towards the dorm. A man on a mission. Monika looked troubled, and Rick knew the reason why.

"I don't know what I'm gonna do, but we at least need to sit down and talk about it. I honestly think I'm about ready to drop the whole matter."

"Well, you know how I feel about it, so I'll keep my mouth shut."

"What are you doing tonight?"

"I told you after lunch, I'm studying tonight. You men don't listen to a word we say."

"It's a genetic defect," he smiled. "Has to do with testosterone levels. Totally beyond our control."

"Well maybe you should get your levels checked then," she laughed back. "Anyway, that's all I've got on for tonight."

"I guess I'll probably do the same. Lord knows I need to."

"You mean after Evan leaves."

"I thought we weren't talking about that anymore."

"You're right. Call me in the morning?"

"You got it. We're still on for tomorrow night, right?"

"Unless I get a better offer," she replied.

"You're just hilarious, you know that?" He could feel himself blushing again, and decided he had better leave. "I'll talk to you in the morning."

"I'm counting on it," she said, turning towards the parking garage.

"Good night."

CHAPTER 11

By nine o'clock, Rick realized he could study no more. He had gone over most of his notes from the previous week, something he planned to make a Friday night tradition. His heart was never really in it, however, as he waited for the phone to ring. It never did.

He decided to give Evan a call, then thought twice and elected a face to face visit. He needed to stretch his legs and get out of the room for a while anyway, and this would be the perfect excuse. He was surprised that he had not heard from him yet, figuring Evan would be beating down his door by six.

Pulling a shirt over his head, he grabbed his keys and headed out the door. As he stepped onto the third floor, three of his classmates walked by on their way out for the night. They invited him along, but he regretfully declined. A little too much on his mind right now.

After the first unanswered knock, Rick knew that Evan was not there. Their rooms were nothing more than oversized coat closets, and if someone didn't answer the door right away, it usually meant there was nobody home. He tried a second time, knowing there would be no response. It bothered Rick that Evan was not in his room. As excited and determined as he had been earlier in the day, it was doubtful he was in the library studying. There was only one thing on the mind of Evan Sanders tonight, and it certainly wasn't homework.

Rick returned slowly to his room, taking the stairs one at a time. Evan's disappearance bothered him. He was undoubtedly off playing detective again. Perhaps he was back up in Shires' office, trying to break into the file cabinet. Or maybe he was paying Mr. Harper a visit, trying to make a connection with the school. Wherever he was, it couldn't be good. Rick was worried.

Back in his room, Rick mulled over his options. He considered an attempt to track him down, but quickly dismissed that notion. The thought of a third night in a row illegally inside the office of Dr. Shires was more than he could stand. He would have to wait until Evan came to him. Further studying just didn't seem possible. What to do on a Friday night?

Then he thought of Monika. Home alone. Studying. Maybe he should give her a call. That thought also sent his stomach spinning, but in a good sort of way. He decided to give it a try. Picking up the phone, he immediately realized he did not know what number to dial.

It had never occurred to him to ask for her number. Never even crossed his mind. And now he had a date with her tomorrow night, wanted to talk with her tonight, and wasn't really sure how to track her down. The frustration level for the evening was escalating.

There was no Monika Reese listed in the phone book. Not a big surprise, since they had only been in town for a week. He tried information, but she had no listing. He was sure she had a phone, or she wouldn't have asked him to call in the morning. There had to be a way.

He pulled out the orientation packet they had all received over the weekend and found the list of student names. It included their undergraduate school and hometown, but no phone number. Then he had an idea. He dialed the medical center operator, and she picked up on the twenty third ring.

"University Hospital, operator 12, may I help you?"

"Yes ma'am, I'm trying to get the phone number of one of the freshman medical students, Monika Reese. Do you have that listing?"

"One moment sir, let me check." Rick waited. "Yes sir I do, but I'm not allowed to give out the home telephone numbers."

"What are you talking about?"

"I'm sorry sir, but I cannot release that number."

"But you don't understand. I'm a classmate of hers and I need to get in touch with her tonight. It's very important."

"What is your name, sir?"

"Rick Stanley." He spelled the last name for her, as if there were more than one way.

"What is your home number Mr. Stanley?"

"My number? Hang on a sec." He looked at the receiver in his hand to be sure he remembered the new number correctly. "293-9908"

"Thank you sir. One moment." He waited once again. "Thank you sir. That number is 291-0293."

"Thank you. Thank you very much." He hung up and scribbled the number down quickly. Now the hard part. He had to make the call.

Following a trip to the bathroom, a snack from the refrigerator, picking out his clothes for tomorrow, and straightening the books on the coffee table, he decided he was ready to try and call. His stomach was up to its familiar acrobatics once again, but he tried not to think about it. Just concentrate on the phone. Just dial the number.

By the third ring, he knew there would be no answer. By the eighth ring he was certain of it. By the twentieth ring, he replaced the phone onto the base. Nobody home. Where the hell could she be?

Maybe she had unplugged the phone to study undisturbed. Maybe she had stepped outside for a bit of fresh air during a study break. Maybe she was out with some guy on a date. The rush of emotion he felt was jealousy, but he did not yet realize that. All he could sense was the anger. She was supposed to be home studying, alone. Yet there was now no answer on the phone of Monika Reese.

By now it was ten o'clock. He had accomplished nothing in the last hour, other than establishing that neither Evan nor Monika were at home tonight. He wasn't sure which missing person bothered him the most.

He thought first of Evan. He knew he had to be out somewhere he shouldn't right now. He considered running up to Shires'office, but finally decided to let it go for the night. He would call him first thing in the morning and hear what he had done. Part of him was glad Evan was out there doing the work. He just wasn't cut out for it. Maybe Evan would solve their little mystery and he could get uninvolved. Seemed unlikely, but one never knew.

Monika would have to wait as well. He certainly wasn't going to run over to her house tonight. For one thing, he wasn't really even sure where she lived. And even if he did, how would it look for him to show up at her doorstep at ten thirty at night asking her why she wasn't answering the phone? Not exactly the look he was going for.

That left sleep or study. His mind was exhausted. Overflowing with data. The combination of a week's worth of minutia, added to a stolen body mystery, topped off by the worry of a potential new romance, made his brain want to explode. One more bit of data might just be the straw to break the camel's back. He had reached his limit for the day. Maybe for the year. It was time for sleep.

It came with surprising ease. He stripped down to his underwear and covered himself with a light sheet. He had feared a long and fitful night, but perhaps the mental overload he was experiencing had forced his mind to clear. His body's way of compensating in order to keep itself sane. Whatever the reason, Rick slept soundly for almost ten hours.

*   *   *   *

Monika Reese was not quite sure what to do. She was deeply disturbed by the events of the last two days. More so than she could let on. She would try her best to discourage any further investigation by her eager classmates, but it would be difficult. They were very persistent. Especially Evan. She worried about him the most. He would not be dissuaded easily. The eagerness of youth coupled with his inevitable immaturity would make him very difficult to handle. He was certainly becoming a problem.

She sat alone in her empty house, sprawled out on the couch with the lights off. This is how she did her best thinking. No interruptions. No external stimuli. Just herself and the darkness. Nothing left to impede the flow of her thoughts. Except the phone.

Monika waited for the ringing to stop. By the eighth ring she sat upright, then stood. She walked slowly over to the socket in the wall and unclipped the cord. Now there was silence. She maneuvered back to the couch in the dark, her eyes now accustomed and pupils dilated. She sat back and closed her eyes.

There had to be a way to keep Rick and Evan from pursuing the matter any further. Cameron should not be a problem, as he had already expressed his profound disinterest. It could be an act, but she didn't think so. He wasn't that clever. That left Rick and Evan. Rick could be led in whatever direction she chose. She was sure of that. Evan, on the other hand, was quickly becoming a significant problem. He was acting as if this were a personal matter, for reasons yet unclear to her. It would be a major undertaking to dissuade him from further investigation. She had sensed his determination earlier today in the lab, and knew they were in for a struggle. Handling Evan would most certainly require a delicate touch.

Her mind explored numerous possibilities and options. None of them sounded very appealing. This would be a most difficult task. Her mind had become clouded by her closeness to all those involved. She felt she was developing a true friendship with both Cameron and Evan. Fellow classmates struggling to beat the system and survive the gauntlet known as medical school. One couldn't help but feel a certain camaraderie with those in the same proverbial boat. It was unavoidable.

And then there was Rick. A friend as well, but perhaps more. She couldn't deny certain feelings she had for him. Feelings she hadn't experienced for a very long time. Not since the accident. She found him entering her mind with increasing frequency. An unwelcome intrusion, but a pleasurable one nonetheless. Their upcoming rendezvous both exhilarated and terrified her at the same time. She couldn't deny her feelings for him, but those thoughts made any decision tonight all that more difficult. She would not make it alone. She needed some help.

Flipping on the light beside the couch, she slipped on a pair of old shoes and grabbed up her purse and keys. She knew he was probably home, and decided not to call first. Spontaneity was much more her thing. She left the house without locking the door, leaving most of the lights on as well. The warm air felt good against her skin, as did the humidity. She lowered the top on the Camaro, dropping both front windows at the same time. This was certainly a night for the wind.

Monika took the back roads through town. She wanted to avoid the traffic tonight. She usually did her best thinking in solitude, but the ride did little to spur on her overworked mind. By the time she arrived at his house, she felt more calm and relaxed, but still had no answers to her questions. Maybe he could help. He usually could. And even if he did not have an immediate answer, he still needed to know what was happening over the last week. Perhaps he did already. She had not discussed this with him yet, but maybe he already knew. She would find out now.

His garage door was up and both cars were in their place. She knew he would be home. He was about as predictable as she was spontaneous. She parked in the driveway behind his truck. She had never really seen him as a pickup kind of guy, but he liked to think that he was. It was almost three years old and still without a scratch. It was used more as a car than a truck, but he still enjoyed having one.

Monika felt strangely nervous outside on the front porch. Sometimes he made her feel that way. It was something over which she had little control. She rang the doorbell, noticing the slight tremor in her right hand as she did. For a long time there was only silence. Then she saw a light come on. Then he opened the door.

"Monika?" He was surprised. "What are you doing out here this time of night?" He motioned for her to enter. "Come in sweetheart."

"I need to talk with you about something." She stepped in and accepted his hug, and then a quick peck on the mouth.

"Come inside and have a seat. Can I get you anything? Something to drink, maybe?" He seemed excited to have a visitor.

"No thanks. I'm fine. I really just need to talk with you for a minute." She followed him into the living room and sat next to him on the couch. "There's a problem at school."

Raymond Shires leaned forward and looked into her eyes. "What kind of problem?"

CHAPTER 12

Rick awoke at eight o'clock without benefit of an alarm. The last five days had been incredibly stressful, both physically and mentally, and last night he decided to allow himself the luxury of waking up whenever his body was ready. The thought of the alarm going off one more morning was almost nauseating.

He had never been a morning person. All throughout college he had arranged his schedule to accommodate his own biological clock. Now he was forced to adapt to the rigid schedule of the school, and it was taking its toll. It felt good to sleep in.

His first thoughts were of Monika. He wondered again where she had been last night. He realized his feelings were those of jealousy, something he would never admit to anyone but himself. It was simply unavoidable.

Breakfast consisted of cereal and toast. He first ran downstairs, barefoot in his shorts, to buy a newspaper from the machine. It had been over a week since he had read anything other than a textbook, and he was beginning to feel a little isolated from the outside world. He ate at a leisurely pace, scanning through the pages one at a time and catching up on the world. He set the sports page off to one side. It was his favorite section, and he liked to save it for last.

By nine his mind was back on Monika again. He wondered if it was still too early to call, then finally decided to wait until at least ten. Didn't want to appear desperate. He found Evan's number written down on a scrap of napkin and tried to call him instead. No answer. Where the hell could he be? Probably sticking his nose out somewhere it shouldn't be. Rick was eager to talk with him, but he had mysteriously vanished.

The next hour was spent cleaning up around the room. It was amazing how such a small area could become so cluttered in less than a week. Part of the problem was that he had never really unpacked. Boxes cluttered the floor, making it difficult move about. He did his best to unpack and organize, and by ten o'clock things didn't look half bad. He sat back on the bed and rested for a moment. It was almost starting to feel like home.

The phone stared back at him from the desk. He sat up slowly and walked over towards it. Monika's number was lying beside the receiver, but he had already memorized it. He dialed it quickly before there was time to contemplate his actions. Monika answered on the second ring.

"Hello."

"Hello, Monika?"

"Yes."

"Hey, it's Rick. Good morning."

"Hi Rick!" Her voice beamed. "I was just thinking about you."

"You must be psychic or something."

"Maybe that's it. I was hoping you'd call this morning."

"I told you I would, didn't I?"

"I guess you did, didn't you. So what are you doing? Been up cramming since six?"

"Hardly. Try up at eight and haven't even made it to the showers yet."

"Sounds like my day. I'm still in a robe and slippers." The image in Rick's mind made him smile.

"Nothing wrong with that, is there? That's what weekends are for."

"I thought weekends were for studying," said Monika.

"That too," he said. "And for going out to eat with certain fellow classmates."

"Which brings us to tonight," she said, following along.

"Are we still on for dinner?"

"Unless you've found some other gorgeous blond to take out tonight."

"So far you're the only one," he laughed. "You found any better offers?"

"Sadly no," she replied. "I guess we're stuck with each other."

"What are you in the mood for?"

"Oh I don't know. I can't think about dinner this early in the morning. Why don't you just surprise me."

"I can do that. I'll see if I can come up with something good."

"Nothing fancy, ok? I don't want you spending a fortune."

"Who said I was paying?" asked Rick.

"You asked me out, you're paying. That's the deal."

"*Now* you tell me."

"Sorry mister. You're stuck tonight."

"All right, you win. I'll see what I can come up with."

"What time shall I expect you?"

"How 'bout seven?" he said. "I'll pick you up around seven."

"You need directions?"

"I guess I do. You're over in Briarwood, right?"

"Yeah. Take that street up from Beck's. Take your second right onto Hickory and I'm the first driveway on the left. You'll see my car in the garage."

"That fancy red thing, right?"

"Yeah, that fancy red thing. I'll see you around seven then?"

"I'm looking forward to it," he said.

They both hung up without saying goodbye. Rick sat back, took a deep breath, and smiled. Their conversation had gone even better than he had hoped. No embarrassing pauses or lagging conversation. Short and to the point. Get in and get out. He congratulated himself for being the master conversationalist. The day was off to a great start.

Now the hard part. He had to somehow wait until seven o'clock before he could drive over to her house. He knew he should be studying, but wasn't sure he had it in him today. The sun shone in through the glass, enticing him to come outside. He settled instead for a compromise , opening the window and stepping out onto the ledge. From eight stories up the world was very peaceful. To his left he could see the downtown buildings reaching for the sky. To his right was the triple A ballpark and beyond that the university football stadium. The air was warm, but not yet smothering, and felt grand as he breathed it into his chest. There would be little studying done on this day.

The next thirty minutes were spent illegally on the balcony, soaking up the sun's rays. A glass of tea in one hand, the crisp new sports page in the other, and thoughts of a beautiful woman running through his mind. Hard to imagine a better morning. Time passed quickly, but he was soon getting warm, and probably sun burned. Time to come inside. Time to start the day.

Rick showered and dressed quickly, electing not to shave for a second day in a row. He thought once again of growing a beard, but knew he would probably shave before tonight. So much for the rugged outdoorsman look. Not really his style, anyway.

With a backpack full of textbooks, he headed out the door for the library. If he left quickly, took the underground tunnel without looking up, and found an inside room with no windows, he just might be able to get a little schoolwork done. Lord knows he needed to. Studying had somehow become third or fourth on his priority list. Not exactly where it needed to be after one week of medical school. Too many distractions made it difficult to concentrate.

He thought about stopping by Evan's room on the way out, then had second thoughts and continued walking. If he was there, Rick would certainly get caught up in something he wasn't ready to confront just yet. If he wasn't there, it would play on his mind as well. Better to simply leave things alone and stick with the studying plan. The elevator actually stopped on Evan's floor, letting on two people he did not know. He resisted the urge to step out, instead riding down three more floors to the basement and heading across to the library.

Things went well for the first two hours. Then the hunger pangs hit, and it became impossible to concentrate. It was already after one now, and he decided to take a quick break and grab a bite in the cafeteria. No sense starving himself. His mind was ready for a break anyway.

The number of people forced to eat at the hospital cafeteria on a Saturday was small. It consisted of nurses, residents, family members, and a handful of students. Everyone else had enough sense to dine elsewhere. They closed for lunch a half hour early on the weekends, one thirty instead of two, and it was nearing that time now. Rick appeared to be the only person on campus who had not yet eaten. The place was deserted.

He walked through the line, getting the baked chicken and a couple of vegetables. They had already closed down the grill, and his usual burger and fries were no longer an option. Grabbing a large Dr. Pepper, Rick headed for the cashier. He was delighted to see a familiar face.

"Hello Dr. Stanley," she smiled.

"Hi Jessie." He set down his tray. "They making you work on a lovely Saturday too?"

"I'm afraid so. Seems like all I do is work."

"I know the feeling. My brain's about to explode from all the cramming I've been doing the last few days."

"Maybe you need to take a break then. Sure is a pretty day outside."

"I'm trying not to notice," he replied.

She glanced down at his tray. "Looks like you're eatin' healthy for a change. Good for you."

"I'm not starting any new diet. I just got here after the grill closed. It was this or the salad bar, and I know my system's not ready for that."

"Well, you're lucky. We happen to be runnin'a special on chicken and vegetables today." She rang up the meal on the register and the drawer popped open against her generous stomach. "That'll be forty two cents."

"Best deal in town," he said, reaching for the change in his pocket. He had all but given up arguing with Jessie over the food. Maybe a token protest from time to time, but it fell on deaf ears.

"So what are you studying today, Dr. Stanley?"

"Anatomy mostly, but I've been kinda flipping back and forth."

"You been up there with them dead bodies again?"

"Not today, Miss Jessie. I've been holed up in the library most of the morning." That was almost the truth.

"That place gives me the willies. I don't like it one bit, thinkin' about all them bodies just laying around up there bein' cut on."

"It's not all that bad. I guess you get used to it pretty quick." He paused for a second. "What do you know about that place anyway, Jessie? You don't have to ever go up there, do you?"

"My son does some of the cleanin' up there on the weekends. Sometimes I go visit him on my break or after work. The damn fool wouldn't come see me at home if I was on my death bed, so it's the only way I get to spend some time with him."

"So you sit up there with all the cadavers?" smiled Rick.

"He's usually downstairs at the offices, but that's close enough for me."

"What offices?" asked Rick.

"Them offices on the fifth floor for all those professors. Like that awful man I told you about the other day."

"You mean Dr. Shires?"

"That's him. I don't like nothin' about him."

"I don't understand. Why don't you like Dr. Shires?"

"I don't need no reason not to like someone. I just don't like him, that's all."

Thoughts of Charlie Ellis flashed into Rick's mind. He was still certain that Shires was somehow involved in the whole matter. He just had to be. Jessie's feelings about the man mirrored his own, but he had more concrete reasons than did she. Unless she knew more than she was letting on.

Rick had a sudden brainstorm of ideas. He looked over at Jessie, not sure if he should open up a rather large can of worms. He was about to open his mouth when two nurses walked up with their trays. It would have to wait.

"What time is your break, Miss Jessie?"

"Anytime I want to I s'pose. I haven't taken my lunch yet."

"I've got something I want to ask you about. You think you could take your lunch in a minute and join me?"

"What you wanna talk about?"

A line had now formed, and the two nurses were reaching into their purses for money. Rick was not about to discuss this with an audience.

"I'll be sitting down there in that corner booth. I'd sure appreciate it if you would join me for a few minutes."

Rick picked up his tray and found a seat in the back. He ate slowly as he thought about how he would approach Jessie. She certainly was no ally of Shires, and appeared to harbor a serious resentment towards him, however unfounded. Rick was thinking about her son, the one who cleaned Shires' office. The one who might just have the key to the famous file cabinet. Perhaps he was their answer.

He could not see the cash registers from where he was sitting. He had finished his lunch and was growing restless. Just as he was about to get up and walk to the front, she appeared off to his left. She carried a Styrofoam container from the kitchen and a large glass of tea.

"Them people in the back thought I was crazy when I told 'em I was havin' lunch with a young white doctor out here." She sat across from him in the booth.

Rick smiled up at her. "I guess it's not something you see every day, is it?"

"It's a first for me, Dr. Stanley. It's a first for me." She opened the lid revealing three pieces of cold fried chicken. Nothing else.

"You're probably wondering what I'm up to?"

"A little," she said, taking a bite from the leg.

"I want to talk to you about Dr. Shires." He waited for her response.

She chewed and swallowed. "What about him?"

Rick quickly debated a final time what exactly to tell her. He realized if he wanted her help, he would have to level with her. It was the only way. "I think he's involved in something bad up there. Something illegal I think, but I can't prove it just yet."

"What makes you say that?" He now had her full attention.

"I think he's somehow getting those bodies up there illegally. One of them that I saw is someone I know was supposed to have been buried a few weeks ago. I was even at the funeral and saw him go into the ground. Two weeks later the same body showed up in our lab upstairs. I think Shires is behind whatever is going on."

Jessie thought for a moment. "Did you ever see the body in the casket?"

"No, I guess not. The lid was always closed."

"What makes you think Shires did somethin'?"

"He's the chairman," he replied with slight hesitation. "He's the one ultimately responsible for that lab. If something's going on up there, then it's his baby."

"That don't mean he had anything to do with gettin' them bodies."

Rick closed his eyes and thought. Should he tell her everything? So far he had mentioned nothing that could endanger himself. Still he realized that if he wanted her help he needed to tell her everything. It was the only way.

"I was in his office two nights ago." He paused waiting for a response, but there was none. "We found a note pad with the name and number of a local funeral home."

"That don't really mean nothin'."

"There's more. I went back and checked on that man who died. He was taken to Harper Funeral Home from the hospital."

"And that's who's name was on that paper?"

"Yeah, it was."

"Could be a coincidence."

"Could be, but it's not. And I bet you don't think so either."

"You don't know what I think, Dr. Stanley."

"I know you don't like Dr. Shires, although I'm not really sure why."

"You wanna know why I don't like that man?" she asked rhetorically. "I'll tell you. And it ain't got nothin'to do with funeral homes and bodies. I don't like him cause the way he treats my boy. He's a God damn bigot, that's what he is. He looks at my boy like he's nothin'. Daryl's been working up there for almost three years now. Sees him every day and hadn't said two words to him. Always lookin'down that long nose at him, like he's somethin' special or somethin'. Well he ain't all that, I promise you."

Rick was a little taken aback by the tirade. He wasn't really sure how to respond to what he had just heard. It was certainly good to know how both Jessie and her son felt about Shires. It might just make them a little more eager to help.

"I see we all share the same dislike for the man."

"If that's what you want to call it," she replied.

"I guess I'm being too easy on him."

"So tell me Dr. Stanley. Why you tellin' me all this, anyways? What's all this dead body business got to do with me?"

"Not a thing if you don't want it to, Jessie. But I could sure use your help on this one. You and Daryl both, really."

"What's my boy got to do with anything?"

"That depends on what you say to him."

"What you want him to do, break into that office or somethin'? Cause I ain't gonna ask him to do nothin' like that."

"And I wouldn't ask you to Jessie. That's not what I need. I can get into the office. The problem comes about once I get there. There's a file cabinet inside that might just have what I'm looking for. But I can't get into it. Not without a key."

"And that's where Daryl comes in?"

"That's right. If he could somehow get me that key, I bet we find some answers locked inside."

"What makes you think he's got a key?"

"I don't know if he does or not. I'm asking. At least I'm asking you to talk with him. If he can't help, or won't help, I'll understand. I realize I'm asking a lot of someone I've never even met."

Jessie thought for a moment. Her eyes never left Rick's. Finally she looked down and took a bite of chicken, chasing it with a large swallow of tea. Then she spoke.

"I'll talk to him tonight and see what he says."

Rick smiled. "I appreciate that, Miss Jessie."

"Hold on now. I'm not done speakin'. If he does decide to help you out, and I'm sayin' if, then I can't let him get in no trouble over this. I want your word that his name will never come up, no matter what happens with this."

"Hey, no problem," he replied, raising his right hand without thinking.

"What is that, scout's honor or something?"

"It's my word Jessie. I've never heard of anyone named Daryl. I found the key in the drawer when I walked inside. Shires must have left it in there and forgot about it." He smiled again. "How's that sound?"

"Sounds like you better keep sayin'that over and over." She smiled back at him briefly, then quickly turned serious once again. "I like you Dr. Stanley. And I want to help you out. I think you're probably right about that man. I know he's no good, and if he's doin'something illegal, I'd love nothin' more than to see him go down. But I got my own family to think of. I've got to protect my boy. It don't matter how bad I want that man hurt. If I think Daryl's in any danger, then the whole thing's done. I hope you understand that." The tone in her voice reminded Rick of his mother's when he had been caught at something he shouldn't have been doing. It sent a slight chill through his body.

"All I want is the key." They eyed each other in silence.

"Then I'll see if I can get it for you."

*   *   *   *

The Mississippi Delta is not the most scenic of locales, but a late summer afternoon was not without its charm, even in the middle of the flat river bottom. The sinking sun played off a few low lying clouds which had settled just above the horizon, creating quite the beautiful landscape. It was wasted on the small group that gathered there, a strange mix of men from a rather large cross section of southern culture. Most entered the building quickly, a thriving feed store in better times, but deserted now and barely standing.

Lloyd Harper and his companion were the last ones to arrive. For them it was a three and a half hour drive, and it seemed that no matter how early they tried to leave town, they were always running late. Today was no exception.

They entered the building and waited a moment for their eyes to adjust to the darkness. The only lighting was from a row of naked bulbs which hung low from the ceiling along the center of the room. Two of the six were blown, and it looked like the others weren't far behind. The heat was overpowering, and the two large fans by the door were doing little to dissipate it. They spotted two seats together towards the front, and excused themselves as they settled into the folding metal chairs. The meeting was about to begin.

"I'd like to welcome y'all this evening and apologize right off the bat for the heat in here. We had planned to get that new window unit put in by now, but it hasn't arrived yet."

"You sure it ain't out in your tool shed, Jimmy?" yelled someone from the back. The crowd laughed loudly.

"You keep your damn nose outta my shed," he shot back smiling. "It's bad enough I gotta keep servicing your wife back there." That one even brought some applause.

"Long as it keeps her from shoppin', you go right on ahead."

"All right, let's get this thing started before we all drop out from the heat. I hereby call to order the Middle Delta Chapter of the Knights of the Ku Klux Klan."

The crowd was now silent.

"Y'all should have a copy of the minutes from last month's meeting. Does anybody have any changes they think need made?"

The thirty or so men took a moment to read over the three pages of notes. Everyone seemed satisfied they were accurate, even those in the crowd that couldn't read.

"If nobody has any changes, we'll accept them as written." He nodded to the chapter secretary to his left, who then initialed his copy for the permanent records. "Does anyone have any old business we need to discuss?"

Someone towards the back stood up. "Did we set a date for initiation next month?"

Jimmy pulled out a pocket calendar. "We're lookin' at September twenty third. That's a Saturday night. We hadn't talked about this yet, but I thought we'd maybe move it up to ten o'clock instead of midnight this year. That way we can all still get up and get to church the next morning."

"You gettin' too old for those late nights, Jimmy?"

"I can't keep up with all you young fellas like I used to?" he laughed back. "Could we maybe get a motion to set that time and date for next month?"

"So moved," yelled someone.

"Second."

"All those in favor of setting initiation for the twenty third at ten?"

"Aye," replied most of the group.

"Any opposed?"

Silence.

"Very good. It looks like we got about ten folks ready to join. If any of you know of anyone else we need to contact, just let me know after the meeting and we can get in touch with them. I'm excited to be gettin' some new blood in here finally."

"What about the new robes?" asked Harper from the front row.

"They should be ready by next month. I talked with nationals the other day. They're runnin' a little behind, but thought they would have the order out by the first."

Jimmy scanned the crowd. "Any other old business?"

Everyone looked around, but nobody spoke.

"Let's move on to new business then. Have any of y'all heard about the rally comin' up in Memphis?" None had. "It's not gonna be until next January, but we need to start thinking about it now. We need to all roll out for that and help support our brothers."

"What's the date?" someone asked.

"January nineteenth. Martin Luther King's birthday." Everyone laughed.

"You mean Robert E. Lee's birthday, don't you?"

"Exactly," replied Jimmy. "We thought that would be a most appropriate time to show to everyone the resurgence of the Ku Klux Klan. As it gets closer, I'll be giving y'all more information, but let's all make plans now to be there and support the Knighthood."

"Our next order of business involves a Mister Calloway Washington. I've received word that he's thinkin' about running for the state senate this fall. Now I'm sure y'all will agree, the last thing we need is another God damn liberal nigger down there at the capital wantin' free handouts for all his brothers and sisters."

Everyone grunted their disapproval.

"I think it's time that Mister Calloway Washington became acquainted with some of our brothers. It's been a while since we've had a good old fashioned cross burning, but if anybody deserves one, then Cal's our man."

"When can we get started?"

"He's supposed to be out of town this weekend, so I thought we might welcome him back Monday night. Let me see a show of hands for everyone who wants to help."

About twenty people threw their arms in the air immediately, then another five or six quickly followed suit. They hadn't burned a cross in almost a year, and it was not something to be missed.

"That's excellent. He just lives about two miles from here, on the other side of old Spencer's place. I thought we could maybe meet up here around nine o'clock and all ride over together. You'll have to bring whatever you want to wear, cause the new robes won't be ready yet."

"What about the cross?" asked someone.

"I'll take care of all that. You boys just bring your lighters," he smiled.

"Does anyone else have any new business we need to discuss?"

The crowd looked around at each other, but nobody spoke up. A few looked at their watches, ready to move on to one of the many local bars and get started on their first longneck. Others had families to get home to, and a few of them even had dates later in the evening. Harper and his friend just had a long drive home, and were also anxious to finish up.

"I know this heat's gettin' unbearable, so in that case, I'll entertain a motion to adjourn."

"So moved." Everyone started to stand.

"Let's not forget about Monday night. We need a big turnout." He had to raise his voice as people started moving. "I'll see y'all here at nine sharp."

The congregation began to disperse. Harper started to follow out the door when he was stopped by Jimmy.

"Lloyd," he shouted. "Can I speak with you a moment?"

He nodded but didn't answer, then turned to his companion. "I'll be right back." They walked back up to the front of the room near the podium and began talking in hushed tones. They spoke for at least five minutes, neither showing much emotion. Finally they shook hands and walked out of the building together.

"I thought you'd run off and left my ass."

"Just waiting for you to finish up. It's too damn hot in there to be standing around."

"Well I'm ready. Let's get the hell out of here."

"What was that all about?"

"It was nothing. Just catching up on a little business. You ready to get out of here?"

"I'm waiting on you. Don't forget your bag over there." They walked towards the car. "What do you have in there, anyway?"

"Mostly camera equipment, and a few other things. None of your damn business, really."

They climbed back in the car, turned on the air conditioning, and headed back to the city.

CHAPTER 13

Rick spent the remainder of the afternoon holed up in the library. He had actually done remarkably well considering the colossal distractions constantly threatening to break his concentration. The sensory deprivation helped, forcing himself to stay in the small room with no windows looking outside or in. By the end of the day he had reviewed all the previous week's material, plus had read ahead through Wednesday of next week. Not a bad day's work.

The library stayed open until midnight every night, but it was nearly deserted when he left at 5:30. Pretty typical for a Saturday night unless a test week loomed ahead. Rick chose the outdoors route for his walk back to the dorm, and was glad he did. The sun was still visible in the sky and beat down warmly on his shoulders. It felt good after a day of air conditioning. The shadows were growing long, and the moon had already begun its ascent over the horizon. It was going to be a beautiful night.

Back in his room, Rick opened the windows and slipped into a pair of shorts. He tuned in his favorite country station on the stereo and twisted the top off a longneck. Every time he thought about his date tonight it sent his stomach lurching, so he tried to keep his mind occupied. It wasn't easy.

Grabbing his toilet kit, a towel, and a clean pair of underwear, he walked down the hallway to the showers. A few of his classmates were scattered about, most preparing to go out for the night, either on dates, or just clubbing with the guys.

"Hey Stanley. You got big plans tonight?" asked the man shaving in front of the mirror.

"Hey Butler. Nothing much really."

"You must have something going on or you wouldn't be gettin' all cleaned up."

"Well actually I've got a date tonight."

"Look at Stanley. Been in town for a week and already got a date."

"I've been here since the first of the summer, remember."

"That's right. You did that ER thing didn't you?"

"That and worked construction."

"So who's the poor unfortunate girl? It is a girl, right?"

"As far as I know she is. It's nobody you know," he lied. "Some nursing assistant I met over the summer. It's no big deal."

"Sounds better than my night. I've got to go out with these slobs."

"Well you ladies have a wonderful time." Rick thought of something. "Hey, have any of you guys seen Evan around this weekend?"

"That Sanders kid? I saw him in class yesterday I think. I guess I haven't seen him since then." Neither had anybody else. "What you need him for?"

"Just need to ask him something. It's no big deal."

"I'm outta here. Hope you get you some tonight, Stanley."

"Always the gentleman, aren't you Butler."

Rick set down his things and looked at himself in the mirror. His dark tan from a week ago had now mostly faded. He was already starting to get circles under his eyes from the long hours. He wondered how he would look four years from now when he would hopefully be graduating and finally realizing his dream.

He rubbed the two day old growth covering his chin. He could grow a thick beard if he wanted, and had actually done so earlier in the summer for a few weeks. The heat had soon made it unbearable, however, and he shaved it off in July. He considered letting it grow once again, but thought about his date tonight, their first date, and reached for the razor instead. Maybe another time. Tonight he wanted to look his best.

He shaved slowly, taking his time with the thick stubble on his chin. He lathered and shaved the area three separate times until the last remnants of beard were gone. He cut himself once and it bled profusely. Five minutes in the shower soon turned in to twenty. He would have stayed longer, but the hot water was beginning to fade. He stepped out, toweled off, and slipped on his underwear and shorts. The cut on his chin was still oozing just a bit, and he stuck a small piece of toilet paper over it to make it stop. A quick brush through the hair, and he was heading back to his room. It was nearly 6:30 now, and he quickly pulled on a pair of khaki slacks and a heavily starched shirt. He held up several ties in the mirror, but finally decided to leave them in the closet. She had said nothing fancy.

By 6:45 he was walking out to the parking lot. The old Honda started on the first crank, not always a given, and he was off. When he found her street it was not even ten till. Not wanting to seem too eager, he drove past her house and kept right on going. The red Camaro was sitting in the garage just as she had said. He drove around for another ten minutes, listening to Garth and Clint and Reba. He finally pulled into her driveway just after seven. Perfect timing, he thought to himself. Not too eager, not too late.

There was no doorbell, so he pounded loudly with the knuckles of his right hand. She opened the door almost immediately. She was breathtaking.

"Hey Rick. Come on in."

"Thanks." He stepped inside. "You look great."

"Well thank you. You look pretty dashing yourself." They walked into the living area. "I see you managed to find your razor."

"Admiring my clean close shave?"

"Actually I was noticing the toilet paper on your chin."

Rick quickly reached up and wiped the paper off his face, turning several shades of red in the process. "I guess I forgot that was there," he said. Off to a rip-roaring start.

"Don't worry about it," she said. "You look nice."

They both took a seat, him on a recliner and her on the couch. "Can I get you something to drink?" she asked.

"I'm fine, thanks, but help yourself if you want."

"I'm all right." She leaned back comfortably. "So where are you taking me tonight?"

"I've got to get some gas, so I thought we'd maybe pick up some microwave burritos and a Coke at the gas station. If that's ok with you." Rick kept a straight face for a moment, and Monika couldn't seem to tell if he was kidding or not. He quickly let her off the hook with a broad smile, which was followed immediately by her own.

"Maybe we could get an ice cream sandwich for dessert?"

"Well, I don't know about all that. I'm living on student loans, remember."

"Maybe I could pick up the dessert then."

"All right, you got a deal."

The five second pause that followed felt like five minutes to them both. There had never been an awkward moment between them since they met last week, but that had now suddenly changed. Now they were on a date.

"Shall we get going?" asked Monika.

"Sure, I'm starving. Don't want those burritos to get stale."

Monika switched off a couple of lights, turned on the answering machine, and followed Rick out the front door. She locked the knob and the dead bolt, each requiring its own key, and closed the screen door. They stopped on the front porch for a moment enjoying the night air. The humidity had dropped a few points today and the heat seemed almost bearable.

"It's gorgeous out here tonight," said Monika.

"I can actually breathe for a change," he said, looking all around. "This neighborhood is really beautiful. I love all these giant oak trees."

"I love it out here. It's a real escape from the chaos over the hill."

"That's what I miss. When you live in the dorm it's like you hardly ever leave the campus. The walls kinda start squeezing in on you."

"Which is exactly why I'm living here," she said.

"You never told me how you got out of staying in the dorm this year."

"You're right, I didn't."

"I'm serious. Who'd you have to buy off?"

"It was really pretty easy," she smiled. "I just wrote the dean a letter and told him I had an attention deficit problem, and that it would be impossible for me to study while living in the dorm. He let me out just like that."

"Is that true?"

"Hell no, it's not true. It worked though."

"Brilliant. How'd you ever come up with that?"

"I know a few people around campus. One of them gave me the idea. Said it had always worked in the past."

They were both bent over leaning on the railing, their bodies nearly touching. Rick was very aware of this fact, and enjoying the hell out of it.

"So how did you get into this place?"

"It belongs to a friend of my dad's. He's off on a sabbatical for a year and I'm sort of house sitting for him. He lets me stay for free in exchange for keeping up the place."

"Sounds like quite a deal. Beautiful house and free rent."

"You see how I couldn't pass that one up."

They looked up at each other at exactly the same time. Neither of them was talking now. The nervous tension was escalating, and Rick could feel it in the pit of his stomach. He felt his face turning red, and stood quickly to conceal it. Monika either didn't notice or pretended not to. She stood as well and began walking towards the steps.

"I guess we'd better get going," she said.

"Yeah, I suppose so," he replied, still slightly shaken.

"Do we have reservations, or are we gonna fight a mob somewhere?"

"I've got everything taken care of. Don't you worry about a thing."

"Who's worried? I'm just asking."

"Well quit asking. It's all under control. Just shut up and I'll tell you when we get there."

"A man who takes charge. My hero."

"All right, enough of the sarcasm, or it's back to the burritos and ice cream sandwiches."

They walked down onto the yard, Monika slightly in front. He resisted the urge to reach up and take her hand, although it certainly seemed the natural thing to do. Maybe not yet. They weren't quite ready for that. One step at a time. Got to get her into the car first.

"I assume we're taking your car?" she asked.

"Of course we are. You don't think I'd be seen in some fancy red convertible do you? It'd ruin my image."

"You have an image?"

"Oh yeah. You haven't heard about my image yet?"

"Guess I missed out on that one. You'll have to fill me in."

They reached the passenger door and she waited for Rick to open it for her. He reached around and pulled on the knob, but it was still locked.

"Guess I don't usually unlock this side," he said, fumbling for his keys. "Here it is." He turned the key and opened her door. She started to climb inside, then stood back up and faced him. She reached around the back of his head with her right hand and gently pulled his face to hers. Rick followed instinctively as she kissed him softly but with passion. It lasted only a moment, but time stood still for Rick. She pulled back and quickly got into her seat, staring straight ahead and not saying a word.

Rick's knees were jello. He stood there for a second, then realized how stupid he looked and pushed her door closed. He walked around the back of the car, pumping his fist in the air once in celebration. This was turning out to be quite the night.

She had already reached across and unlocked his side. Rick opened the door and took his seat. He started not to say anything, but couldn't resist.

"What was that for?"

"Just a little ice breaker."

"Try ice melter." They both laughed.

"I just thought we were both a little nervous, and that's something I've wanted to do since last week when I met you, so I thought 'what the hell'?"

"Well, you've got great instincts."

He started the car and they drove off. The tension had vanished with the kiss. They talked much more freely now, about school mostly, but other things as well. Rick felt very comfortable with her, not like most of the first dates he had been on before. He was genuinely having a good time.

Mazatlan's was a sort of upscale Mexican restaurant, known mostly for their fajitas and frozen margaritas. They arrived shortly before eight, the time of their reservation. Rick was immediately glad he had called ahead, as they had to fight their way through a rather large crowd. He took Monika's hand as he led her to the front. It felt very comfortable inside his own.

"Reservations for Stanley?" he asked the hostess.

She scanned down her list and found his name almost right away. "Will that be smoking, non, or first available?"

"We'll take first available," he replied without asking.

"It'll be just a few minutes sir. You can either wait over there or at the bar and we'll call your name shortly."

He started to ask her for a menu to read over, but she had already moved on to the next couple. They stepped back out of the way and scanned the restaurant.

"I don't know about you," he said, "but I'd much rather wait at the bar."

"Lead the way," she replied.

He took her hand once again and she followed him up the steps to the large rectangular bar. There were three people at work behind the counter, all frantically taking orders and mixing drinks. Saturday was no doubt their biggest night. Rick soon caught the eye of one of the girls and she leaned over to speak.

"What can I get you?"

He looked at Monika. "Frozen margarita?"

"Make mine a strawberry."

He turned back to the girl behind the bar. "Two frozen margaritas. One regular and one strawberry." She ran off to pour.

"Kind of a girly drink, isn't it?" he asked her.

"I am a girl, in case you hadn't noticed."

"Believe me, I've noticed."

She was already back with their order. "That'll be eight dollars."

He handed her a ten, and kept both dollars when she returned with his change. He didn't believe in tipping at the bar. There were no stools available, so they stood off to the side together and to wait for a table. A moment later their name was called over the loudspeaker.

"Stanley, party of two. Stanley."

They walked with their drinks back down to the hostess, then followed their waitress right back up the steps to a table for two towards the back of the restaurant. They took a seat and she disappeared, promising to return shortly for their orders.

Rick picked up both menus and handed one to Monika. They opened them up and read for a moment in silence.

"What are you getting?" she asked.

"The fajitas are great here. I think I'll have to go with them."

"That sounds pretty good. This taco salad doesn't look bad either."

"It's good too. I tried one a few months ago."

"I'm getting the feeling I'm not the first girl you've ever brought out here."

"I've been here a time or two before." He smiled up at her. "Jealous already?"

"Hardly. Just trying to figure you out, Rick Stanley."

"And how's it coming?"

"Not very well, I'm afraid. I've still got some work to do."

"You're not exactly an open book yourself, Miss Monika Reese."

"And what makes you say that?"

"Do you realize you've managed to dodge and evade every personal question I've ever put to you?"

"I thought we were talking about you."

"There you go. You did it again."

"I'm just mysterious, that's all. Most men find it charming."

"Well, I'm not sure charming is the word I would use."

"So what word would you use then?"

"Frustrating maybe?" He thought for a moment. "Or how about unusual? Or possibly irritating."

"I said one word," she interrupted. "I get the point."

A young man stopped at their table and bringing ice water, chips, and hot sauce. He informed them that their waitress would return shortly, then headed back for the kitchen. Monika dipped a chip in the sauce, took a bite, then looked up at Rick.

"So tell me what you want to know."

"I'm not even sure where to start. How 'bout where are you from?"

"Lots of places, but Minnesota most recently. Finished my undergrad at U of M."

"The Golden Gophers," said Rick.

"That's us. Nice place in the summertime, but the winters are hell!"

"So why the move so far south? You hate the cold that bad?"

"That was part of it. Plus I've got some family around here."

"You told me you were divorced, right?"

"Yeah, I guess so."

"What does that mean?"

"Nothing," she stammered. "I've been divorced for a couple of years." Rick could tell he had hit a nerve, but decided to press a little further.

"And you never had any kids, married all that time?"

Monika was silent for a moment. "I've never told anyone down here any of this."

"Any of what?"

"Any of what I'm about to tell you now. You've got to swear not to tell a soul."

"Don't worry about me. Not a word."

"Have y'all decided what you want?" The waitress startled them both.

"Um, yeah," said Rick, fumbling with his menu. He looked over at Monika. "Did you decide yet?"

"I guess I'll try the fajitas."

Rick looked back to the waitress. "We'll both have the fajitas. How 'bout one chicken and one beef." She wrote down their order on a small green pad.

"Anything else from the bar?" She picked up the menus waited patiently.

"Another one?" Rick asked Monika.

"Please."

"We'll have two more margaritas, one regular and one strawberry."

"Ok, I'll get those right out to you."

She walked away and Rick reached for the chips. "You were about to say?"

"Now I've lost my train of thought," she lied.

"Tell me about your ex-husband."

"Not much to tell really. He beat me and I finally left him."

Rick was a little taken back by her sudden forthright honesty. "How long did you say you were married?"

"Seven years. He didn't really get violent until the last two though. He blamed it on pressures of work, but I don't know."

"What does he do?"

"He was a cardiac surgeon in Minneapolis."

"Was?"

She paused once again, tipping up the last of her drink. "He was killed in a car wreck shortly after the divorce was final. Had a few too many drinks one Saturday afternoon and crossed the center line into an eighteen wheeler."

"Yikes," said Rick. "I don't know what to say."

"There's nothing to say really. Our son Zach was in the car with him. In the front without a seat belt or child seat. They were both killed instantly."

Now Rick really didn't know what to say. Monika was looking down at her empty drink, not wanting to make eye contact. Rick was wishing he had never asked a question now, but that ship had long since sailed. They sat in silence for too long.

"It's ok Rick. It was two years ago. I'm ok talking about it." She still had not looked up.

"You left me pretty speechless with that one. I'm sorry. I don't know what else to say."

"Like I said, there's nothing else to say. I've moved on. I don't even think about them that often anymore."

"Now I wish I'd never brought it up."

"Actually I think I'm kinda glad you did. I haven't really talked to anyone about it much since the accident. Except for my dad. He thinks I need to see a shrink."

"What'd you tell him?"

"I told him I wasn't crazy. That I'd work through it on my own."

"And have you? Worked through it, I mean."

"In my own way, I think I probably have. It's kind of hard to know how to feel exactly. I mean I don't want to forget them, but you gotta move on with your life."

"Is that why you went to med school?"

"No. I went to med school to pick up guys."

Rick smiled. When she smiled back he started laughing, and she immediately followed suit. "It doesn't work the same for women, you know. Most men aren't looking for a doctor wife."

"Well they should be. Find someone who can bring in two hundred grand a year so they can sit at home and sleep on the couch and drink beer with the guys."

"You know, you may have a point there. Maybe I'm going about this all wrong."

"You just might be."

"I'm starving," said Rick. "I wish they'd hurry with our food."

"Have some more chips."

"I hate filling up on those. Then I don't want to eat the meal I paid for."

"You're paying for the chips too, you know."

"You know what I mean."

"I think it's your turn to talk now. Any deep dark secrets in your past? Ever been in prison or anything like that?"

"Actually I have, if you can believe that."

"I'm not sure I do."

"It was only for a few hours, but I had cuffs on and everything."

"They let you out early for good behavior?"

"They let me out early with bail money. It was down in Florida a couple of years ago. Spring break in Daytona Beach. Me and a few friends got busted for disorderly conduct."

"I'm sure alcohol had nothing to do with it."

"Maybe just a little. We were up on one of the balconies looking over the pool. The cops were out there arresting minors for drinking, and we started hollering at 'em from three stories up. I guess they had some of their buddies with them cause all of a sudden two of 'em came up behind us slapped the cuffs on us."

"What happened?"

"Well, they took us downstairs, put us in the back of their car, and hauled us down to the police station or jail or whatever it was. Made us sit in there for a couple of hours, then let us post bail and leave."

"What did that cost you?"

"Just fifty bucks bail money. We all got fined five hundred dollars, but none of us ever paid it."

"How'd you get out of that?"

"Oh we didn't get out of anything. We just didn't pay. I don't figure they're gonna extradite me to Florida for five hundred bucks."

"So you're telling me that you're wanted in at least one state."

"Just the one, as far as I know."

"So I'm out on a date with an ex con. My father would really love that one."

"How 'bout we keep that one to ourselves. Let's just make this a night of secrets."

"No problem there," said Rick. "We'll put it all in the vault."

"Anything else you wanna tell me about now while we're being all open and everything?" asked Monika.

Before Rick could answer their waitress appeared with their food. The fajitas looked great and were still sizzling on the hot plate. She set everything down in the middle of the table. It smelled incredible.

The conversation waned as they devoured the food. It was already way after eight o'clock, much later than either was accustomed to eating.

They were well into their third margarita by the end of the meal, both of them feeling the effects, but neither realizing it.

"I tried to call you last night," said Rick.

"Couldn't wait till morning to hear my voice?"

"I guess not. Actually I was tired of studying and looking for any excuse for a break."

"I unplugged the phone. It's the only way I can get any work done."

"Aren't you afraid you might miss an important call?"

"I'm a freshman medical student. What could be so important?"

"I don't know. Family emergency or something I guess."

"They know where I live."

"Anyway, I was bored and tired of studying and couldn't find an excuse to stop. Even Evan was out doing who knows what."

"That's right. Weren't you and he supposed to be out playing Sherlock Holmes last night?"

"He was supposed to call me so we could talk about some things."

"And he never did?"

"Never heard from him. I don't know where the hell he is. I've gone by his room a couple of times this weekend, but he's not been around."

"Maybe he left town for the weekend," she suggested. "Went to see his folks or something."

"Maybe so. I just thought he might have called me first."

"He's got to clear his calendar with you now?"

"Of course not. It's just that we kind of had plans for last night, that's all."

"What kind of plans?" she asked.

"Just plans. You've already expressed your disapproval and I don't want to hear it again."

"Aren't we getting a little edgy."

"Sorry, I didn't mean for it to sound like that. I just know your thoughts on the whole matter, so it's probably better that we don't even discuss it."

"Too late now, Sherlock. That can of worms is now officially open."

"Well I vote we close it right back up."

"What were you two gonna do last night anyway?"

"Nothing. Nothing at all. We just wanted to put our heads together to try and sort this out, that's all."

"How 'bout you and I put our heads together?"

"I thought you didn't want to get involved in this," he said.

"I don't. And hopefully I can convince you to do the same. Tell me what you've got."

"I'm not sure this is such a good idea."

"What's the matter, Stanley? Afraid I might figure it out for you and blow your whole conspiracy theory?"

"All right then. You tell me how that body got into our anatomy lab when it's supposed to be buried in Lawson's Cemetery."

"You saw it buried?" she asked.

"I saw the casket go into the ground. I didn't actually see the dirt thrown on top of his body."

"You mean on top of the casket."

"You think the casket was empty and he meant for his body to go to the school."

"Why is that so unbelievable?"

"I just don't see it happening. Why would he go through all that money and effort to fake a funeral."

"He didn't fake a funeral," she said. "He had a very nice funeral and burial for his friends and family. They're all happy as they watch him go into the ground, and he's happy cause he's donated his body to science and is helping educate a student doctor."

"See I just don't buy that. I knew this guy pretty well. He didn't have any close friends, and he hadn't seen his family in years. It just doesn't seem like something he would do."

"So what next?"

Rick had to once again decide how much of this story to share with her. "If I tell you, it can't leave this table."

"Hey, this is kind of the night for secrets."

"I'm serious Monika. Not a word. Even to Cameron."

"I'd be afraid to tell this crazy story to anyone. Now tell me what you're talking about."

"I've got to get back inside Shire's office again. Inside that file cabinet."

"Will you listen to yourself?"

"I'm serious. It's the only way. I want to see what's in there."

"And just how do you plan to get into the files?"

"I may be getting the key shortly."

"How are you gonna manage that?"

"I'm not ready to say just yet. But I've got a pretty good lead. Hopefully I'll find out tomorrow."

"And break in tomorrow night?"

"If I get the key."

"What if you get caught, Rick? You know how serious this is."

"I know. It's just something I've got to do. I know you don't understand, and I'm not asking you to."

"Can I show y'all a dessert menu tonight?" Their long lost waitress finally returned.

Rick looked at Monika. "Do you want anything?"

"I'm stuffed. Go ahead if you do though."

"I think I'll pass too. We'll take the check when you get a chance."

"I've got it right here. You can pay me whenever you're ready."

Rick reached for his wallet. "Here, let me give you this now." He handed her his credit card.

"Great. I'll be right back."

"I'm ready to change the subject," said Rick.

"Fine with me," she replied. "I didn't want to talk about that to begin with."

"I'm sorry I brought it up."

The waitress returned quickly with the check. Rick signed his name, writing in a few extra dollars for a tip. He promised himself when he was rich doctor that he would start tipping more. Right now he just didn't have the money.

"You ready to get out of here?" he asked.

"Sure. Let me just swing by the ladies' room on the way out."

"I'll meet you out front then."

They stood up and walked in opposite directions, Monika towards the restrooms in the back, and Rick to the main entrance in the front. He thought about their conversation, wishing now they had never talked about the cadaver. He did not want her involved in any of this, and it had certainly put a damper on the end of their evening. Short of that, he felt their first date had gone extremely well. Better than he had expected, really. His mind still lingered on their kiss at the car. Quite a shock, but most definitely welcomed. He hoped for an encore performance tonight.

She didn't take long, and they were soon out the door, into the car, and headed home. They briefly debated a movie or drinks, but were both pretty exhausted from the week and decided to call it an early night. The conversation coming home was sparse, as they seemed lost in their own thoughts. It wasn't quite awkward, but a definite change from most of their evening. They pulled into her driveway precisely at ten.

"I had a great time," said Monika.

Rick came around and helped her with the door. He reached for her hand as they walked slowly up the drive. "I really did too," he replied truthfully. "I had a feeling I probably would."

"Oh you did, did you?"

"As I'm sure you did too."

She left him hanging without a response. "Thanks for dinner. It was very good."

"I'm glad you enjoyed it. The margaritas were good too." Rick could feel the uneasiness returning as they struggled for conversation. They cleared the top step onto the porch, and he decided to follow her example from earlier in the evening.

He turned to face her. She looked incredible under the full moon and street lights. An alluring silhouette against the brightly lit sky. He cupped both hands around the back of her head and pulled her gently to him. They kissed softly at first, then deeper as their passion escalated. Their tongues entwined and their hands roamed. Rick was incredibly aroused, and could sense the same in his partner. He finally, reluctantly, pulled back to catch his breath.

"Wow," she said. The flush in her cheeks was noticeable even in the dark of night. She was breathing hard and finding it difficult to speak.

"My sentiments exactly." Words did not come easily to him either.

"I'd invite you up, but I don't think I'm quite ready for that just yet."

"That's ok. I can understand that." Rick hid his disappointment well.

"Call me tomorrow?"

"Sure. You gonna be around all day?"

"Most of it. I've got a few errands to run, but mostly plan to spend the day in the books." They started moving towards the front door. "What about you?"

"Pretty much the same, I guess."

"I wish you would reconsider about Shires. I don't want to see you throw your career away over something so stupid."

"I thought we weren't talking about this anymore."

"Call me in the morning?"

Rick was glad she let it go. The last thing he wanted was to end this evening in a fight. "I'll try, as long as you don't unplug your phone again."

"I'll leave it hooked up just for you."

They now were standing in the doorway. She had the door unlocked and opened while they talked, and appeared ready to go in for the night. She leaned forward and kissed him one final time, this time more platonic than passionate. He gave her a hug, then turned to leave.

"Good night Monika Reese."

"Try not to think about me all night long," she replied.

Monika watched as he hopped into his car and drove away. When she was certain he was gone, she turned and went inside, locking the door behind her. Grabbing a longneck from the fridge, she went to the bedroom and stripped down to her panties. She admired her long naked body in the closet mirror, dancing by herself with her hands in the air. For a woman of thirty, she was exceptionally fit and was very proud of that fact. She found it difficult to remain humble in public, and when she spent time home alone, humility went out the window.

Before she left the closet, she pulled on a pair of shorts and an old sweatshirt. The beer accompanied her to the couch, where she settled in with the phone, remote control, and this week's television guide. She used the phone first. He answered on the second ring.

"Hello?"

"It's me."

"How was your date?"

"Quite interesting really. On several levels."

"I'm not sure I want to know what that means. Did you find out anything?"

"More than I was expecting to. There's some things we need to do."

"Tonight?"

"I think it can wait until morning."

"I'll call you when I get up," he said.

"Ok. I should be here all morning."

"Get some sleep sweetheart."

"I will. Good night daddy."

"Good night baby doll. Sleep tight."

Raymond Shires hung up the phone and went on to bed. He did not sleep well.

CHAPTER 14

Rick went to church the next morning. It was the first time in over six months, except for Charlie Ellis' funeral. He wasn't really sure why he went. It just seemed like the right thing to do. It was actually a spur of the moment decision. He woke up, took a quick shower, and was flipping around the channels on the small TV in his room. All that he could find on was church services.

Rick found the number for one of the large Methodist churches to get the time of their late service. He went alone and sat in the back, hoping to keep to himself and not be disturbed. He was quite successful, and other than a few nods to strangers that he passed entering the building, he was able to sit in solitude.

After the service, he again left quietly, not wanting to be asked about Sunday school or becoming a member. He drove back to the dorm and slipped up the back stairwell to his room. He didn't really want to be seen wearing his only suit. He changed quickly into khaki shorts and an old college t shirt, putting the suit back up for what would probably be another six months. It was time for lunch, but he wasn't hungry. Too much on his mind.

Thoughts of Monika flashed through his head. He considered calling her, knowing he had told her he would, but for some reason just wasn't in the mood. He knew he should be after the time they had last night, but really just wanted to spend the day alone.

The one person he did try to call was Evan, who was still nowhere to be found. If Rick had a suspicious mind he might have been a little bit worried, but he knew there would eventually be a logical explanation for Evan's disappearance. It just wasn't very forthright in coming, that was all. He would have to move along the investigation without him. And the first step was getting that key.

He thought of Jessie of course, and decided a trip to the cafeteria wouldn't be a bad idea, both to get a bite for lunch, and to find out if she had talked with her son yet. Mainly the latter, but he wouldn't quite admit that to himself.

He changed clothes for the third time that day, putting on a pair of jeans instead of the shorts. It was always cold in the cafeteria regardless of the conditions outside. The day was hot of course, but he didn't seem to notice or mind. He would take the heat over the cold any day of the week. He found the typical weekend lull inside the cafeteria. It was almost one o'clock and the place was deserted.

Jessie was in her usual spot. He grabbed a burger and fries and headed to the back. Her gold tooth sparkled as she smiled widely.

"Good morning Dr. Stanley."

"Morning Jessie. How's your weekend going?"

"I can't complain. Just wish I could get outside and enjoy some of that sunshine."

"You and me both. I'm gonna try to get some studying done today."

"I admire your dedication, Dr. Stanley. If it were me, I think I'd be runnin' around outside."

"Well I did take a little time off yesterday. Actually had a date last night."

"You don't say. Tell me, who's the lucky lady?"

"Just a girl I know around here."

"It ain't that pretty blonde I seen you with in here, is it? I think you two sure look nice together."

"It's nobody you know," he lied. "Just a girl I met. It's no big deal really."

"Well I hope you had a nice time. You need to take a break every now and then. I think you're workin' too hard."

Rick looked back towards the food, making sure they were still alone. "Miss Jessie, you haven't had a chance to talk with your son yet, have you?"

"As a matter of fact, I have."

He waited for her to elaborate, but she did not. "Did you talk with him about the key?"

"I been thinking on that some," she said. "I don't wanna get you in no kinda trouble. I know you're talkin' about breakin' into that man's stuff. I don't like him a bit, but I sure don't wanna see you get into no trouble over him."

"I know Jessie. But it's something I've gotta do. Having that key will help, but I'll get into there one way or another. You giving me that key won't decide whether or not I go through with all this. It will just make it easier, that's all."

She reached into her pocket and pulled out a small key on a safety pin. She looked around as well, then placed it into Rick's hand. He smiled.

"This is the original," she said. "It sits in the mouth of some big fish he's got on top of some bookcase. I never seen it, but that's where Daryl says it's from."

"You don't know how much I appreciate this, Miss Jessie."

"You just stay out of trouble Dr. Stanley. I don't want to hear about you getting busted snoopin' around up there. Now he got that key last night. If you're smart you'll do what you need to do soon and get it back before he sees it missin'."

"Don't worry, Miss Jessie. It'll be back in its place by morning."

"You be sure that it is. I don't want none of y'all gettin' in no trouble."

"I really appreciate all your help," he said sincerely.

"You just go on now. I'll see you tomorrow."

"What about the food?" he asked.

"Burgers and fries are free today. Freezer broke and they're tryin' to cook it all up before it gets bad."

"Thank you Miss Jessie. For everything."

Rick ate quickly in the cafeteria, alone with his thoughts. He set the key on the table in front of him, running through various scenarios as he fondled it with his right hand. He knew he would have to make another trip tonight, but was desperately trying to come up with another plan. Much to his dismay, nothing else would come to mind.

Once he had finished, he dropped his empty tray off on the non-moving conveyer belt and headed back to the dorm. A quick stop at Evan's room produced the same result, and he rode the elevator back up to eight, becoming increasingly concerned.

His thoughts were once again of Monika, and he knew that if he didn't call he would not be able to get her out of his head. Probably wouldn't be able to anyway. He had written her number down in several places, just in case, but had memorized it last night as soon as he heard it. He picked up the phone and dialed.

"Hello," she answered on the second ring.

"Good morning," he said, immediately realizing it was after noon.

She recognized his voice right away. "Don't tell me you're just getting out of bed."

"Of course not. I've been up for hours. I didn't wake you did I?"

"Hardly. I've been up since eight."

"Good for you," he said. "Getting any studying done?"

"A little. How 'bout you?"

"Not yet, but I'm thinking hard about it."

"It sounds like it. You just been goofing off all morning?"

"I actually got up and went to church today. First time in forever."

"I'm impressed. What brought all that on?"

"I don't know," he answered truthfully. "Just something I wanted to do."

"So what's up for the rest of the day?"

"I don't know. Studying I guess. How 'bout you?"

"I think I'm gonna get together with my dad for a while tonight. Do that family thing."

"Did you tell him about your big date last night?" Rick asked.

"Not yet," she laughed. "I thought I'd spring that on him tonight. He'll be so excited."

"Not as excited as I was," he responded, making himself blush over the phone.

"It's nice to know I have that effect on you," she said, with a hint of tease in her voice.

"Promise you won't tell anyone."

"Don't worry Stanley. Your secret's safe with me."

"Are you up for a repeat performance sometime?"

"Sure, I'd love to. What'd you have in mind?"

"Oh, I don't know. I guess let's just see how the week goes. Maybe dinner one night later in the week or something?"

"Sure, that sounds great. Let's just leave it open for now and we'll play it by ear."

"Do you care if people know we're dating?" he asked.

"Is that what we're doing now?"

Rick feared he had overstepped his boundaries. They had just made a second date. That was dating, wasn't it? Maybe she didn't think so. Fortunately she let him off the hook with minimal pain and suffering.

"We probably shouldn't walk in to class tomorrow holding hands and making out, but if it comes up I'm certainly not going to deny it. What do you think?"

"That sounds like a good idea. Don't get me wrong, I sure don't mean to...uh...I mean I'm not.....well, you know what I mean. I'll just never hear the end of it from some of the guys, that's all."

"You mean like Cameron?"

"Well, for starters, yes. Cameron."

"Rick, if you want to keep this to ourselves for a little while and see what happens, that's fine with me. I promise not to be offended."

"That really doesn't bother you?"

"Of course not. I know what you're talking about. You think Cameron's gonna ride me any less?"

"He'd just be jealous, that's all."

"You're probably right," she said with sigh.

"All right, it's settled then. I guess I better run. It's already two thirty and I haven't opened a book."

"I've finally met someone who studies more than I do."

"I just hope it pays off someday."

"It will, don't worry. I guess I better run to. I'm meeting dad before long. Big cookout over at his house this afternoon."

"Sounds like fun."

"Not really, but I can't get out of it now. I'll tell you all about it tomorrow." She paused for a moment. Rick could sense there was something else.

"I hate to even bring this up," she said, "but what ever happened with that file cabinet key and all that nonsense?"

Rick thought for a moment, then lied. "My lead on the key didn't pan out. I guess I'll have to put the detective work on hold for a little while."

"I'm glad to hear it," she said. "You're nuts for even thinking about it in the first place."

"Let's not get this all stirred up again."

"All right, I'll be quiet. You already know how I feel about it."

"Thank you," he said. "If anything develops, I'll let you know."

"I'll see you in the morning then."

"Looking forward to it."

Rick hung up the phone and laid back on the bed. He wondered why he had lied to her, and decided he didn't really know. Maybe not to worry her. Maybe to avoid any more interrogation. There was no question how she felt about him making another unauthorized trip into Shire's office. Truth be told, he didn't care for the idea much himself. But he had to remember Charlie.

The next couple of hours were well spent. Rick chose to remain in his room, but was actually quite productive. The amount of material they had accumulated in just one week was legion. The thought of an entire semester was beyond overwhelming, and he tried not to think about it. One day at a time.

He felt comfortable with the material they had covered up to this point. However, the weeks ahead would most certainly be an uphill climb, as the detail and quantity of work grew exponentially. At least they were gradually eased into the meat of the semester, moving more deliberately through the first couple of weeks. Even that pace was frenetic.

By five o'clock he was ready for a break. Just as he was getting up from the bed, the phone rang. He caught himself wishing it would be Monika.

"Hello."

"I figured you'd be holed up in your room studying, chief."

"Cameron?"

"What the hell's going on?"

"Like you said, holed up in the room studying."

"Sounds pretty damn exciting. Is that where you've been all weekend?"

"Not the whole weekend. I've been out and around a bit."

"The library doesn't count there, chief."

"I've actually been off campus twice in the last day or so," Rick said defensively.

"So what'd you do? Hot date or anything fun like that?"

"Not really, just out running around."

"Did you and Evan wind up playing Hardy Boys Friday night?"

"I don't know what the hell happened to Evan. He was supposed to come over Friday, but I haven't been able to find him all weekend."

"Maybe he went home or something."

"I don't know. He didn't sound like he was going home on Friday. I'm kind of worried about him if you want the truth."

"Shit Stanley, you wouldn't be happy if you weren't worried about something."

"Bite me, Cameron." They both laughed.

"So what did you do all weekend?" Rick asked.

"I ran back to the farm for a while yesterday. Took care of some business stuff and caught up with a few friends."

"I'm sure you got lots of studying done too."

"Exams are too far away for me to start studying yet. You just worry about your own grade point. I'll take care of mine."

"Fair enough."

"What are you doing tonight?" asked Cameron, quickly changing the topic.

"I don't know yet exactly. I've got some things I need to take care of."

"You wanna get a bite to eat or something? That is, if you can work it into your busy study schedule."

"Yeah, sure, why not. It's gotta be cheap, though."

"How 'bout I come up and we order a pizza? Doesn't get much cheaper than that."

Thirty minutes later Cameron was knocking at the door. Before Rick had a chance to get up, he was already turning the knob and letting himself in.

"I called Domino's and gave 'em your room number."

"And what did you order?" asked Rick, a little perturbed that he wasn't consulted.

"Big supreme thin crust. I figured everyone likes that." He glanced over at the television. "What ya watchin'?"

"The end of the local news. I wanted to see if the Travelers are in town this week."

"Thinking about catching a ball game on a school night? Surely not."

"I really don't just study all the time, despite what you believe."

"Sure Stanley, whatever you say. You study about as much as I don't study, and that's saying a lot."

"We'll see who's around at the end of four years," said Rick.

"I'll be the one walking right in front of you picking up my diploma."

Rick wanted to argue, but knew that Cameron was probably right. He was that annoying type of person who somehow always managed to find his way to the top while putting forth the minimal effort required.

"So what's happening with your little dead body mystery, anyway?" asked Cameron.

"Unfortunately, it remains a mystery."

"Did you look into it any more? Been out digging up any graves or anything gruesome like that?"

"Haven't done any grave robbing yet, but who knows what this may lead to."

"Sounds like it's still burning a hole in your brain."

"I've been thinking about it this weekend. I just wish I knew where the hell Evan was. He kind of left me hanging on this one."

"I'm sure he'll turn up tomorrow. You know he's not gonna miss a class. He's more compulsive than you are."

"Yeah, you're probably right."

"So what are you gonna do about all this stuff?"

Rick started to say something, then changed his mind. "Forget it, Cam. You don't really want to know."

"What do you mean I don't want to know?"

"I know how you feel about all of this. You're not the least bit interested in my little witch hunt."

"Hey, I'm interested. I'm here aren't I? I'm asking? Tell me what's going on."

"Why the sudden change of heart?"

"I don't know, Stanley. I guess I thought about it a little while I was home. Some of that stuff you were saying kind of makes sense. It is kind of hard to explain how that guy's body ended up in our lab."

"It's impossible to explain legitimately. I've thought about this a ton, and there's just no legal, legitimate way it could have happened."

"So what are we gonna do about it?"

"We?"

"Sure, we. I've decided to give you a hand. Somebody's gotta keep your ass out of trouble."

"And you think you can do that?"

"Sure, how hard could it be," he smiled.

"You're really serious about this, Cameron?"

"As serious as my brain allows me."

"Cause I've got some plans for tonight, and I could use some help."

"What kind of plans?" asked Cameron.

"Breaking and entering kind of plans."

"You're not going back to Shires' office again, are you?"

"That's exactly where I'm going. Evan was supposed to be my lookout this weekend. You interested in filling in for him?"

"I thought you already searched that office?"

"There's still one place we didn't look."

"The mysterious file cabinet. Was it locked or something?"

"It was."

"So what's different about tonight?"

Rick reached into his pocket and pulled out the small key. Cameron took it and looked closely. "The key?" he asked.

"The key."

"How'd you get it?"

"I'd rather not reveal my sources."

"Don't give me that crap, Stanley. If you want me to help, you can come clean. Where'd you get this?"

"One of the janitors that works up there."

"How'd you manage that one?"

"I'm sort of a friend of the family in a way," answered Rick.

"What about the office door?"

"He's been leaving it unlocked. We should be able to just walk right in."

Cameron thought for a moment. "I'm still not sure about all of this, Rick. This is some pretty serious shit you're talking about."

"Nobody's forcing you to help. If you're not interested, I'll just go by myself."

"It's not that I'm not interested. I'm just not sure I want to jeopardize my career for the sake of some indigent bum."

"It's more than that, and you know it. If something like this happened once, you know it's happened before and will happen again. I'm telling you Cam, Shires is a dangerous man, and I want to take him down."

"You sound like some stupid teenager playing laser tag or something. If you get busted, your career is over. I know you say you understand that, but I'm not sure you really do."

"Like I said, I'm going with or without you. It's just not something I can drop with a clear conscience."

"Screw your conscience!" said Cameron. "You need to start thinking about your ass."

"I've thought about my ass plenty," Rick said calmly. "You're not changing my mind."

The silence that followed was deafening. Rick got up and walked to the tiny refrigerator. It was nearly empty, but it gave him something to do. He knelt there with the door open, staring at a stale bottle of Dr. Pepper and half a six pack of Miller Lite.

"You want a beer?" he asked Cameron.

"Sure."

Rick pulled off two of the cans, leaving the final beer inside attached to five empty plastic rings. He tossed one over to Cameron, who looked up just in time to block it from smashing his forehead.

"How 'bout a heads up or something?" he asked.

"Sorry. Thought you were paying attention."

Cameron popped the top and looked up. "I'm in."

"Excuse me?"

"I said I'm in. For your little reconnaissance mission tonight. I'll play the lookout, or whatever the hell you want me to do."

"You sure you want to do this?"

"Hell no I'm not sure. But if you go up there by yourself tonight, you're liable to get busted. If you get kicked out of school, that means one less person at our table in anatomy lab, which means more work for yours truly. So I'm in."

"I'm touched by your motivation."

Cameron flashed a smile. "I knew you would be."

The knock at the door made them both jump. Rick first emotion was paranoia, wondering who could have been out there listening to their devious plan. Then he remembered the pizza.

"Dinner's here," said Rick.

"I knew that."

"You got any money?"

They pooled their collection of small bills and came up with just enough. The total was $11.53 and the 47 cent tip was all they could cover. The delivery kid didn't seem too surprised. The dorm was probably not his biggest source of tips every night.

The food was hot and they dug right in. The first beer went quickly, and Rick got out two glasses so they could split the remaining one. They ate and planned for the next thirty minutes, working out the details for their evening. Rick brought Cameron up to speed with everything that had occurred over the last week. He spared no details, other than Jessie's name and how exactly he got the key. For some reason he just didn't feel right exposing her at this time. If Cameron wondered about that at all, he showed no signs of it to Rick.

It was only eight o'clock when they finished their meal. Still another hour of daylight left. They felt safer going in after dark, although it probably didn't matter one bit. They spent that time going over a hundred different scenarios, trying to sort out just what could have really happened. None of the legitimate ones made sense. They kept coming back to the bodies for cash scam. Selling bodies against the deceased one's wishes to make a quick profit.

By nine the sun was gone. Inside with the air conditioner at full blast, it looked like the perfect night, but they knew the hot thick evening air lied waiting on the other side of that thin piece of glass. They walked out together, each carrying a few books and notes to avoid appearing suspicious. A few other students were outside walking around, most on their way back from the library, which shut its doors at nine. They moved with confidence, resisting the temptation to look over their shoulders. Once inside the Education Building, they rode the elevator up to the fifth floor and stepped out into the empty hallway.

Cameron smiled. "Nice and quiet up here," he whispered.

"Let's just get moving. I don't want to be up here a minute longer than we have to."

"Lead the way, chief."

Neither spoke again as they made their way down the long hallway to the suite of offices at the far end. Rick stepped inside first, with Cameron right on his heels. Every office was dark and quiet. The doors were left open on all but one. The one belonging to Raymond Shires.

"You said it would be open," said Cameron, a little too loudly.

"Shhhh," Rick whispered back. "I said it should be unlocked. Let's check."

They crept over together. Rick tried the knob. It turned easily.

"Bingo," he smiled.

"You want me to wait right here?" asked Cameron.

"You really need to be watching the hallway," Rick whispered back. "Ok, get busy. I'll be out here."

Cameron the sentry took his post by the front door. He stuck his head out into the hallway and looked about, seeing no movement in either direction. In the meantime, Rick got to work.

With Cameron watching his back, he felt pretty comfortable turning on the main overhead light. It would probably allow him to move along more quickly, and the added risk was minimal. He and Evan had searched the room pretty thoroughly the other night, so he went straight to the file cabinet. Four stacked drawers, one of which might just hold the answers to some very difficult questions. The key fit perfectly, and the button popped out as he moved it a quarter turn counter-clockwise. He left the key in place and started with the bottom drawer. It was empty. Closing it quickly, he moved up to drawer number two.

Fortunately Dr. Shires was a compulsive man, and each file was labeled neatly at the top. Rick scanned them quickly, but found little of interest. Mostly notes from some research projects he was involved in. There were several folders filled with journal articles which pertained mostly to his work. It would take hours to read every page, and Rick decided to move on for now.

The third drawer was just as organized, and Rick's eyes widened when he saw their contents. Every test for the entire semester was laid out before him. Weekly quizzes, major exams, lab practicals, even the semester final. Everything. There were even multiple copies of each one. It would be so easy to just slip one out of each folder and fold up into his pockets. Nobody would ever know. Without thinking, he abruptly slammed the drawer closed, shutting out all temptation. The noise brought Cameron into the room.

"What the hell are you doing in here?" he whispered loudly. "It sounds like a damn bowling alley!"

"Sorry. The drawer kind of slipped out of my hand."

"Well keep it down in here! Have you found anything?"

"Not yet. I've got one more drawer to look through. You better get back out there before someone walks up."

"All right, but hurry up. I'm getting a bad feeling about this."

Rick put the test file out of his mind. He knew he would never really be able to steal a test, despite the overwhelming temptation. It wasn't his style. He would leave them as they were and continue on with the search.

The final drawer was the top one. If it wasn't in there, then the night was wasted. It was also packed tight with neatly labeled files, just as the two below had been. It seemed to contain a wide assortment of papers, from personal documents to business invoices. He didn't really know what he was looking for, but stumbled across it about a third of the way back. A plain manila folder marked 'CADAVERS'. This had to be it.

Rick pulled the file and sat down at the desk, first carefully noting the label on either side so it would be properly replaced. It took him a moment to look through the papers, but this was definitely it. It started with two pages, stapled together, containing a list of cadaver names, all of which had apparently been procured through the state. Following this was a stack of consent forms, one for each body. Some were signed by the deceased themselves, no doubt part of some type of will. The others were authorized by someone else's signature, probably the next of kin as many of the surnames matched those of the deceased. Rick scanned through each page, but Charlie Ellis was not listed anywhere.

Following this was a second list containing only three names. Charlie Ellis was the first of the trifecta, followed by two more names that he didn't recognize. These had to be the three latecomers to the class, the ones added after the first lab. The next three pages were their consent forms. Each of the signatures matched the same name as the body, including Charlie's. The forms were identical to the first batch, and neither gave any mention as to the source of the bodies. Everything seemed to be in order, much to Rick's dismay.

He left the file lying open to Charlie's page and went back to the cabinet. He scanned through the remaining folders, but found nothing else of interest. The consent form of Charlie's was the only pertinent finding, and it did nothing but disprove his theory. Not exactly the purpose of tonight's mission.

Rick took the form and walked out of the office to show Cameron. He found him rummaging through the secretaries desk in the outer foyer.

"You're supposed to be keeping watch! What the hell are you doing?"

"I'm listening, and I run out there every minute or two. I'm just searching around out here a little bit."

Rick softened. "Any luck?"

"I haven't found dick. What do you have there?" he asked, pointing to the single piece of paper in Rick's hand.

"The consent form that Charlie Ellis apparently signed to donate his body."

"Apparently?"

"Well, it's got a signature on it. It may be his, but I'm gonna check it out to be sure."

"You just gonna take it?"

"There's a copy machine over here in the corner," Rick said, walking towards it. On his way across the room he stuck his head out into the empty hallway, then walked up to the copier.

"Damn, it's not turned on." He fumbled in the scant light, feeling the sides of the machine until he located the power button. A loud hum filled the room as it roared to life.

"That thing's loud as hell," said Cameron.

"It should be warmed up in a sec and we can turn it right off again." Rick looked around nervously. "Check that hallway again, will ya?"

Cameron did as instructed and again saw nothing. He shut the door most of the way to help muffle the noise, which also darkened the room significantly. They both stared at the copier, using all their mental telepathy to hurry it along. After an eternity the humming stopped and the green 'ready' light flashed on.

Rick had the paper already loaded, and hit the print button right away. He hit it a second time, making an extra copy. They both came out perfectly. He removed both copies, as well as the original, and killed the power.

"You got it?" asked Cameron.

"Yeah." He held up the original. "Let me get this put back."

"Put it up and let's get the hell out of here."

Rick was already inside the office. He carefully replaced the form in its proper place in the file. He saw the other two names below Charlie's, and wished he had made a copy of that page as well. Finding a pen in the front drawer, he jotted down the names of Charlie's companions on the back of one of the copies. With everything back in order, he replaced the file in the top drawer and closed it tight. Through the door he could see Cameron nervously pacing, and couldn't resist cracking a smile. It took a lot to shake him, but tonight he was nervous as a cat. Rick seemed less bothered by the whole situation, probably the result of spending two previous nights snooping around the office. Sad to say, but the whole breaking and entering thing was becoming old hat.

Rick locked the cabinet and pulled out the key. He had already spotted the fish on an earlier visit, and placed the key carefully into its mouth. Quite an ingenious hiding place, really. He gave the exam drawer a final fleeting thought, then listened to his conscience and let it go. His only justification for his many recent illegal activities was that he was taking the moral high ground. Stealing a test would nullify that argument, leaving him a mere petty thief. The choice was clear.

They left the building unnoticed, and walked quickly back to the dorm. Both were tired and ready to call it a night, and they split off to their own separate rooms at the elevators. Once inside, Rick kicked off his shoes and laid out on the bed, stolen paper in hand. It looked legitimate enough, but anyone could forge a signature. He studied the other two names, wondering if they had similar stories. Did their families think they were safely buried in some lovely cemetery full of birds and squirrels, or were they all meant to be sprawled out in the eighth floor lab? There was definitely work to be done, but now he at least had something to go on. There would be plenty of tasks to fill the day tomorrow.

Before being overtaken by sleep, his final thoughts were of Evan. He wanted desperately to find a logical explanation for his disappearance, but none were forthcoming. He tried to convince himself that nothing was wrong, and pictured Evan showing up early for class in the morning in his usual seat. Yet he couldn't fend off the eerie feeling that something was just not right. Consciousness faded and thoughts of Monika filled his wandering mind.

CHAPTER 15

The second Monday. They had survived the first week of medical school. Their numbers had shrunken by a few, but for the most part they remained intact. Of course they had yet to see their first exam, but it still felt good to be starting a new week.

Rick was actually almost thirty minutes early to class, a rare feat for him. He had awakened even before the alarm made its first noise, and never really could get back to sleep, another rarity. Too many thoughts and ideas running through his overworked mind. Rather than fight it, he got up, showered, and ate a couple of untoasted Pop-Tarts. He left the room a few minutes early to allow time for a coffee stop in the cafeteria. He had hoped to run across Jessie, but she was not at her usual register and nowhere to be seen.

Several classmates had already taken their seats in the lecture hall. Rick made some small talk with a few, but most were focused on reviewing the day's lectures before they got started. There were all types of medical students found in any given class. Those in the room thirty minutes early were the gunners. The top of the top. The most intense of an already intense group. While Rick was serious about his grades, he was not in their league. He finally decided to take a seat and wait for class to begin.

Monika walked in around ten till. She spotted Rick immediately, and took the seat to his right. She looked stunning in a casual sort of way, understated yet elegant. He felt very fortunate to be sitting by her side.

She smiled at him as she opened her books. "Decided to stick around for another week?"

"I thought I'd give it a few more days. Stick around until they decide to throw me out of here."

"Yeah, me too I guess. I figure I'll hang around for the first round of tests anyway."

"We may all leave after that week."

Monika quickly changed the subject. "I tried to call you last night."

"Oh you did?" Rick found it very exciting that she was calling him. "Missed me that much, huh?"

"Couldn't bear another moment without the sound of your voice in my ear," she replied.

"I was home studying most of the night. Cameron and I ran around for a little while. You must have called when we were out."

"And just what were you two gentlemen up to?"

"I'd tell you, but I don't think you really want to know."

"Try me," she said.

"Let's just say we were out doing a little research."

"What kind of research?" she asked suspiciously.

"Just research, that's all." Rick really didn't want to get into a big discussion about the cadaver matter this morning. He knew how opposed she was to their sleuthing, and was actually growing tired of defending his actions to her.

"You weren't out digging up bones or anything gruesome like that, were you?"

"It hasn't quite come to that yet." Rick wished she would drop the matter.

"So you're not going to tell me?"

"I told you Saturday night what I was planning to do."

Monika lowered her voice. "Tell me you didn't break into Shires' office again?"

Rick looked around the room and saw that several more people had begun to file in. The entire row behind them was now full, everyone readying their notebooks for the lecture ahead.

"Let's walk and talk for a minute."

He stood and got out of his chair, and Monika quickly followed suit. They walked down the steps and out the door at the front of the auditorium. The hallway outside was empty. Rick led her into a small vacant classroom and shut the door behind them.

"Too many ears out there," said Rick.

Monika leaned back against one of the tables. "So you did go through his office again, didn't you?"

Rick didn't answer right away.

"I can't believe you talked Cameron into something like that. Did you find anything up there?"

He paced the small room nervously. "I guess I might as well fill you in, since you know the rest already."

Monika sat silently and waited for him to go on.

139

"I got that key for the file cabinet and we went through it last night. Not much in there really, but we did find the consent form that Charlie supposedly had signed."

"So maybe he did mean to donate his body," she said.

"I don't know, maybe he did. Still doesn't really add up. It's easy enough to fake a consent form."

"More conspiracy theories?"

"I guess if that's what you want to call them."

"Sounds to me like you're getting a little paranoid."

"It's not paranoia if they're really out to get you," he said. Neither laughed.

"So how'd you ever drag Cameron out there? I thought he was dead set against all of this."

"I think he was worried about me out there alone. I was supposed to be working with Evan on all of this, but his sorry ass still hasn't shown up."

"I'm sure he'll make it to class this morning."

"Speaking of class," Rick said, "They're probably in there starting without us."

Monika looked up a the clock and saw it was nearly five after. "Oh shit, we'd better get back up there." She moved towards the door. "Let me know what you dig up next."

Rick smiled. "Starting to get a little interested?"

"Just don't want you getting yourself in too deep."

"I'm flattered by your concern."

"Well, don't be," she flirted back. "I just don't want my lab partner kicked out of school. It means I'd have to do twice the work."

"That's two days in a row that someone's told me that. I'm starting to feel unappreciated as a person."

Rick smiled and playfully shoved her out the door. They walked back into the classroom from the front and saw Dr. Shires had already started his lecture. Hoping not to be noticed, they snuck quietly back to their seats and opened their notebooks.

"Dr. Reese and Dr. Stanley. How nice of you two to join us this morning."

They both blushed. "I'm sorry sir," said Rick. "It's my fault."

"That was never in question, Dr. Stanley. I expect you to be seated on time, or do not attend at all. Do you think you are capable of doing that."

Rick heard the sound of muffled amusement spread across the room, all at his expense of course. He quickly cut his losses.

"Yes sir, it won't happen again."

Dr. Shires returned to the class and nothing more was said. Rick and Monika settled in and took a few notes. Rick scanned the room looking for Evan, but he was nowhere to be seen. He decided to run to the Dean's office between lectures and let them know he was missing. Maybe he had some kind of family emergency or something. If so, they would probably know there. If not, then they should be made aware of his disappearance.

Unfortunately, the Dean's office was little help. They were not aware of anything unusual regarding Evan Sanders, and did not seem all that interested in helping him track down a student who had missed one lecture on a Monday morning. Apparently this was not the first time that a medical student had skipped class. Rick saw their point, but was unable to make them see his, and eventually gave up trying. He was able to talk them out of Evan's home address and phone number, although even this took some effort. Confidentiality was a serious issue, as well it should be, and it was next to impossible to gain access to another student's files.

Rick placed the number back into his wallet and headed back to class. He paid little attention to Dr. Williams's ramblings, as he began formulating a new game plan for his investigation. He thought first of calling Evan's parents, but picturing the worry and fear they would no doubt experience upon hearing of their missing son, elected to postpone contact for now. Perhaps there would be something in his room that might be of help. Lead him in some direction. Any direction. It meant breaking into another room, but the risks were minimal and his motives just. Besides, what was one more illegal entry to an accomplished thief such as himself?

Rick made a quick excuse to Monika at the end of class, promising to explain everything this afternoon in lab. He walked briskly back to the dorm and straight to his room, dropping off his books and returning immediately down the elevator to Evan's floor. He had thought of several options for getting into the room. One was from the balcony. It was only three floors up, but he would have to get out there somehow, perhaps through a bathroom window. Another possibility was finding a key. There must be any number of master keys floating around, it was just a matter of convincing someone to let him use it. That would be Plan B. Thinking and walking, Rick soon arrived in front of Evan's room. Just to be thorough, he tried the knob. It opened easily.

Who would have thought it? It actually bothered him a little that someone as compulsive as Evan would leave his door unlocked. Didn't exactly fit the personality. Nonetheless, he was glad that he had. He wasn't too fond of Plans A and B.

The hallway was empty, unusual for the middle of the day, and Rick stepped into the room unobserved, locking the door behind him. A sense of normalcy filled the room. Everything was neatly in its place. The bed was made. All the books were neatly shelved. Not a single piece of trash was found anywhere except in the wastebasket. It looked just as it had the other night, when they sat and reviewed their conquest from the earlier raid on Shires' office.

The red light on the answering machine was blinking, and Rick hoped for a break. He pushed the 'message' button.

"You have three messages.....beeeeeeep."

"Hi Evan, it's mom and dad. It's Friday evening about five o'clock. I guess you must be up at the library studying tonight. We just wanted to see how the first week of school went. Give us a call tonight if it's not too late. Your father and I have a brunch with the Henderson's in the morning, so we won't be up too late tonight. Good luck with your classes and remember we love you."

Rick smiled. Just like the Ward and June, he thought.

"Beeeeeeep........Hi Evan. It's me, Monika. I need to talk with you tonight. I just got in from lab. Would you please call me when you get in. My number is 291-0293. It's kind of important. Thanks."

His smile quickly faded. Why was Monika calling Evan on a Friday night? She hadn't mentioned anything to Rick about it, and there had been plenty of opportunity to. Very strange.

"Beeeeeeep........Hi son, it's mom and dad again. It's Sunday night about seven o'clock. We haven't heard from you all weekend and were getting a little worried. You mustn't study too hard. It's only the first week. We don't want you getting burned out too soon. Remember to take some time off for yourself. Please call us when you get in, even if it's late so we don't have to worry. We love you."

Very interesting indeed. This confirmed that Evan had not gone home for the weekend. His parents were looking for him too. Rick was concerned, for this blew the one good theory he had for the missing Evan. Other than spending the weekend with mom and dad, Rick could think of no other place that he might be.

And then there was the call from Monika. What was she doing calling Evan Friday night? Possibly a question about school, but the tone in her voice didn't sound like homework. He would ask her about the call this afternoon, if he could figure out a way to do it without letting her know how he found out.

Rick went to work looking through the small room. He started at the desk, searching each drawer carefully. In the top drawer he discovered a journal. Actually it was more of a diary, like the kind most kids had in junior high school. It came with a lock and everything. No key in site.

If he didn't think, know even, that Evan was in trouble, he would have let it lie. After all, this was a serious invasion of privacy. But he had already broken into his room, listened to his phone messages, and searched through his most personal belongings. Reading the diary was the next logical step. Now if he could just figure out a way to open it up. It was almost laughable that a ten cent lock was keeping him out, but without a key there was no way to open it, short of dividing the strap with a pair of scissors.

It cut rather easily really, using a pocket knife he found in the top right hand drawer. This would be difficult to explain now if Evan was just on some road trip somewhere. But there had to be more to it than that. Rick sat on the edge of the bed and began to read.

He flipped back to the weekend before medical school. Evan wrote about some of his fears with starting school. Fears of making the grades. Fears of fitting in. Fears of living in a new place. Rick felt bad for invading his life this way, but continued on. The next few days talked mostly about school itself. Evan had found it challenging but not overwhelming. He also wrote about his excitement in developing a friendship with Cameron, Monika, and Rick. Seeing his name turned the guilt meter up a few notches, but he forced himself to move along.

The rest of the entries were pretty routine until Thursday night. He had devoted four pages to the big cadaver mystery. He talked about their trip to Shires' office and what they had found there. He wrote how Shires was certainly into some type of illegal activity, probably involving Harper and his funeral home. He basically reviewed everything that Rick already knew, save the findings of the weekend.

The last page, however, gave Rick some answers. Answers that he didn't like very much. It appeared that Evan had plans to continue the investigation alone, not wanting to endanger Rick or anyone else. He talked about going to the funeral home himself to search for clues, making plans to drive out there the next day after class. The same evening he was supposed to come by and meet with Rick. And that was the last time anyone had seen Evan Sanders.

Rick set down the journal and lay back on the bed. What had Evan done? More importantly, what had he done to Evan? He had filled his head with crazy ideas. Ideas which he had apparently acted upon, and now perhaps gotten in harm's way. His last words spoke of plans to investigate Harper and his business, and since he had now been missing for three days, one had to assume that something very bad had occurred. And Rick felt personally responsible for whatever that was. He said a brief silent prayer for Evan.

Finishing up the search, he found nothing else of interest in the room. It was getting late, but there would still be time for a quick bite before anatomy lab this afternoon if he left now. Besides, there was nothing more to do in the room. He wanted to determine if anything was missing, but not knowing what was there in the first place made this very difficult. He took the journal with him, but left everything else as he had found it. He decided to lock the door on his way out to discourage anyone else from doing what he had just done.

Back in his room, Rick ate a quick sandwich of peanut butter and jelly and drank a glass of milk. He looked back over Thursday night's entry for a second and then third time. It sounded more ominous with each reading. He thought about going to the police at this point, something he had avoided until now. Police involvement frightened him on several fronts, not the least of which was his own guilt. With the police involved, his activities of the past few days would no doubt come under scrutiny. He didn't want to jeopardize Evan in any way, but at the same time, he couldn't quite bring himself to make the call. Not just yet, anyway. Perhaps soon, but not just yet.

Rick put the journal away, actually hiding it between his mattress and box springs. Nothing like a healthy dose of paranoia. He made it to lab with a few minutes to spare, and leisurely changed into his work clothes. Stepping out of the dressing room, he saw that Cameron and Monika were already at the table and ready to start.

"Any sign of Evan?" asked Rick, already knowing the answer.

"Haven't seen him since Friday afternoon," answered Cameron. "What did he say in class this morning?"

"I don't think he was there, was he Rick?"

"No, he wasn't. He's been missing since Friday."

Monika frowned. "It's not like him to miss class, especially a lab."

"I'm pretty damn worried about him. He's completely vanished." Rick considered telling them about the answering machine and the journal, but held his tongue. Mostly out of contempt for what he had done.

"You don't think anything might have happened to him, do you?" asked Monika.

"Oh, he'll be fine," said Cameron. "He probably just ran home for a long weekend to see mommy and daddy."

"I don't think so," said Rick. He had to tell them everything.

Monika looked puzzled. "Why do you say that?"

He looked at them both. "I got worried when he didn't show up this morning. I went over to his room to look for him. He wasn't there, but the door was open."

"Open?" asked Cameron.

"Well, unlocked. Like I said, I've been worried about what might have happened, so I went inside and looked around a little bit."

"And?"

"There's a couple of messages on his machine from the weekend. His folks called twice looking for him. He didn't go home."

"You probably heard me on there too, then," said Monika.

"That was the other message," he replied, waiting for her to explain.

"I called Friday after class when I got home. I wanted to talk with him about this cadaver business. Try and discourage him from pursuing it. He was so damn intense about the whole thing after class Friday, I just wanted to try and talk some sense into him."

Rick accepted her response. "Pursuing it is exactly what I think he might have done."

"What do you mean, Stanley?" asked Cameron.

"I found some stuff he had written down. Kind of a journal actually. He talked about going out to the funeral home to poke around."

"That Harper place?" said Cameron.

"Yeah. The proverbial scene of the crime."

"If there was any crime," said Monika.

"Anyway, he talked about going out there to look around and now he's missing."

"So what do you think we should do?" asked Monika.

"What do you guys think?"

"I wonder if we should go to the cops," said Cameron. "Report him as a missing person or whatever it is you do?"

"I thought about that. The problem is, if we go to the cops then we've got a whole lot of explaining to do. Including our little field trip last night." He looked directly at Cameron.

"I can't believe you guys broke into Shires' office again last night."

"Shit Monika, a little louder!" whispered Cameron.

She lowered her voice. "I'm sorry, I just think it's a mistake."

Rick jumped in. "Well, it's over and done with. At least we got something out of it."

"You mean that consent form?"

"Alleged consent form. It's got Charlie's name on it, but I'm not totally convinced it's his."

"I think you're losing it, Rick," said Monika.

"Maybe you're right." Rick was growing tired of justifying his suspicions.

"That's a tough call about the cops, chief."

"What do you think?"

Cameron mulled it over. "I don't want to jeopardize old Evan, but if we go to the cops now, we may be going to jail."

"Or at least get kicked out of med school," added Rick.

"You realize this means we're gonna have to do this ourselves."

"Do what yourselves?" asked Monika.

"Find Evan," they said simultaneously.

*   *   *   *

Evan Sanders couldn't remember ever feeling this tired, and was certain he had been drugged. Probably in the food, or perhaps the water they gave him to drink. He didn't recall any type of injections, but the last few days contained such a bizarre collage of images that he couldn't be certain of anything.

His head was actually the clearest at this moment than it had been in days. He tried to take advantage of that fact by surveying his surroundings and coming up with some kind of plan. His thought processes were very restricted, but he forced himself to concentrate on the situation at hand.

Focus on the doorway, he thought. Start with the known and work towards the unknown. It had worked for him all through school, and hopefully wouldn't fail him now. The door was solid oak and nine or ten feet tall. At least it looked that tall from his vantage point on the small bare mattress which he now called home. He had caught a glimpse of a strange little man through the door once or twice, his only human contact since he began his captivity. The man brought his tray of food through the door, laying it on the floor and backing out quickly. Usually it was just there when he woke up, but twice while lying there awake, he had seen him slip in and out . He had tried to get up and speak both times, but the foreign substance coursing through his body kept it from listening to his mind.

It was dead bolted from the outside, that much he could tell. A few times he had managed enough strength to try the knob, which of course was always locked. There were no windows anywhere in the room, which made it impossible to keep track of time. The only light came from a small simple fixture in the center of the ceiling. If it was controlled from inside the room, Evan had yet to locate the switch. It was switched off and on at different intervals. In his mind this represented night and day, but there was no way to know this with any certainty.

Sitting up usually made the room spin uncontrollably, so he spent most of his waking hours, the few that there were, lying on his back. The room was small, maybe fifteen feet across, and almost barren. His bed, if you could call it that, was the only piece of 'furniture' present. There was an ancient white commode sitting alone in one corner. Apparently toilet paper was considered a luxury. The ceiling, which he had become quite acquainted with, was blown. It was full of cracks and water spots, and did not appear very stable.

He felt like he had been there for two or three days, but it was difficult to tell. He was judging mostly by the amount of stubble on his face. He thought back to Friday, when this strange, awful ordeal began. His memory was filled with gaps, however, and he struggled to recall just what had occurred.

He had been to class Friday, that much he knew. There was the anatomy lab in the afternoon, then back to his room. He was supposed to have stopped by Rick's room, but for some reason had left without him. Obviously a mistake in hindsight.

The next images skipped ahead a bit. He remembered walking up to the front of the funeral home, then having second thoughts and moving around to the back for a look around. It was an older building, but of considerable size. It seemed pretty deserted, and Evan recalled only one other car besides his own in the parking lot that afternoon.

Somehow he had ended up inside the building, but didn't think it was through the front door. There were steps, long wooden, unstable steps that he had walked down. Perhaps a back door leading to a basement of some sort. He had definitely gotten into the building, but then what? His mind refused to cooperate as he fought with his failing memory. Something had happened inside the building.

That was it. The pain. He remembered the pain. It had been intense, burrowing into his right neck and shoulder. Had he been hit? That must have been it. Someone had come up from behind and struck him in the neck, rendering him unconscious. That had to be it. Somebody had heard or seen him enter the building and attacked him from behind. But who? And where was he now? How long had he been there? What would happen next? Plenty of questions raced through his mind. None of them had answers.

CHAPTER 16

"Why do you think Monika's so opposed to all of this?" asked Cameron.

"She's just worried about everything, that's all," replied Rick.

"I guess so. You'd think she'd at least try to give us a hand. Especially with Evan missing."

"I think she's just afraid to get involved. You weren't exactly jumping all over this last week, either. What caused your big turn around?"

"I don't know. I thought about it some over the weekend and realized you had some good points. Then you suckered me into that little trip last night. I figure I'm in for the duration now."

"Well, I appreciate the help."

Rick and Cameron were sitting across from each other in a booth at Beck's, waiting on their burgers to arrive. Lab had run late, and it was almost five before they completed the day's dissection. Their's was the last table to finish, in part because they were a man short, but mostly because they spent so much of the afternoon talking. Not about their work, but about how Evan was missing and how Charlie had been found. They had gone straight from the lab to Beck's, dragging their books along with them. Monika wasn't coming.

She had played the devil's advocate throughout the afternoon, discouraging most of the plans they had formulated. She told them she had family plans that night, and they went their separate ways at five. Rick and Cameron continued their brain storming over a cold beer.

"We've got to check out Harper's House of Horrors, don't we?" said Cameron.

"Is that what we're calling it now?"

"Kind of fits, doesn't it?"

"I guess so. I think that's where we've got to look. It's the only direction this thing seems to be pointing."

"What exactly do you propose we do once we get there?"

"I'm not sure really. Depends on who's there when we arrive. If it's deserted, I think we need to poke around a little bit."

"You mean more breaking and entering."

Rick smiled. "It sounds so much worse when you say it like that."

"Well, that's what it is, whatever you want to call it."

"I know. Believe me, I know. I'm not sure we'd be able to do it anyway. Walking into Shires' office is one thing. This place has probably got real locks and real alarms. Unless there's more to your past than I know, we'll never be able to break into something like that."

"So what's the point in going out there then?"

"We've at least got to look. Who knows what we'll find out there."

"You know, this whole thing could be a wild goose chase. The only thing we have tying Shires in with Harper is that he might have scribbled his name down on a scrap of paper.

"We know that Evan was going out there Friday night and that's the last time anyone has seen him."

"Maybe we ought to think about calling the cops again," said Cameron.

"If something doesn't turn up soon, we'll have to. For now I'd still rather do this ourselves. I guess that's kind of selfish, huh?"

"I think as long as we're doing what we can, it's not."

"Let's give it another twenty four hours. If we haven't come up with something by then, we're gonna have to suck it up and get the police involved."

"That doesn't exactly make my day."

The cheeseburgers arrived and the conversation came to a screeching halt. They each ordered one more beer, hoping to take the edge off of an anxious night. They paid their bill and kept all of the change, sharing none with their waitress for the evening. Both their cars were still back at the dorm, and they walked back up the hill to campus together, still carrying their books with them.

"Do we need to wear dark clothes and ski masks?" asked Rick.

"That won't look suspicious in the middle of summer."

"So what are you wearing then?"

Cameron pointed to his jeans and t shirt. "You're looking at it."

"I guess I'll do the same. You want me to drive?"

"Sure, why not. I'm out of gas, anyways."

"I need to run up to the room for a second and drop all this stuff off."

"Yeah, so do I. Gotta unload some of this beer, too."

"How 'bout I meet you down in the lobby in five minutes?" said Rick.

"You got it, chief."

They split and each made a quick run to their rooms and to the bathrooms. They arrived in the lobby at the same time and headed out to the parking lot. Rick's car was close, in the very first space in the whole lot. It had been there since yesterday morning when he got back from church. It was such a perfect spot, he hated to move it.

"So where's this place at?" Cameron asked, as they were pulling out of the lot.

Rick thought for a moment. "This is stupid, but you know, I'm not sure I know."

"You don't know?"

He slowed the car. "I don't think I do."

"I thought you did all that stuff for the funeral earlier this month."

"It was all over the phone. I never went to the funeral home. And the funeral itself wasn't there, it was at a church."

"Well don't we make a couple of fine private investigators," said Cameron.

Rick accelerated to the next intersection. "Hang on, I've got an idea." He made a U-turn at the stop sign and headed back into campus. "There's a pay phone right up here by the hospital. The address should be in the phone book."

"Where exactly were you gonna drive, Stanley?"

"I guess I was concentrating on everything else and wasn't thinking about where we were going."

Both men laughed. It was hard not too, really. They pulled up to the phone booth and Cameron got out. Rick watched as he found the page, then ripped it out of the book and ran back to the car.

"You could have just written it down," said Rick.

"With everything that's happened in the last few days, you're worried about stealing a page out of the phone book?"

"Forget it. What's the address?"

"Hang on." He unfolded the paper and scanned it with his finger. "12300 Jackson Parkway."

"That's out west of here, isn't it? Out past where the freeway stops?"

"Yeah, that's it. I know where this place is now. It's just before you get to the golf course out there. I've driven past it a few times."

"Oh, I know where you're talking about. That older looking white building with the big pillars out front."

"That's the one. I guess we knew where it was all along."

They left campus for good this time. Rick pulled onto the freeway heading west. The sun was not quite down, making it very difficult to look in that direction and drive. He slipped on his sunglasses and pulled down the visor, but still had to hold his left hand up to shield his eyes.

"Guess we should have waited till dark," he said.

"Having a little trouble seeing?"

"That sun's bright as hell. I can't see a thing."

"Well don't get us in a wreck. We've got things to do."

They eventually made it safely off the freeway. Another five minutes and they had reached their destination. Rick slowed the car as they both looked out his window for any sign of activity. There was none.

"Let's just drive around it for a second and scout this thing out," said Rick.

"I don't even see a car there," said Cameron. "Let's just pull on in."

The lot was indeed vacant. They had already driven past the turn off, so Rick pulled into a drive ahead on the right, turned the car around, and headed back towards the home. He pulled off the road again into the front drive. The building loomed up ahead of them. It was an older structure, probably built in the forties or fifties. It was two stories tall, maybe three in one place, and looked to be around ten thousand square feet. It had held up to time and nature very well, probably the result of a bit of remodeling and a fresh coat of paint. They pulled up to the front and parked the car. It sat in solitude on the steaming asphalt.

"Doesn't look like anyone's home," said Cameron.

"Shall we go and have a look?"

"I'm not sure what we're gonna be able to see. I'll bet you fifty bucks this place is locked up tighter than Alcatraz."

"Well, it's worth a look around. That's why we're here, isn't it?"

"I'm right behind you, chief. Just making an observation."

The two men stepped out of the car and walked cautiously towards the main front entrance. The landscaping was immaculate. Each and every plant was trimmed just so, and there wasn't a weed in sight. The mulch looked as if it had just been put out. Some of the crepe myrtles were still in bloom.

"You think there's a doorbell or something?" asked Rick, stepping onto the front porch.

"Who's gonna answer it?" said Cameron. "Remember, yours is the only car out there in the lot."

Rick was ignoring him as he walked up the steps to the front door. He tried the knob first, which of course was locked. There was indeed a doorbell, but pressing it brought no reaction from within. He slipped over to one of the front windows and peered inside, cupping his hands around his eyes.

"See anything?" asked Cameron.

"No, it looks deserted. Just a bunch of fancy looking furniture."

"No dead bodies lying around, are there?"

"You're hilarious, you know that Cam?"

"So what do we do now?"

"I don't know. Let's walk around the building and see if we can spot anything."

They left the porch and together walked around the right side of the building. They eventually came upon a side entrance of some sort, but the door there was locked as well. Continuing on to the rear, they found another driveway which led to a large five car garage, each slot having its own door. This was no doubt where the hearses were stored when they were not in use.

Rick nudged Cameron and pointed toward the doors. "Maybe we could get in through the garage using one of those doors."

"They look locked to me."

"How can a door look locked?" asked Rick. "Let's get down there and give them a try."

They walked down a small slope towards the garage area. Both were crouched down low for no apparent reason. Rick led the way with Cameron a reluctant follower. At the bottom of the hill, they jumped over a small drainage ditch, then walked quickly up to the back of the building. They both felt a little safer once they were out of the open.

Rick pointed to the far door. "You start at that end, and I'll check over here."

Cameron jogged off to the last big door in the row, looking over his right shoulder twice along the way. Rick started on the opposite end. He grasped the handle on the aluminum garage door, turned, and lifted. It glided smoothly up on its tracks.

"Cameron!"

He looked over, saw Rick was in, and quickly joined him.

"That was easy enough," said Cameron.

"Let's get inside and shut this door before somebody sees us." He was whispering now.

"Hang on. Let me turn a light on in here before you make it pitch black."

He searched the walls for the switch, eventually finding it towards the back next to the entrance into the building. He flipped on the first one and a giant fluorescent flickered to life above their heads. Rick dropped the door back to the floor and they were in.

Three large hearses occupied the stalls on the other end of the room. The two closest to them were empty. The room was immaculate, almost compulsively so for a garage. The back wall was lined with tools of every imaginable shape and size, each in its own assigned position. The floor looked like one could eat off it, and didn't even have any visible oil stains. The air smelled less like a garage and more like formaldehyde, a rather odd mixture of olfactory stimuli.

"So now what?" asked Cameron.

"I guess we start looking around."

"We're in a garage, Stanley. What the hell are we gonna find?"

"Let's start with the hearses over there."

"You want me to search inside a hearse?"

"You did realize we were coming to a funeral home, didn't you Cam?"

"All right smart ass. I'll search the damn hearse. But they better be empty, that's all I've got to say."

"I doubt that they store the bodies out here in the garage."

They walked over to the first car and Rick tried the handle. It was locked.

"Try the next one over there while I check these other doors."

The result was the same with every door on every car. Locked. They tried peering into the windows. There was nothing visible in the front, and the back of all three was shielded by curtains.

"There's got to be a key around here somewhere," said Rick.

"You know Stanley, I'm starting to get a really bad feeling about this. Maybe we ought to get out of here."

"We're just getting started. Don't quit on me now, Cam. Let's look around for a key."

They searched the car itself first, looking for a hidden magnet box underneath the frame. Rick then walked over to the long workbench along the back wall, leaving Cameron to check the other two vehicles. In no time at all he saw them. A row of car keys, each with its own hook. The first two sets were gone. The last three were there hanging.

Grabbing the first one, Rick walked back to the car and tried it in the lock. Bingo.

"Come here. I'm in!"

Cameron looked up and saw Rick standing by the open door and smiling.

"Where'd you find those?"

"They're all hanging up by the wall over there. Here's the set for the next one. Go have a look."

Rick tossed him the keys, then got in the front seat of the first hearse. Nothing out of the ordinary as far as he could tell. The glove box was locked and took a different key than the ones he had. Nothing under the seats or in the doors. An old Clint Black tape was left in the stereo.

Rick got back out and walked around to the back. He noticed Cameron searching through the front of the next car. The large door swung outward as he first turned the key and then the knob. Inside was a large casket.

"Cameron, come here!"

He stepped out of the car and walked over. "What ya got? Yikes!" He stared down at the large wooden box. "You think that thing's loaded?"

"I think we're gonna have to check."

Cameron waved his hand towards the car. "You just go right ahead. I'll be back here for moral support, right behind you."

Rick looked for a latch of some kind, but there was none. He grabbed the corner of the casket and lifted upwards. It moved easily and was not as heavy as it appeared. Probably pine or some other cheap, lighter wood. Once it was up where he could see, he almost dropped it back down. Inside was a body.

"Holy shit! There *is* somebody in here."

"Now what do we do?" asked Cameron.

They stared down at the dead man. He was a young black man, probably no more than thirty years old. His face was badly bruised, as if he had been beaten. He was completely naked from the waist up, wearing a pair of faded old jeans. No shoes or socks.

The initial shock wore off quickly, and Rick was the first to speak.

"Why would they keep a body out here in the garage like this? It doesn't make any sense."

"Maybe they just got him ready for a funeral in the morning."

Rick frowned. "Like this? He's hardly dressed. I can't imagine why they would just leave him out here like this."

"It doesn't make a lot of sense, does it?"

"Sure as hell doesn't."

A light bulb flicked on over Cameron's head. "What if this is another illegal body? Like our man Charlie."

"You think he's hiding 'em out here in the garage?"

"Who knows. I can't imagine they would put a legitimate body out here like this. Maybe our good friend Dr. Shires has put in another order and we're looking at his next shipment."

"I guess it's possible." Rick was thinking hard. "But why would he need a body now? The lab is set. Especially now after the three new ones came in and a couple of students have dropped out."

"Maybe he needs them for other stuff?"

"Like what?"

"I don't know, research or something. I'm sure they use cadavers for other things besides teaching us. Or maybe it's for Weddington?" he suggested, referring to the small private medical school across town.

"I wish we could find out where this is going."

"Check the address on the casket," smiled Cameron.

Rick thought for a moment. "That's it."

"What's it?"

"An address. They've got to keep some kind of records around here."

"How we going to find something like that in a place this big?"

"We're gonna look, that's how."

"Can we close that lid now?" asked Cameron.

"Yeah, I think we're done in here." He closed the lid and shut and locked the door in the back. "Let's check out the other two cars first, then have a look around."

The remaining two hearses were not nearly as interesting. No caskets. No dead bodies. Nothing. The only excitement came when Cameron accidentally backed into the car horn, stopping both of their hearts for several seconds. They found nothing in either of the remaining two vehicles, and decided to move the search elsewhere.

Rick returned the keys to their hooks, and they split up to check out the rest of the garage. Twenty minutes of diligent searching yielded nothing but a sore back from too much bending.

"There's nothing in here," said a tired Cameron. "I'm ready to get out of here."

"I think we need to get inside the main building."

Cameron looked up in disbelief. "You're seriously considering breaking into this place?"

"What do you think we've been doing for the last hour?"

"The garage is one thing, but inside is a whole different matter?"

"Why?" asked Rick.

"Why? Cause that's inside the building. The garage doesn't really count. Besides, they may have an alarm system, you said that yourself."

"I don't think so. I didn't see any signs posted, and there's not a control panel over there by the door."

"What if it's some kind of silent alarm? One that rings straight to the cops?"

"Are you coming or not?" Rick asked, already heading for the door.

"Shit Stanley, you're nuts, you know that? Nuts."

Despite the protests and against his better judgment, Cameron followed him up to the door. Rick tried the knob, which of course was locked. They searched around the door for a key, checking every nook and cranny but coming up with nothing.

"Now what?" asked Cameron.

"You know, the door's half glass. It would be easy enough to just knock out a pane and unlock it from the inside." He was thinking aloud, trying to convince himself as much as Cameron. He wasn't sure he was quite ready to literally break and enter. There was no doubt in Cameron's mind.

"No way Stanley. This is where I draw the line. I am not breaking down that door to get into there. I'll walk home if I have to, but I'm outta here."

Rick's shoulders slumped. "Maybe you're right."

"You know I am. Come on. We've done enough detective work for one night. Tomorrow you can check out those names we found last night. Maybe we can even call this Harper guy and see if we can rattle him a bit."

"I've got an idea before we go," said Rick. He took down the first set of hearse keys once again and they walked back across the garage.

"What are you doing?"

"I'll show you," he smiled, tossing him the keys. "Open it up and let's have a look at our man once more." As Cameron went to work, Rick spotted a small piece of plastic lying on the floor. He picked it up and joined his friend.

"Hand me that rag over there," said Cameron.

He took it and wiped the plastic firmly on both sides, being careful not to touch it directly.

"Fingerprints?" asked Cameron.

"There's hope for you after all," he replied. They both climbed into the back of the hearse.

Rick lifted the dead man's arm and placed the piece of plastic in his hand. He pressed his fingers against the surface, careful not to smudge, and gently removed it.

"Brilliant Stanley."

Rick looked closely at the surface. "I don't know. I'm not sure it's picking up on here very good. He stepped out and looked around again, spotting something on one of the workbenches.

"Grab that glass over there," he said, pointing.

Cameron retrieved it and Rick wiped it clean with the same rag, sticking the piece of plastic into his pocket first. "This is gonna work much better."

They wrapped the dead man's hand around the glass, pressing each fingertip down firmly. Actually, Rick did the pressing while Cameron held the glass, as he refused to touch the dead man. They were much more satisfied with the results the second time.

Rick held the glass up to the light with the rag, admiring their work. "Just like in the movies."

They locked the hearse back up, returned the key, and headed for the door. Cameron was wearing a pair of khaki shorts with large pockets, and they slid the glass inside the left front. They quietly made their exit, walked back around the building, climbed into Rick's car, and drove out of the lot. Neither of them noticed Lloyd Harper, who turned into the drive right after they pulled out. Lloyd Harper, on the other hand, most certainly noticed them.

*   *   *   *

The lucid interval that Evan had experienced was long gone. His mind was once again a spinning blur. It had to be something in the food, or maybe the water. He thought about not eating or drinking, but knew he wouldn't last long without nourishment. Those were his choices. Starvation or delirium. He chose the latter.

His world had once again become surreal. Everything was in slow motion, or maybe sped up, perhaps both, he couldn't really tell. He sometimes heard a voice, but many times realized it was his own trying to speak. Now it was the footsteps. He was sure he had heard them, but perhaps they were his own. No, he was not walking. And barefoot. These were definitely heavy shoes that were walking. Couldn't be his own.

Then the voices. Men's voices, but different than the familiar ones. New voices, but to whom did they belong? Two men talking to each other, but hard to hear the words. Then a car horn. Definitely a horn, there was no mistaking that. He tried to speak, to yell out to whoever was outside his door, but couldn't manage anything more than a whisper. At one point the door to his cage rattled, as if someone might step inside. But then there was silence again, for at least several minutes. The last noise he heard, as his unstable consciousness faded, was the sound of a garage door being pulled shut. Then there was only darkness.

CHAPTER 17

Lloyd Harper first thought of the kid. He came through the front door, turned off the alarm, then headed straight for the garage. A quick glance through the building as he walked did not reveal anything out of place. He went to the back of the garage and saw that the door was still closed and locked. Just for assurance, he unlocked the dead bolt and opened the door just a crack. Evan lay sleeping on the mattress undisturbed. He quickly closed it back before he awoke. He hadn't yet decided on the fate of the young snoop, but if he ever opted to grant him his life, he must not be able to identify him.

Back inside, he rode the elevator down to his private room. As the door opened, he breathed deeply and felt his tension ease. This was home.

In the opposite corner of the dark room sat all the surveillance equipment. The building's alarm was designed to detect any motion or entry. If activated, it rang not to the police, but to a beeper on his belt. He had been almost an hour away when it rang tonight. The screen showed there had been entry into the garage, but not the building itself. He found the exact time, then went to the video collection and found the proper screen. He had seen the two men leaving his property, but wanted to see exactly what they had been doing in his garage.

He watched without emotion for the next forty five minutes. When it was over, he carefully placed the tape back in its proper slot and verified that everything was once again up and running. He sat back at the desk, then without warning, slammed his fist down hard atop the metal file to his right. This was not the first dent it had seen.

Sitting was difficult, and pacing felt better. How dare they break into his house. Touch his personal belongings. Not to mention touching the body. His body. Even the niggers he considered his own. It had been foolish to leave him in the car, but he had planned to move him out later tonight. He cursed himself for being careless. It mustn't happen again.

Lloyd Harper could feel his blood pressure rising. He could always tell when it was getting out of control. He could feel it in his ears. The pounding, the flushing, the ringing. All signs that it was approaching a dangerous level. He found his pills in the top right desk drawer and placed one under his tongue. They tasted awful, but it was better than having a stroke.

After a few minutes he felt a little better. His head began to clear and he was able to think now. He had been careless tonight, and knew he had gotten himself into some trouble. Nothing he couldn't get out of, mind you, but trouble nonetheless. He decided to give Dr. Shires a quick call and spread the misery around a little bit.

"Hello," he answered on the first ring.

"We've got big problems, Raymond."

"Harper?"

He ignored the question. "Two of your boys were snooping around my place tonight. Found one of the bodies."

"My boys? You mean two of my students?"

"Hell yeah. Got 'em right here on video."

He now had his full attention. "Which two are you talking about?"

"Hell, I don't have the damn class roster. Come see for yourself if you want."

"What do you mean they found one of the bodies?"

"Oh, I had some nigger thrown in the back of one of the trucks. They broke into the garage and found him back there."

"What else did they find?" asked Shires.

"That's about it, as far as I can tell."

Shires paused for a second to process everything. "So why the hell are you telling me all this, Harper? Sounds like you've got a security problem. I'm not sure what that's got to do with me."

"Don't play that bullshit with me, Raymond. It's got plenty to do with you."

"Look, Harper. I've got my bodies and I'm out. Whatever trouble you're having out there now, well that's your's to deal with and doesn't concern me."

He could feel his ears again. "They're your damn students! You need to keep them under control!"

"If you'd remember to lock your doors, we wouldn't be having this discussion."

He popped another pill into his mouth and bit down on it hard. "Don't forget that I keep very careful records over here, Raymond. Every body that comes and goes through here is very well documented."

Shires laughed. "What is that, some kind of threat?"

"I'm just telling you how it is, that's all."

"You would do best not to threaten me, Mr. Harper. Now I suggest you tighten down your security, destroy whatever needs to be destroyed, and lay low for a while. And I don't expect you to be calling me again. I hope I'm making myself clear."

"You're a real piece of work, you know that Shires?"

"I'm serious, Harper. Don't screw with me."

And with that, Raymond Shires hung up the phone and ended their engaging conversation. Harper stood and resumed his pacing. He replayed their conversation in his mind. Maybe he had a few good points. Maybe he did need to lay low for a while. Stay up on the legitimate side of his business until the smoke cleared. It would be difficult to do. His clients had come to depend on him. Plus he would definitely miss the money. He needed the money.

Before he had a chance to make any major decisions, the phone at his desk rang. It was the private line, or he would have let the service take care of it.

"Yeah?" he answered.

"Lloyd? It's Jimmy Wilkins."

"Hello Jimmy."

"Lloyd, I appreciate y'all comin' out to our meeting last weekend. I know it's a long drive for y'all to get there. You know how we depend on your services."

"You sound like you're about to ask another favor."

"Well, we've got a little problem. I appreciate your help Sunday night. But we've got another job for you this week."

"I'm not sure that I'm gonna be available for a little while."

"I'm sorry, you said you're not available? That's not exactly what I want to hear from you, Harper. We're already committed to this job. It's not something I can just pass on. What the hell's goin' on up there, anyway?"

"It's nothing really, Jimmy." Harper was now a little nervous, and it showed in his wavering voice. "We've just had some unwelcomed interest in our work here recently. It's not anything I can't handle, but I feel like we need to lay low for just a little while. Let the dust settle and that sort of thing."

"What the hell are you rambling about, Harper?"

"Well, I've had a couple of break-ins since Friday. Nothing major, but I think I need to run legit for a couple of weeks until things settle down."

"Look Harper. I wish I could give you that luxury, but we've got a deal. Now I've got another job this week down here, and it can't be finished without your cooperation. Now you do whatever you have to do, but I need you by Friday."

Harper hesitated, not certain he wanted to tell him no again. "Look Jimmy. I'm sorry, I really am. But I just don't think that's smart right now. Let's hold off a couple of weeks and then we'll be right back in business. I swear."

"Harper, you don't understand. We've got a deal. You're leaving me in one hell of a spot, you know that? We need to get this done."

"And I wish I could help you. But not for a couple of weeks."

"Is that your final word?"

"I'm afraid it is."

"Dammit Harper, you know how important our work is. Without your help, we're shut down. I want you to think about that tonight. I'll call you in the morning after you've had a chance to sleep on it."

Harper was left with a dead phone pressed to his ear.

*   *   *   *

"Daddy, what was that all about?"

"That Harper is a damn lunatic. I'm starting to regret ever doing business with him."

"Why?" asked Monika. "What did he say?"

Shires stood back up. It felt better to pace. "He says two of your classmates broke into his place tonight."

"Did he say who?"

"Said he didn't know their names. I don't know what the hell he expects me to do about it. It's his problem with security"

"What did he say after you told him that?" asked Monika.

"Started talking about all the records he had lying around. Almost like he was trying to threaten me, but I don't know what he thinks I can do about it."

Now it was Monika's turn to pace. "What kind of records does he have on you, anyway?"

"Who knows what that crazy bastard writes down. All I've done is buy a few bodies from time to time. I guess he's got some kind of records showing that."

"He can't do anything to you without implicating himself anyway," said Monika. "Surely he's not that stupid."

Shires walked over to the bar and mixed himself another drink. That is if adding ice to bourbon is considered mixing. Monika was drinking bottled water, and seemed content with that. "Like I said, he's crazy. I wouldn't put anything past him."

"So what do we do?"

"*We* don't do anything. *I* am going to wait him out and see what's his next move."

"Isn't there something I can do to help," she asked with genuine concern.

"What you need to do, young lady, is get your butt home and get to bed so you can be fresh for class in the morning. You just worry about medical school, and I'll take care of everything else."

She knew that was his final word, and didn't bother arguing. "Will you let me know if I can help?"

"You'll be the first person I call," he said. "Now get on out of here and get to bed. I'll see you sometime tomorrow at school."

Monika stood with reluctance. The matter was closed and the discussion over. She had been in enough encounters with her father to know when he had made up his mind, and this was one of those times. He walked her to the front door, and received a hug and a kiss on the cheek. "Good night, daddy."

"Good night sweetheart. I'll see you in the morning."

He watched her drive away, then returned to the den to think. There would certainly be some storm clouds ahead.

CHAPTER 18

Rick awoke the next morning with a list of things to do. Unfortunately, attending class wasn't one of them. He sat down with some orange juice and a couple of cold Pop Tarts and wrote out his schedule for the day. He always felt better once he had his day down on paper.

The body in the hearse had to be identified. The glass with the fingerprints sat in front of him, wrapped in a handkerchief to keep anything from getting smudged. He had decided to call his dad and figure out the best way to match the prints without getting the police involved quite yet. They had agreed to call them in today, but he remained hesitant. If he could get the glass to his dad, he could probably get it checked at the sheriff's office over in Corman County. Maybe he could do it himself and keep it quiet for now.

The next item of business was following up on the alleged signature on Charlie Ellis' body donor consent. It should be easy enough to do. There had been numerous emergency room visits and hospital admissions over the last several months, and there had to be signatures on his old chart down in medical records. Rick knew they wouldn't match, but wanted to be thorough.

He also had the other two names from Shires' office. The two bodies that arrived along with Charlie. They too had similar consent forms, but their validity was also in question. Rick cursed himself for not copying those forms as well, but at least he had the names. He would need to find out how they died and whether or not they had funerals. And most importantly, what was their connection with the notorious Harper Funeral Home? Rick had spent some time thinking about this one, and decided the best place to start would be the city paper. They would have everything on microfilm, and it wouldn't be difficult to look back through the obituaries from the last few weeks.

He knew his dad would be up by now, and decided to start there. He answered after the first ring.

"Hello."

"Dad?"

"Rick? Why are you calling so early?" Always direct and to the point.

Rick smiled. "I thought I'd just call and wish you a good morning. Can't a loving son do that every once in a while?"

"Do you need money or something?"

"Yeah, I'm in jail and I need ten thousand for bail. Can you wire it down?" He hoped he wouldn't be having this conversation for real anytime soon.

"I'm sorry, you're just going to have to find a good bail bondsman. Now can I go? My oatmeal's getting cold."

"I've got a quick question for you. I guess it's a favor, really."

"And it's not money?"

"It's not money."

"Great. Anything I can do to help."

"It's kind of a weird story, but I don't really want to explain it all right now. Can we just leave it at that if I promise to tell you all about it in a day or two?"

"Depends on what you need, I guess. You're not in any kind of trouble, are you Rick?"

"Not really. But a friend of mine may be. I need to check some fingerprints out, and I'm not sure how to do it."

"What do you mean, fingerprints?"

"Just fingerprints. On a glass. I'm trying to identify someone and I know they've touched this glass."

"Why all the mystery?"

"I promise I'll fill you in on everything in a day or two, after I get this all sorted out. I just need your help with the glass."

"It'd be easy enough to match the prints. You know we just got that new computer up here last year. Nothing to it now, really. Assuming your man's been fingerprinted before."

"I don't know if he has or not. How can I get the glass up to you?"

"I've actually got one of my deputies coming down there this morning to drop off a prisoner. He could probably pick it up from you and bring it back up here later today."

"That would be great. Where can I meet him?"

"How about I have him come by the dorm, say around eleven or so this morning?"

"That'll work out perfectly. I should be just getting back from class then," he lied. "You remember my room number?"

"Eight twelve, isn't it?"

"That's it. I'll just meet him there around eleven then. When do you think you'll have something for me?"

"Probably by late afternoon if the prints are good and if he's on the computer. You sure you don't want to tell me what this is about?"

"I will soon, Dad. I've got a few more things to check out first."

"Well study hard, son. Try to leave the nurses alone for now."

"I'll try and control myself. Thanks Dad."

Rick hung up the phone and finished his breakfast. He had hundreds of thoughts running in and out of his head, and was finding it difficult to concentrate. Class was about to start, but he just wasn't up to it this morning. Too many things to contemplate, too many errands to run. He was considering a quick trip to the hospital cafeteria for a cup of coffee when a loud knock on the door startled him. Before he could respond, the visitor turned the knob, pressed into the door, and was halted by the deadbolt. Rick heard the thump of cranium against metal.

"Crap," he heard from the familiar voice in the hallway.

"Cameron?" he asked, turning the lock and opening the door.

"When the hell did you start locking your door, Stanley? I think I've got a subdural."

"You don't even know what a subdural is yet."

"And I suppose you know all about it now, don't you?"

Rick ignored his response. "What are you doing out of bed this early in the morning?"

"Pretty amazing, huh? I've been known to get up early on occasion."

"And just what is the occasion?"

"I thought we'd do a little more detective work this morning."

"Actually I could probably use the help." Rick picked up the glass using the handkerchief. "One of Dad's men is coming down this morning to get some prints off of this."

Cameron frowned. "You think that's a good idea? I thought we weren't talking to the police just yet."

"It's not the police, it's my Dad. He's just doing me a favor."

"What if that turns out to be a missing person or something. Then he'll have to get involved."

"If that's what's going on, then he needs to be involved."

"I guess you've got a point. You gonna meet him somewhere today?"

"One of the deputies is coming by the room at eleven to pick it up. Dad said he'd have an answer later this afternoon."

"So what else do you have planned today?"

"We need to match up Charlie's signature from the consent with the ones on file in medical records. Just to prove he didn't sign that form."

"What if they match?" asked Cameron.

"They won't." Rick put his dishes in the sink and headed towards the door. "Let's run over to the cafeteria and grab some coffee. We can talk on the way."

Cameron followed him out, then watched as Rick locked both the knob and the deadbolt. They headed for the elevator.

"So what else we gonna do?"

"We've still got these other two names to follow up on. The other two bodies that arrived with Charlie. I'd like to show that they came from Harper as well. I'm willing to bet they both had big funerals within the last couple of weeks. Probably with nice big empty caskets."

"How we gonna find that out?"

"I thought I'd run over to the paper and read through the obituaries. If they were sent to Harper's, we can call up there to confirm there was indeed a funeral and burial."

"Sounds like you got this under control. Hard to believe he'd actually be selling dead bodies like that. One hell of a way to make a living."

"The only thing I haven't figured out is Evan."

"I guess he's still missing, huh?"

"As far as I know. I tried calling his room again this morning."

"Where do you think he is?"

"I don't know," replied Rick. "But we're gonna have to call the cops soon if he doesn't turn up."

"I still think we need to give him a little time. Hell, he may just be off doing something stupid that has nothing to do with any of this."

"Evan's not the type to be off doing something stupid."

They arrived at the cafeteria and were met by a large crowd of hungry hospital workers. Both men had already eaten, so they bypassed most of the mob and headed for the coffee. Rick saw Jessie working off to the left, and they steered towards her register. They stood for a minute or two before reaching the front of the line. She smiled when she saw Rick.

"Good morning Dr. Stanley."

"Hi Miss Jessie. How have you been?"

"I'm makin' it all right. I was wonderin' what happened to you though. I hadn't seen you down here since last week."

"Oh, I've been around. Just keeping busy I guess."

"Who's your friend?" She seemed oblivious to the growing line behind them.

"This is Cameron Sharp, a classmate of mine. Cameron, this is Jessie." Rick suddenly realized that he didn't know her last name.

"Nice to meet you, Dr. Sharp. How are you liking school so far?"

"It's not too bad, I guess. Keeps me off the streets."

"Well, you study hard and learn everything you can. We need more good doctors around here." She finally started to ring up their coffee.

Cameron smiled at her. "I'll see what I can do."

"I seen that pretty young girlfriend of yours in here a little earlier, Dr. Stanley."

Rick felt his pulse quicken. "What girlfriend?"

"Yeah Stanley, what girlfriend?"

"That pretty blonde in your class. Now you know I don't know her name. She was in here with her daddy. I hope she didn't inherit none of those genes."

"Her dad was here?"

"She's not talking about Monika, is she?" Cameron was confused. "Since when is she your girlfriend?"

Rick ignored him. "Are they still around, Miss Jessie?"

"I saw her leave a little while ago. I think he's still in that big conference room in some kinda meeting."

Now Rick was confused. "Wait a minute. Her dad works here?"

"You know her dad, that horrible man." Her tone had suddenly changed, becoming quieter and more serious.

"What horrible man?" Rick already knew the answer.

"You know, that Dr. Shires. She seems so sweet to come from somebody like him. I hope you don't hold that against her, Dr. Stanley. After all, we can't choose our families now, can we?"

Cameron finally jumped back in. "You're telling us that Monika and Dr. Shires are father and daughter?"

"I thought you already knew that," she said to Rick. "But by the look on your face, I would say you probably didn't."

"Are you sure about this?"

"Sure I'm sure. My sources are pretty reliable," she smiled.

"Well I'll be damned," said Rick.

"Excuse me," said the junior med student behind them in line. "I'm kind of in a hurry."

"Oh, sorry," said Rick. "I guess we better move along Miss Jessie."

"Y'all go right on ahead. I'll get you for the coffee next time around."

Rick knew that was a lie. "Thank you Miss Jessie."

"I hope I didn't tell you something I wasn't supposed to be tellin'," she said as they walked away.

"Don't worry about it. I'll see you tomorrow."

She waved to them. "Nice to meet you, Dr. Sharp." He waved back.

They walked in silence to one of the booths in the back and sat across from each other. Cameron reached for the sugar and creamer and began to load up his coffee.

"So what's this girlfriend stuff, Stanley? You been bangin' Monika all this time and not sharing it with your best buddy?"

"Did you know that Shires was her dad?" he asked, ignoring the question.

"Not a clue. She's sure had plenty of opportunities to tell us about it too, hasn't she?"

"I wonder what that's all about? You realize we've been telling her all these bad things we think Shires has been doing. Along with breaking into his office. She knows about all of that."

"You don't think she's involved in any of this too, do you?" asked Cameron.

"I hadn't even thought about it before, but I guess she could be."

"She knows about everything?"

"Pretty much. I've told her quite a bit. Sometimes she acted like she didn't want to hear anything, but we always ended up talking about it."

"Have you two really been dating?"

"We went out once over the weekend. Saturday night. I wouldn't exactly call it 'dating' yet."

"I'll bet you fifty bucks that they're both caught up in this thing," said Cameron.

"Kind of looks that way, doesn't it." Rick wasn't sure what to believe now. This news was a bombshell, and it would take a minute to sort through it. He tried to remember exactly what he had told her. She knew of his suspicions. That he thought Shires was involved in something illegal in the way he obtained the cadavers. She also knew about his forays into the office after hours. He had even told her about the return trip to examine the file cabinet. Her dad's file cabinet.

"She planted it," said Rick.

"Planted what?"

"Charlie's consent form. She must have planted it. I told her we were going back there to look for it. She had plenty of time to either warn her father or take care of it herself."

"We still gonna try to match up that signature?"

"It's on the list of errands for the day."

"What about Evan?" asked Cameron.

"What do you mean?"

"You think she could have had something to do with him disappearing?"

"I hadn't thought about that. Surely not."

"I don't know why not," said Cameron. "Think about it. She knew about what her father was up to. She knew we were on to him. And she knew Evan was going out to Harper's Friday night to nose around."

"So what do you think happened?"

"I don't know, Stanley. But whatever it was, I bet you Monika's involved."

"Are you two gentlemen lost?"

Both Rick and Cameron nearly jumped out of their seats. Behind Cameron's left shoulder stood Dr. Glenn Williams. They had been so engrossed in their discussion that neither of them had seen him approach. Rick wondered just how much of their conversation he had heard, hoping he had not been standing there long. Looking up, he saw several other professors from the anatomy department leaving the cafeteria together, apparently all coming from the same meeting. Shires was not among them.

Cameron was the first to find his voice. "No sir, Dr. Williams. We're just grabbing a quick cup of coffee before we get to class."

"Well son, class started almost thirty minutes ago."

"Yes sir, I guess we're running a bit tardy today."

Since arriving at the table, his eyes had never left Rick. "So tell me Mr. Stanley, how are your studies going thus far?"

"Quite well," he stammered, "thank you sir."

"I hope you are spending your time wisely. Nights and weekends in the library and that sort of thing."

"I'm doing my best sir." He looked over at Cameron, who seemed delighted to be left out of the conversation.

"Well, I guess that's all we can ask of you now, isn't it?"

"We've both been working very hard."

"Yes, I'm sure you have. I hope you will concentrate your energies on the schoolwork at hand, and not get sidetracked by any other misadventures."

"Yes sir. We're leaving right now for Dr. Robbins lecture this morning."

"If I'm not mistaken, Dr. Robbins locks the doors of the lecture hall at the start of class, and doesn't open them until he has finished speaking. I'm afraid you two gentlemen may be out of luck this morning."

Cameron finally jumped in. "Well then we'll spend the time studying sir."

"I think that would be wise," he replied, still staring at Rick. "Good day, gentlemen."

"Thank you Dr. Williams," they said in unison.

They watched him leave, then waited another thirty seconds to be sure he was really gone. It appeared that he was.

"That sucked," said Cameron.

"You're telling me. What was all that crap he was talking about with the 'misadventures' and all that? You don't think he was listening to us, do you?"

"How would I know? You were the one facing his direction. Didn't you see him walk up?"

"I guess I was too busy talking. He just appeared out of nowhere."

"Scared the crap out of me."

"He was acting awfully weird, don't you think?"

"I don't know, I guess so," said Cameron. "All I know is we better get out of here before he decides to come back and chat some more."

"Yeah, let's get the hell out of here." They both stood to leave. "You still up for a little detective work this morning?"

They started walking back towards the dorm. "Where do we start?"

"I need to run over to the paper and look up those two names out there. How'd you like to go to medical records and try and match up that signature on Charlie?"

"You got it on you?"

"Yeah, it's right here." Rick reached into his backpack and pulled out the form. "Be careful with it. It's the only copy."

"This shouldn't take too long. Anything else I can be doing?"

"I think that's it until I get some more information together. I need to run so I can get back to meet that deputy at eleven."

"Why don't you let me do that? I'll be around here and that way you can finish up what you need to over there."

"That would actually help," said Rick. "Let me give you the room key. I guess just drop it off in my mailbox when you are done with it." He was working the key off the chain as he talked.

"No problem. Just give him the glass, right?"

"Yeah. Just be careful you don't smudge it or anything."

"Thanks Stanley, I never would have thought of that one."

"You gonna be in your room later this morning?"

"Unless I get a sudden urge to rush over to class or something, but I don't really see that happening."

"I tell you what. Why don't you just hang on to my key and I'll come by your room later this morning when I get done with this stuff."

"That'll work. I should be there, as far as I know."

They split up once they got to the dorm, with Rick heading straight for his car in the parking lot, and Cameron heading back to his room. Rick had looked up the address of the newspaper's main office last night, and headed out for the downtown area. It was a short drive from campus and he was pulling up to the front door within a few minutes.

The building was relatively new and consisted mostly of windows. The bright morning sun bounced off the glass and reflected back onto his face, both warming and blinding simultaneously. It felt good to be outside, but missing class still bothered him. Even if it was for a good cause.

The lobby was nicely decorated with lots of newspaper antiques, accented by a large number of beautiful green plants. The huge windows gave an airy, outdoors feeling to the room. The furniture and fixtures all appeared brand new. Not your typical front office.

The main desk was long with several people standing behind it, almost like you would see in the lobby of a nice hotel. Rick walked up to the closest person there, an attractive woman in her mid thirties.

"Good morning," said Rick.

"Good morning. Can I help you with something?"

"Yes ma'am, I need to look up some things from your paper around two or three weeks ago. Do you have that on microfilm somewhere around here?"

"Actually files that current won't be copied yet. But we've got copies of the actual paper you can look through if you like."

"That would be great."

"If you'll go all the way down that hallway to the last door on the left. There should be somebody in there who can help you pull up what you need."

"That's great. Thank you very much."

Rick walked down to the other end of the building, found the room, and settled in next to the rack containing the last month's worth of news. Each paper had a long wooden rod running through the middle, making them easy to hang but difficult to read. He started with a paper from three weeks ago and quickly found the obituary section. There were a lot of names, several of whom were taken to Harper Funeral Home, but none matched the two on his list. He set it down and reached for the next in line.

Twenty minutes later he found what he was looking for. Both people had died on the same day. Both of them were listed in the same paper. Both bodies were taken to Harper Funeral Home. Bingo. He had his first answer. Now it was only a matter of proving that they had supposedly been buried, and he would have his first piece of hard evidence.

Rick made a copy of the obituary page from that day. The listings were side by side, so it only cost him a dime to copy them both. He replaced the newspaper in the rack, folded up his page, and headed out the door. He thanked the lady at the counter on his way out. It was just after ten o'clock and he decided to head straight back to the dorm. He knew one of his dad's men was coming to meet Cameron, and he wanted to be there if he could.

At ten fifteen he pulled into the dorm lot. He was just in time to see a Corman County Sheriff's car pulling away. He tried to flag him down, but the driver never saw him. He parked the car and walked up to his room. Cameron was sprawled out on the bed reading yesterday's USA Today.

"Comfortable?" asked Rick.

"This paper's two day's old, chief. How do you expect me to read this?"

"I don't expect you to read it. And besides, it's yesterday's. They don't put one out on Sunday."

"Ok, whatever. Did you find anything good?"

"I matched those names with Harper's place. They were both taken there on the same day, about two weeks ago. I haven't checked yet, but I'll bet they were both supposedly buried last week too."

"Sounds like we've found a clue, Velma."

"Did somebody come by and pick up that glass?"

"Yeah, he just left out of here a few minutes ago. One of your dad's goons."

"I'd hardly call a deputy a goon."

"Did you see this guy?"

"Well, since I wasn't here, I guess I probably didn't."

"I thought you might have bumped into him in the elevator or something. You just missed him. He was heading back home to run those prints for us."

"So you gave him the glass?"

"I'm not a moron, Stanley. It wasn't that complicated of an assignment."

"I know. I just want to be sure he gets it today. Did he tell you when he might have something?"

"He was gonna report in to your Dad, but said it shouldn't take long once he gets back."

"How'd you do with that signature?"

"Well, I didn't quite get to that yet this morning."

Rick stared at his friend. "What do you mean you didn't get to it?"

"I just got sidetracked with some stuff, that's all. I thought we could run down there after lunch and check it out."

"You're a huge help, you know that, Cameron?"

"Hey, I'm here for you, Stanley," he replied, seemingly missing the sarcasm.

"We still need to check out the funeral home. See if they buried these two guys last week."

"How you gonna do that? You think they'll give you that kind of info over the phone?"

"I don't know. I would think they would. It shouldn't be any kind of confidentiality thing. Why don't we give them a call right now."

"Sounds good to me."

Rick looked up the number in the book and dialed, not really sure what he was going to say when they answered.

"Good morning, Harper Funeral Home."

"Good morning. I'm calling to find out about a couple of people who died and were sent to your funeral home. They're friends of the family, and we'd like to find out where they were buried."

"Yes sir, do you have their names and approximate dates when they were brought here?"

Rick looked down at his copy of the newspaper. "Their names are Elmer Schwartz and Claire Saddock. They both died on the same day and were there about two weeks ago."

"If you can hold on for a moment, I'll go check on that for you."

"Thank you."

Rick waited patiently while she put him on hold. Cameron looked up when he heard the silence and saw Rick was waiting.

"They gonna tell you?" asked Cameron.

"She's checking right now, but it doesn't sound like it's gonna be a problem."

"Where we gonna eat for lunch?"

"It's not even eleven o'clock yet. Are you hungry already?"

"Starving. Why don't we run across the street and grab something."

"How 'bout a peanut butter sandwich here in the room. I'm broke, and besides, I don't really want to run into a bunch of people from class and explain why we're not there."

"You mean why you're not there. They don't expect to see me."

"Hell, Cameron, half of them don't even know who you are."

"Sure they do. I'm a legend."

"I've heard you called a lot of things, but a......yes ma'am."

"Yes sir, I'm sorry for the delay. It's sort of chaotic around here this morning."

"At a funeral home?" asked Rick.

"Unfortunately so, what with the death of Mr. Harper and all."

Rick was floored. Speechless. He must have misunderstood. "I'm sorry, could you repeat that?"

"Well, I guess it's not any kind of secret. Mr. Harper was found dead in his office this morning. It's made for quite a day."

"What happened to him?" Rick was still in shock.

"I'm sorry, I've probably already discussed more than I should have. I have that information you requested."

Rick had forgotten for a moment why he had even called. "Oh, right. The two bodies. What can you tell me?"

"Well, we did take care of both of the funerals here at the home. On the same day, as a matter of fact. Mr. Schwartz was buried at Lawson's cemetery around two weeks ago and Ms. Saddock was cremated and the remains released to her family after the funeral."

Rick's mind was still on Harper. "Can you tell me how he died?"

She paused briefly, as if she wanted to tell, but was not sure if she should. "I'm sorry sir, but I really don't think I should give out any more information over the phone. This place is run over with police and a few reporters. I'm sure there will be an official report out soon."

He decided to let it go. "All right, thanks for your help."

Rick sat in silence. Harper dead. This had to tied in to this whole mess. The more he dug, the weirder it all got. And now one of the key figures, maybe *the* key figure, was lying dead in his own mortuary. Almost ironic, in a morbid sort of way.

Cameron looked up from his day old paper. "What was that all about?"

"It seems our good friend Mr. Harper was found dead this morning in his office."

That got Cameron's attention. "Dead how?"

"I don't know. I thought she was about to tell me, but then she wouldn't say. Said the place was full of cops and reporters, so I'm sure there'll be something on the news this morning."

"You think he got whacked?"

"It's hard not to think that, with everything that's going on." Rick got up and walked towards the door, mostly to pace. "This thing keeps coming back to the funeral home, and now all of sudden he shows up dead. Pretty damn big coincidence, if you ask me."

"She wouldn't tell you how he died?"

"Just said he was found in his office."

Cameron finally put down the paper. "Seems like he was the man we needed to talk to."

"I guess that won't be happening anytime soon."

"We need to find out what happened out there. You think they'll show it on the news this morning?"

"Probably. It's almost eleven now, let's see if it's on."

They spent nearly a minute searching for the remote to the television that was three feet away. The eleven o'clock news was just coming on, and the death of Lloyd Harper was their lead story.

"Good morning. For Action News Four, I'm Wendell Raymond." He straightened the papers in front of him. "Death returns to the city today, and this time it was in a most fitting place. Lloyd Harper, owner and general manager of Harper Funeral Homes was found dead in his office this morning, the apparent victim of a grisly suicide. Our Kristin Murphy is at the scene live. Kristin?"

The camera cut to a young tall blonde woman, sharply dressed in a white blouse and navy jacket. The front of the funeral home could be seen over her right shoulder. "Thank you Wendell. Things are just beginning to unfold here at Harper Funeral Home on West Jackson Parkway. Lloyd Harper apparently was found slumped over the desk in his office this morning by a concerned employee. Authorities report that he had a single gunshot wound to the temple. They will not confirm whether or not they think the injury was self-inflicted, although it certainly appears to be a successful suicide. Little else is being released at this time, pending further investigation."

"Kristin, do the police mention anything about a motive? Possibly a suicide note left by the deceased?"

Her hand was pressing the small speaker further into her ear to block out the surrounding noise. "Not at this time, Wendell, but again, little information is being released until the police are able to complete their investigation."

"Thank you Kristin. We'll have more on this breaking story to lead off our twelve o'clock broadcast. Meanwhile, down in Corman County the search continues for Calloway Washington, the candidate for state senate who has been missing since Sunday night. Authorities there have little to go on, and are asking for your help."

Rick reached for the remote and pressed the Mute button. "Suicide my ass," he said.

"You think somebody got to him?" asked Cameron.

"I'm sure of it. It's too much of a coincidence to think he suddenly just up and killed himself. Somebody's trying to make it look like that, but I'll bet you my college degree that he was murdered."

Cameron finally set down the newspaper. "Shires?"

"It's gotta be. Something must have happened between him and Harper that set him off."

"How are we gonna prove that?" asked Cameron.

"That's been the problem all along. Finding proof."

"I've got a better idea. I think it's time we went to the cops and told them everything. Let them sort it all out."

Rick thought about this for a second. "As much as I hate to admit it, I think you're right. We're talking murder now, and Evan's still missing. I don't think we can keep this to ourselves anymore."

"You think we're gonna be in trouble?"

"I don't know for sure. I would think with everything that's happened that we're not gonna be the ones they're after."

"Maybe you're right. Hell, we're solving they're murder case for them. Surely they're not gonna prosecute us for a little snooping around."

"What about Monika?" asked Rick. "You think she's involved in all of this?" He was afraid what the answer would be.

"Hard to say, I guess. She sure seems to be in the center of everything. Maybe it's just coincidence though."

"I hope you're right. I really don't want her to be involved."

The phone rang and startled them both. Rick somehow knew who would be on the other end.

"Hello?"

"Rick? It's Monika."

Rick mouthed her name to Cameron. "Oh hey. How ya doin'?"

"I'm fine. How are you? I didn't see you in class this morning and got a little worried. You're not sick or anything, are you?"

Rick forced a laugh. "Can't a guy skip class every now and then?"

"Not if he's Rick Stanley. You're just not the class-skipping type."

"Maybe it's the new me." He tried to joke, but felt very uncomfortable. "Really I just overslept is all. I was up late studying and I must have forgot to set an alarm. I've just been hanging around here this morning."

"I tried to call you earlier and nobody answered."

"I must have been in the shower or something. I thought I heard the phone ring."

"Well, just don't let Cameron's bad habits start rubbing off on you."

Rick looked over at his friend. "Now don't start comparing me to Cameron. I don't plan on making this a habit."

"Well I hope not. What are you doing for lunch? You want to meet somewhere and get a quick bite. I can fill you in on what you missed this morning."

Rick knew there was no way he could sit down with Monika today. One part of him did want to see her. He couldn't deny he still had certain feelings for her. What had occurred over the last twenty four hours could not just make that go away. But what was her involvement in this bizarre cascade of events? Did she have a role in the cadaver cover up? In Evan's disappearance? In Harper's death? He doubted she was merely an innocent bystander.

"I'm afraid I'll have to take a rain check. I'm just gonna fix something quick here in the room and then I've got some personal matters to take care of this afternoon."

"Skipping class again?"

"I don't think one day is going to affect my medical career. Will you take notes for me?"

"I suppose I could do that. You're being awfully secretive, Rick."

"It's no big deal, really. I've just got some things to check on after lunch today. I'll try and call you tonight."

Monika wasn't giving in just yet. "Why don't you let me help you out then? It wouldn't kill me to miss one afternoon of class."

"I'm sorry, but it's really a personal matter. I promise I'll call you later tonight. Just take notes for me and I'll see you in the morning." He hung up before she had a chance to respond.

"Kind of rude, don't you think?" said Cameron.

"She wasn't taking no for an answer," answered Rick, not the least bit apologetic. "I want to figure out what she and her dad are up to before I talk with her anymore."

"So what's the plan, chief?"

Rick knew the right answer. It was the only place they could now turn. They were getting in too deep, and people were starting to show up dead. "We've got to call the cops."

CHAPTER 19

Neither Rick nor Cameron was exactly sure how you went about calling the police. They thought about dialing 911, but decided that while this was probably an emergency, it was not that kind of emergency. Rick looked up the number for the police station, but there were almost a dozen scattered throughout the city. He found the one that seemed closest to Harper's Funeral Home and started to dial the number. Then he had another thought and hung up in the middle of the first ring.

"Maybe we should call my dad first."

"He doesn't have any jurisdiction over here."

"I know, but he might be able to help us out. Plus we could make sure he thinks we're doing the right thing."

"You know we're doing the right thing. I say we just call the local boys."

Rick thought for a moment, but had already made up his mind. "I'm calling dad first."

It took a few moments to get through, but his dad finally came on the line. "Hello Rick, I don't have anything back for you on those prints yet. Eugene just pulled in a minute ago."

"That's ok. I need to run something else by you first anyway. I may be in a bit of trouble here, and I want to know what you think I should do."

His voice lowered, as if there were others nearby. "What kind of trouble? I knew you were acting strangely this morning."

"You didn't happen to hear about the suicide at that big funeral home here, did you?"

"As a matter of fact, I just watched it on the news a few minutes ago."

"So did we," said Rick. "That's what I need to talk to you about."

"Why? How does any of that involve you?"

Rick hardly knew where to start. "It's kind of a long story. I know some things that make me wonder if Mr. Harper really killed himself."

"Does this have anything to do with those fingerprints you're being so secretive about?"

"That's a small part of it, yeah. You got a few minutes to listen to this?"

Rick heard what sounded like a door closing, then the squeak of a chair. Finally his dad answered him. "Start from the beginning and don't leave anything out."

Rick took a deep breath, looked over at Cameron, then began telling his dad about the first week and a half of medical school. The only interruptions were an occasional one from Cameron with a comment or question, but mostly he talked straight through. Fifteen minutes later, he finished his tale, held his breath, and waited for a response.

His dad spoke quietly and without anger. "Why didn't you tell me about any of this before now, Rick? How could you possibly have allowed yourself to get so involved in something of this magnitude without asking for help? For Christ's sake, you're a medical student, not a detective."

"I know I should have told someone, but I thought I could figure things out myself. And after a while I guess I was a little afraid that I'd get myself in trouble too."

"Damn son, you've got one man missing and now another one dead. You're neck deep in horse shit and I'm not sure I can get you out."

Not exactly the comforting words he wanted to hear. "So what do we need to do now? Me and Cameron."

"You need to do now what you should have done a week ago. You need to talk with the police. And I'm not talkin' about me. You need to talk to the city police."

"That's what we were about to do, but I wanted to call you first."

"Roger Mulholland is who you need to speak with. He and I were at the academy together, and he'll still do me a favor from time to time. He'll probably be over the case anyway. Just be sure and tell him who you are. Tell him I'll be calling later today to find out how things are going."

"I'm sorry dad. We just kind of got deeper and deeper into this thing and I guess didn't realize it until now."

"Well, you're doing the right thing by going to the police. Tell Mully I'll call him when I get these fingerprints back."

"I'd appreciate it if you'd still let me know, too."

"If you're not in jail yet, I'll call you this afternoon."

Rick didn't laugh. "Not a very comforting thought, dad."

"I think everything will work out fine, but you're in for one hell of a mess for the next few days."

"Couldn't get any worse than it's been."

"It can always get worse," said Mr. Stanley. "Always."

Rick hung up the phone and stared at Cameron.

"Call the cops?" asked Cameron, already knowing the answer.

"Call the cops," replied Rick. "Dad gave me the name of a buddy of his up there for us to talk to. Maybe that'll help."

"We need something. I sure don't want to spend Christmas in prison. Makes my butt hurt just thinking about it."

"Very funny, but nobody's going to prison. Where's that number we started to dial?"

Cameron leaned over, grabbed the phone book and tossed it to Rick. He looked up the number once again, and this time dialed it without hanging up. A bored sounding younger man answered on the first ring.

"Fourth Precinct, how may I help you?"

"Hi," said Rick, already feeling stupid. "I'm calling with some information about the incident at the funeral home this morning."

"Can I have your name?" Still bored.

"Rick Stanley." He looked over at his friend. "And Cameron Sharp."

"Which one of you is speaking, please?" Now more annoyed than bored.

"I'm Rick. And Cameron is right here with me. We need to talk with Roger Mulholland please."

"Is he expecting your call?"

"Not yet," he answered. "My father is Jim Stanley, the sheriff over in Corman County. He told me to speak with Lieutenant Mulholland about this matter."

"The lieutenant's awfully busy this morning. Why don't you just tell me what you know and if it seems important I'll have him call you back later in the day."

The man seemed quite underwhelmed and Rick was getting nowhere. He decided to try and pull rank. "Look dammit, this is Dr. Rick Stanley. It's very important that I speak with Lieutenant Mulholland right away, and if you can't help me on the phone, then I'll leave the hospital and come down there personally and let him know just how uncooperative you've been." Rick looked over and saw a shocked surprise on Cameron's face. "Would you give me your name, please," Rick demanded.

His strategy obviously worked. "I'm sorry Dr. Stanley. It's just that we get a lot of crackpots calling in, and I have to try to filter them out as much as possible. Let me get the lieutenant for you. If you'll hold on just one second." He never gave his name.

"Thank you very much." Rick waited on hold for several minutes, listening to the Spice Girls put to Muzak. "You think we're doing the right thing?" he asked Cameron.

"I don't know what else we can do. I just hope we don't get swallowed up in all of this."

"I doubt that they'd want to bust us for some misdemeanor when people are showing up dead. And Evan's still missing. I think we owe it to him."

"You don't think we need to find us a lawyer, do you?"

"I thought about it, but it sure would make us look guilty if we go running to one of those weasels. I think we're better off just going in cold."

"I think you're right." Cameron had obviously given this question a lot of thought already.

"I'm just ready to come clean and get all this crap behind us."

"You don't have to convince me. The sooner we bring Shires down, the better as far as I'm concerned."

The voice on the other end of the line jumped out so loudly that Cameron could hear every word, as if the receiver were to his own ear. "Mulholland here. Is this Jim Stanley's kid?"

Rick pictured a man of six foot four and pushing two eighty. Probably could twirl him on his finger. He found himself a little intimidated by the gruff voice on the other end of the line. "Yes sir, Lieutenant Mulholland. This is Rick Stanley. I appreciate you taking my call."

"What is it that you need, son?" The man didn't believe much in small talk. Not unlike his father.

Rick's voice sounded nervous to himself, but he continued on. "Well sir, my friend and I have some information about the Mr. Harper that was recently found dead. We know of some possible illegal activity that he may have been involved in, and would like to discuss it with you."

Rick could sense the man was glancing up at a clock somewhere. "You think what you got's all that important?"

"Yes sir, and my dad does too. I just got off the phone with him and he agreed that I needed to talk with you. In fact, he said he'd be calling you later today as well."

"I'll tell you what. I was just about to break for lunch. How 'bout you and your friend join me and you can tell me all about it?"

"Yes sir, that would be great."

"All right then. You know that new Popeye's chicken place that just opened up over on University?"

"Yes sir, I know where it is."

"I'll meet you boys there in about fifteen minutes and we'll have us a little sit down."

"That'll be great. Thank you sir."

Rick hung up the phone and looked over at Cameron. "He wants to meet us for lunch."

"Right now?"

Rick had already stood and was looking for his keys. "Why, you got something more pressing to do?"

"I'm just asking a question. Let me go take a leak and I'll be ready to go." He walked down the hallway to the bathroom and returned in less than a minute. "You got any money I can borrow?"

Rick pulled his empty wallet from the back pocket of his jeans and rummaged through it. "Looks like we gotta stop by the money machine on our way out."

They did just that. Rick withdrew twenty dollars from the ATM, loaning Cameron half of it that he knew he'd never see back. They climbed into Rick's car and drove off the campus toward University Avenue. Both men were extremely nervous, but they hid it well. They pulled into the Popeye's lot right on time.

"I don't see any cop cars out here," said Cameron.

"It's probably unmarked, dumb ass," replied Rick. "He is a lieutenant, remember?"

"I'm just saying he must have come alone."

They walked into the restaurant with Cameron leading the way. The place was full, and they scanned the crowd trying to find their man. He approached them from behind, and they both jumped as a massive hand landed on each of their shoulders.

"Rick Stanley?" the man asked.

Rick turned slightly and looked up at a rather intimidating figure. He was a black man, at least six foot three, heavy without an ounce of fat. He looked to be about the same age as his father, as expected, but that was about the only trait they seemed to have in common. Rick finally found his voice.

"Lieutenant Mulholland?"

"Call me Roger," he said, extending his right hand. Rick shook it firmly, noticing the power in the man's grip.

"This is a classmate and friend of mine, Cameron Sharp."

"Good to meet you, sir," said Cameron, shaking hands with the vice grip.

"I just sat down with my food. Why don't you boys get you something and meet me over there." He pointed to an empty table in the far corner, where the restaurant turned into a convenience store and gas station. He walked over with his food without waiting for their reply.

Cameron grabbed Rick's arm. "You never told me he was black."

"How was I supposed to know? It didn't exactly come up when I called him this morning."

"Your dad didn't tell you?"

"Didn't mention it. What does it matter?"

"I guess it doesn't, really. Just kind of caught me off guard, that's all."

They waited in line for several minutes, then finally ordered, paid, and got their food. They sat down at Mulholland's table in the two swivel chairs. He took up most of the booth across from them.

"So what's your old dad been up to lately?" he asked.

"Just working, mostly. He bought a little cabin over on Lake Belle Taine last year. He spends most of his free time trying to get it fixed up."

"What's your momma think about all that?"

Rick laughed. "I think she's just happy to get him out of the house."

"I could see that," said Mulholland. "Jim's a good man, but he can sure be a pain in the ass sometimes."

"I won't argue with you there," said Rick.

All three men started eating. "So what is it that you boys know that's so important about our poor Mr. Harper this morning?"

"We know who killed him for starters," blurted out Cameron.

The lieutenant stared down at him. "Is that right?" He seemed unimpressed. "Now it's my understanding that he did all that to himself."

"No sir, we think he was killed and we know who's responsible."

Rick looked around the restaurant to be sure nobody was eavesdropping. They seemed to be alone. "Why don't we back up a little and tell you how all this started."

"That sounds like a good idea," he replied. "How did you boys get involved with this guy in the first place?"

For the second time that day, Rick recounted the last week and a half of their lives, actually beginning with Charlie's death almost a month ago. Lieutenant Mulholland was not quite the listener that his father was, interrupting frequently to clarify a statement or ask another question. For the most part, Cameron remained silent, allowing Rick to tell the tale.

185

When all was told, Mulholland and Cameron had finished their meals. Rick's was barely touched.

"You realize you boys may be in a good bit of trouble over this?"

"Yes sir, we do. I guess that's why we haven't come forward until now."

"I'm gonna have to go over this with the detectives working the case. I'm afraid I can't really let you know where you two stand with this just yet."

"We understand, sir," said Cameron. "We just want to get this thing solved and hopefully find our friend."

"Well, what you've told me should certainly help. Like I said, we're gonna have to put our heads together and decide what to make of all of this. I can't go off half-cocked accusing a faculty member at the medical school of murder. We'll have to spend some more time with it."

Rick spoke with a mouthful of food, having just started eating his lunch. "What do we need to do now?"

"Nothing 'cept be available. Don't be planning no trips cross-country anytime soon, if you know what I mean."

"Will you let us know how things are moving along?" asked Cameron.

"As much as I can without jeopardizing the case. But I'll be in touch." He looked over at Rick. "You said your daddy's gonna be calling me this afternoon?"

"Yes sir, that's what he told me this morning."

"I hadn't talked with ol' Jimbo in probably five years. He still working in Corman?"

"Oh yeah. Been sheriff there for almost fifteen years now. I'm sure he'll stay as long as they'll have him."

"Well, I'll talk with him this afternoon if he calls." He reached into his pocket and pulled out a small note pad. "You two write down your name and numbers for me, and plan on being available if we need you."

Cameron took it from him. "It's ok to go to class, isn't it sir?"

"I think that'll probably be all right. Like I said, just don't be takin' any big trips without talking to me first."

Rick had not quite finished his meal, but left the rest of it sitting when Mulholland stood to leave. They followed him out to the parking lot and watched him drive off.

"So what do we do now, chief?"

"I guess we head back to the dorm and make ourselves available." They started walking towards Rick's car. "I can't see making it to class this late in the day."

"Can't say that was ever really an option in my mind," said Cameron. "I may just go back to the room and chill for a while."

Rick started the car quickly and turned the air on full blast. They both rolled down the windows and sat there with the doors open as the stifling heat bellowed out. "I guess that's where I'm headed too. Maybe try a little studying, if I can get my head focused."

"You're actually gonna sit in your room and study after the morning we just had?"

"What the hell else am I gonna do, holed up in that broom closet of a room. Might as well accomplish something while I'm sitting there."

"You're a machine, Stanley. A fucking machine." He pulled his door shut and rolled up the window. "We gonna go anytime soon, or you wanna sit at Popeye's all afternoon?"

Rick closed his door. "What's your hurry, you got a hot date or something?"

"I just got better things to do than sit out here in this tanning booth."

"All right, we're going, we're going." Rick secured his seat belt and pulled away. They drove back without speaking, each man lost in his own thoughts. He tried to remain calm and rational about the whole matter, but Rick Stanley was worried. It wouldn't take much for the whole matter to explode in their faces, ending a promising career in an instant. Perhaps they would even be prosecuted for their confessed illegal activities. The thought of retaining a lawyer once again crossed his mind. And finally, and foremost in Rick's mind, was the missing Evan. The longer he remained missing, the more Rick worried about his safety and well-being. This was his primary motivation for doing what he had done this afternoon.

When they arrived at the dorm, they split and went their separate ways, promising to call each other if anything came up. The elevators were slow in coming, and for the first time Rick walked the stairs up to the eighth floor. He was embarrassed at how winded he was at the top. School was already taking a toll on his body. He rounded the corner and nearly knocked down the woman coming towards him.

"Damn, I'm sorry. Are you ok?"

"I'll be all right," replied Monika. "I was just coming to see you."

CHAPTER 20

It felt like he had been imprisoned for at least a week, but time had little relevance in his new world. Without a clock or a window, there was simply no way to know how long he had been held captive. The drugs made it even worse. It had to be coming in the food and water, and short of starving himself, Evan knew there was no way to avoid them. Perhaps he was building a tolerance, however, and his lucid intervals seemed to be growing longer. He had even spent some time examining his new home, hoping to find a way out. It seemed hopeless.

The circumstances of his capture were also becoming more clear. He could now remember slipping inside the building through an unlocked window. He had been searching for anything that might shed some light on the cadaver mystery, and vaguely remembered going through an office when the sharp pain in the back of his neck exploded through his body. The details at the end were still a blur, but would hopefully return with time. Time was certainly the one thing he had in abundance right now.

Evan was in such a deep thought that he didn't hear it initially. Then it grew louder and finally caught his attention. His first thought was the drugs. They had blurred the line between reality and illusion, and the voices he heard were most certainly coming from inside his head. But soon they became louder yet, and eventually unmistakable. Two male voices, garbled to where the words could not be heard, yet definitely there.

Evan's mind was clear enough to realize he had to make his presence known. He stood up and tried to yell.

"Hello? Can anyone here me?" He hadn't spoke in days, and what was supposed to be a yell was more of amplified whisper, cracking and splitting with each syllable. He tried again.

"Hello out there. Can anybody hear me? This is Evan Sanders. Is anyone out there? Somebody please help me!"

It was no use. His voice was shot, and not about to project through the thick walls. He stopped and listened again. The voices were still there, but fading away. He panicked as his chance for rescue slipped quietly away.

Out of desperation, he beat on the door with both fists. The sound echoed in the small room, but it did not make the voices come back. The folding chair in the corner of the room caught his eye, and he launched it against the wall. It fell harmlessly to the floor, just missing his right knee on its way to the ground. He pounded once more, but his energy was spent and there was little effect.

The voices were gone now, and he questioned whether they were ever there. His sanity was slipping away with each passing moment, and a sense of despair filled his mind. It was almost as powerful as the hunger coming from his empty stomach. He remembered eating supper last night, three cold pieces of pizza which were no doubt leftover from his captor's last meal. But he had slept since then, which was usually followed by oatmeal or some other type of cereal, and then a sandwich a few hours later. Neither of those great feasts had made it down yet, and he wondered if they were coming at all. He laid back down on his cot and watched the walls spin.

* * * *

"Did you hear something?"

"Like what?"

"I don't know, like somebody knocking or something?" He paused. "There it is again. Did you hear that?"

They both stood for a moment and listened. Silence.

"I think you're losing it, partner. I don't hear nothing."

"Come on, just humor me a second and let's go look around back there."

"You realize it's almost two o'clock and we still haven't eaten lunch? I say we tell 'em the garage is clean and let's get out of here."

"Just five minutes. Let's have one more look around over on that side. What if I really did hear something?"

He began to follow him, but continued the argument. "Maybe it's the ghost of one of these dead guys that got whacked."

"This place really bothers you, doesn't it?" he asked.

"It doesn't bother you? All these dead people lying around in here?"

They were walking back to where the knocking originated. "What are you, scared, Phil?"

"Hell no I ain't scared," he lied. "It just ain't natural being around all these dead people, that's all." He wanted to change the subject. "Now where did you think you heard something?"

"I thought over at this end somewhere, but I couldn't really tell for sure."

"You know we've looked through there twice already." Phil's stomach was directing the conversation.

"Everywhere except that little bathroom that was locked."

"What are you gonna do, break down the door to see if somebody's knocking from inside the commode? It's just a damn suicide. We're gonna get our asses chewed if we go bustin' up the place."

"Not as bad as we would if we miss something important."

They walked back over to the far end of the garage to the bathroom. A unisex toilet sign was stuck to the door, slightly off center. There was a faint light coming out from underneath. They bent down to look at the locks.

"Kind of strange having two deadbolts on a bathroom door, don't you think?"

"Maybe he liked to whack off in there and didn't want to get caught," replied Phil.

They tried the door, but the knob and both deadbolts appeared to be locked

"Hello," shouted Phil. "Any dead people hidin' in there taking a dump?"

His partner ignored him. "We gotta get inside there."

"How you gonna do that? This don't look like the kind of door we're gonna just kick in."

"Isn't that locksmith place right down the street?"

"Christ Bill, you know how long that's gonna take?"

He wasn't giving in. "What if there's something important in there. Mulholland called back and said search every inch of the place. If he finds out we left out a room just cause the door was locked, he'll be all over our ass."

Bill seemed to be winning the argument, as he most often did. "You think we could maybe eat lunch first?"

He had an answer ready. "Why don't you run out and pick us up some burgers while I get a locksmith down here to get us inside?"

"As long as we eat, I don't give a rat's ass what we do." He was already heading back towards the car. "You want cheese on yours?"

"Yeah."

"How 'bout fries?"

"Now how am I gonna eat a cheeseburger without fries?"

"Hey, I'm just askin'"

"If you forget the ketchup again, I'm sending you back." They were yelling across the garage now. Once he was gone, Bill found the phone and dialed the locksmith, first getting the number from information. Fortunately he was there in the office and volunteered to drive right down. He arrived just as Phil returned with their lunch.

"We gonna eat first, or open locks?" he asked, already knowing his answer. Unfortunately, Bill had a different one.

"Put your food down for two seconds. Let's clear this room and then you can eat whatever you want."

Phil wasn't giving up. "You two get started," he said, reaching into the bag. "I'll be right here for moral support." He pulled out one of the burgers, opened the paper, and put nearly a third of it into his mouth.

Bill looked over. "You're disgusting, you know that?"

He smiled back. "Just hungry, that's all."

They watched the locksmith as he opened up a cloth pouch containing thirty of forty tiny odd shaped screwdrivers and wrenches. He tinkered with the upper deadbolt first, trying several different tools. Five minutes later it was open, and he directed his attention to lock number two. Another three minutes and it was done too. He then pulled a credit card out of his wallet and slid it into the crack of the door.

"A credit card?" asked Phil between handfuls of fries.

"Best tool I own," he replied. "Works wonders for these older locks in the knob."

They watched as he slid the card down to the last lock, pulled towards himself, and twisted the knob. The door swung outwards. They were shocked by the size of the room inside.

"Holy crap," said Phil from the back. "That ain't no bathroom."

"Is he always that observant?" joked the locksmith.

"Only after lunch," Bill replied. "I think we can get it from here. Appreciate you coming over pronto like that. Just send the bill to the department."

"Hey, no problem. Give me a call anytime I can help." The police department was always good about paying their bills, and made up a significant percentage of his income. He was more than willing to make himself available anytime.

Bill looked over at his partner. "You wanna put that burger down for a second and come have a look?"

"I'm right behind you," he replied, taking one last bite to finish it off.

They walked together into the room. From the doorway it was obviously more than just a bathroom. It apparently went back into the wall, and the part that was visible from the outside was some type of foyer into the larger room. They stepped inside cautiously side by side. Neither man reached for his gun, but they both made sure they knew exactly where it was.

The room was large, probably forty by forty, but unusually barren. The floor was concrete, and sheet rock hung on the walls. There were no windows, but the room was dimly lit by two bare bulbs hanging from each end of the ceiling. Two folding lawn chairs sat in one corner, placed on either side of a flimsy-appearing card table. It barely supported a small black and white television with rabbit ears. A long counter top with a sink lined the wall behind the table and chairs. There was a small refrigerator sitting at one end of the counter, the kind you might find in a college dorm room. There was also another door, held shut by a single deadbolt lock. It was made of solid wood and nearly reached to the ceiling. It looked conspicuously out of place in this odd room. They pushed against the door, but it held firm.

"You think Smitty's taken off by now?"

"I bet he has," replied Bill. "We may have to call him right back. We're gonna have to see what's inside here."

They looked around the room again. "I'll bet this Harper guy was one weird dude," said Phil. "What do you think's up with this room?"

"Kinda bizarre, isn't it?" he replied. "I'm just wondering what's behind curtain number three over there."

"You don't think there's a key around here somewhere, do you?" asked Phil.

"Who knows," he answered. They walked back over to the counter. "Let's have a look through these drawers."

They opened the one on the top right first, and inside was a ring with four keys. Three of them looked too small, but the fourth had potential. Bill picked it up and walked over to the door. He slid it into the lock and turned. It opened easily.

"Better to be lucky than good."

They walked inside, into a much smaller room. It was no more than twelve by twelve, and was also lit by a single bare bulb. There was a commode in one corner next to the door. The only other thing in the room was a small cot up against the opposite wall. On it lied a young man they had never seen before. He was breathing, but appeared to be unconscious. When he would not arouse, they ran out to call for an ambulance.

*　*　*　*

Rick had to invite her inside. He didn't see any way around it. Monika was the last person in the world he wanted to talk with right now, but she had given him little choice. His feelings toward her were very ambiguous, and he didn't have the time to sort through them right now. Her involvement in this case, whatever that would turn out to be, scared Rick. She may not be the one who killed Harper, or did Lord knows what to Evan, but she was most certainly caught up in the middle of this chaos in some form or fashion.

But damn she looked good in those shorts.

"You want something to drink?" he asked, opening the refrigerator. "It looks like your choices are beer or water."

"I'm fine, thanks. I just had something from the cafeteria."

Rick looked at his watch. "Shouldn't you be in class right now?"

"We all have the same schedule, remember? At least I made it to the morning round."

"All right, give me a break." He sat down on the chair, across from the bed where she had already perched. "I miss one day and I'll never hear the end of it."

Monika was fishing. "I just can't help but wonder what could be so important to make Rick Stanley miss a whole day's worth of class. You aren't seeing another woman behind my back now, are you?" She was flirting, but serious at the same time.

"You know you're the only woman for me, Ms. Reese." Rick had already decided he wouldn't reveal anything just yet. No matter how hard she tried to get it out of him.

"Come on Rick, tell me what's going on. I don't like that you're keeping secrets from me." She was persistent.

"I promise it's no big deal. I've just got some personal business to take care of. Family stuff that I don't really want to talk about right now."

"Nobody's hurt or sick or anything, are they?"

"No, it's nothing like that."

"Have you heard any more about Evan?" she asked, trying to change the subject.

"Nothing. I'm getting pretty worried about him. We talked with the cops, but they weren't much help." Not exactly a lie.

"When did you talk with the cops?"

"Earlier this morning. They're gonna keep a lookout for him, but didn't seem too interested, really."

"What do you think happened to him?" she asked.

Rick was tired of the question and answer game. He stood and headed back towards the door. "I'm sure he'll turn up soon with some stupid story." She watched him get up, but remained seated.

"So why don't you come back to class with me this afternoon. Micro lab's just getting started."

"I told you, Monika, I've got some things I've got to finish up. Now get on out of here and I'll see you tomorrow. Quit worrying about me. Everything's fine."

She stood reluctantly, obviously not happy that she wasn't getting her way, but not knowing what else to do. "Will you call me tonight?" she asked.

"I'll try my best, but I'm not making any promises."

She finally walked toward the door. "Do I get a kiss before I leave?" she asked seductively.

Rick smiled. There was simply no way he could turn down a request like that. "I suppose. If it will make you feel better."

She pressed against his body, wrapping her arms around his waist. Despite her tall stature, Rick still looked down on her. Their heads turned slightly as their lips met. The electricity was every bit as strong as it had been the other night, and he had to concentrate to keep his knees from buckling. It lasted no more than five seconds, but seemed an eternity. They finally stepped back, Rick reminded himself to breathe, then opened the door for his guest.

"Please call me tonight," she said.

"Ok, I will."

"And let me know if I can help with whatever it is you are doing. I wish you wouldn't shut me out of this, Rick?" She had to try one last time.

"I'll be fine. Quit worrying." He was ready for her to leave before he said anymore. "I'll see you in the morning."

Rick had the last word, and she reluctantly walked away. The phone rang just as he closed the door, slapping him back into reality. Lieutenant Mulholland was on the other end.

"I've got some good news I thought you might like to hear."

"I could sure use some."

"That Sanders buddy of yours turned up this afternoon."

Rick nearly dropped the phone. "Evan? Is he all right? Where is he?"

"They think he's gonna be just fine. Couple of my boys found him while they was out searchin' Harper's place this afternoon. Looks like he had him locked up in some hidden little room somewhere. I hadn't been out to see it yet. They're goin' over every inch of it right now."

"You mean he kidnapped him?"

"Hard to know just what happened yet. They say he might have been drugged or something. Had a real tough time wakin' him up. He's over there at your Med Center right now, but they think he's gonna be fine."

Rick didn't know what to say. He realized now that their decision to call the police had been the right one. With Harper dead and Evan locked up in his building, he would surely have died otherwise. He was anxious to tell Cameron.

"Do you think we can get in to see him?" asked Rick.

"It's fine with me, if the docs will let you in. I'll have to ask that one of my detectives be with you though, in case anything comes up that might help with the investigation."

"Sure, that'll be fine. I'll probably run over there right now."

"Oh, I almost forgot. I talked with your daddy a few minutes ago. I wish you would have told me you were runnin' prints on somebody."

Rick realized he hadn't mentioned that at lunch. "I guess I just forgot, with everything that's happened. It wasn't intentional."

"Well, anyway, he got a match. Anthony Shackleford. A forty eight year old black gentleman from the Delta. I checked with the funeral home just before I called you, and they said he was buried this morning. Died over the weekend in a car wreck. Who is this guy, anyway? Some stiff you found in the morgue?"

Rick took a second to process this new information. It wasn't exactly the huge break he was hoping for. He kept his disappointment hidden well. "We found him inside one of the hearses when we were out there. Just seemed like he was a bit out of place, that's all. I guess it was nothing."

"Well, anyway, your buddy's up at the hospital if you want to go see him. I thought you'd like to know."

"Yes sir, I appreciate your call. I'm headed that way just as soon as I hang up."

"Remember, stay close in case we need you."

"You know where I live. I'll either be here or in class."

They hung up without saying goodbye. Rick was exuberant at the thought of seeing Evan. His disappearance had worried Rick more than he had let on to anyone. He didn't want to say it, or even think it for that matter, but he had feared something terrible had happened. He wondered if he would ever see his new friend alive again. He grabbed his wallet and keys and headed out the door. Once downstairs, he walked back down the dorm hallway and knocked on Cameron's door.

"Who is it?"

"Open the damn door. I've got good news."

"Rick? Hang on a sec."

It took nearly thirty seconds for him to finally open the door. "You hiding a girl in there or something?"

"I was actually trying to study and had everything laid out on the floor in front of the door. What's up?"

"They found Evan," he blurted out. "He's up here in the hospital, but they think he's gonna be ok."

"What happened to him?" asked Cameron.

"I'm going over to talk to him right now, if you want to come along. Mulholland said they found him locked up in a room somewhere over at the funeral home. That crazy son of a bitch must have kidnapped him or something."

Cameron stepped back into the room. "Hang on, let me get some shoes on." He found a pair of old Reeboks and put them on without socks. "You said they brought him here to the hospital?"

"That's what he told me."

"Is he hurt or something?"

"Mulholland said he'd been drugged, but it didn't really sound like he'd been hurt." Cameron locked the door behind them and they headed towards the hospital.

"You know what room he's in?" asked Cameron.

"He never said. We can ask at that big information desk out front."

"I hope you know your way around that place better than I do." Freshmen medical students rarely saw the hospital or real live patients.

"I think I can get us there. I took patients up to the floor some nights when I worked the ER this summer."

They walked through the automatic doors at the main hospital entrance. The cool dry air was a stark contrast to the sauna outside. They walked over to the desk for guidance.

"Can I help you?"

Rick was their spokesman. "Can you tell me what room Evan Sanders is in, please?" She was cute, so he decided to be polite.

She typed in his name on the keyboard and looked up at the screen. "I have him listed in the emergency room. Evan Q Sanders? Is that him?" she asked, looking up at them.

"They must still be working him up down there," said Rick. "Thank you for your help."

"Your welcome. It's right down this hallway, then left, then take the elevators down to G and follow the signs."

"We got it, thank you," replied Rick, not really listening. They walked off quickly towards the ER.

"What do you suppose the 'Q' stands for?" asked Cameron.

"Queen, if you can believe that. Some sort of family name, he told me once."

"Evan Queen? Poor kid never had a chance." They both laughed. The fact that Evan was found and alive and hopefully well had lifted a tremendous burden off their shoulders. Everything else seemed almost inconsequential to them now. Evan's kidnapping had made it personal, and now they had him back.

The ER was running about average speed. Rick took them in through a back door and they headed for the big board at the front of the department. They could no longer write a patient's full name out where all could see, due to concerns about confidentiality, but he was the only EQS initialed up there at the present time. Cameron started walking towards the room, but noticed he was alone, leaving Rick still staring at the board.

"Hey Stanley, it's this way." When he didn't respond, he walked back over to the board and poked his right arm. "You with me, Stanley?"

"Room 5," said Rick.

"Yeah, I got that already. Let's go see him."

Rick finally looked up. "That's the same room where Charlie Ellis died last month. Room 5."

Cameron gave him a second. "You haven't been back here since then, have you?"

"I've been through a couple of times. I guess it just kind of hit me today."

"Well, it's just a room. Come on. Let's go see Evan."

They walked down to the room, together this time, and were met by two uniformed officers standing at the door. They looked like bouncers at a club, and didn't appear too interested in letting anybody pass.

Rick thought about calling himself Dr. Stanley, but was dressed in shorts and a t shirt and didn't think he could pull it off. Through a crack in the curtain he could see Evan's legs, as well as another person, probably a detective, sitting at the foot of the bed. They didn't appear to be talking, although he could only see Evan from the waist down. He didn't realize he was staring until the officer spoke.

"Can I help you two with something?"

Rick looked at him. "Yes sir, we're classmates of his and would like to get in to speak with him for a minute if we could."

The taller of the two mountains continued speaking. "I'm sorry, but nobody is allowed in there right now. You'll have to come back later."

Neither Rick not Cameron was accepting that for an answer. "Look, we'll just be a few minutes. He's been missing for days and we need to talk with him."

Now Andre the Giant stood. "Maybe you didn't hear me correctly. I've got orders to let nobody in here, and I ain't making an exception for you two." He remained standing to punctuate his statement.

Rick looked over at Cameron. "I guess we're gonna have to call Lt. Mulholland back and tell him we couldn't get through."

"He's not gonna be happy," said Cameron.

A look of doubt flashed across Andre's face. "How do you two guys know the lieutenant?"

"I just got off the phone with Roger," he said truthfully. "We're sort of helping him with this investigation and he asked us to come down and speak with Evan. See if we could find out anything else since we know him so well."

Now Andre was confused. He looked down at his partner for help, but he just shrugged up at him. Then he had an idea. "You guys wait right here a minute."

He walked into Evan's room and closed the door behind him. They could see the two men talking, but couldn't hear a sound. Thirty seconds later, they reemerged together.

"I'm Detective Sparks," he said, extending his right hand. "You two must be Rick Stanley and Cameron Sharp."

Rick was impressed as he shook the man's hand. "You must have spoken with Lt. Mulholland," he deduced.

"He called a minute ago and said you two might be coming by. You're welcome to come in and see him, but I'll need to be in the room with you."

"Is he doing ok?" asked Cameron.

"They said he's gonna be fine. He's still a bit groggy from whatever they drugged him with out there." Sparks opened the door and they followed him in. Andre scowled, but didn't say a word. "He's sleeping now, but he'll wake up for you."

Evan looked awful. He was lying there asleep, but shook every few seconds with some type of tremor. His eyes appeared sunken, and were underlined with black. He hadn't shaved in nearly a week, but the only hair was some around his chin and sideburns. He had an IV in each arm, with two bags of fluid hanging from poles at the head of the bed. He was hooked up to the heart monitor, and Rick noticed that his vital signs all appeared normal. He was almost afraid to touch him, which was apparently noticed by Detective Sparks.

"The doc said he's not as bad off as he looks. Just shake him a little and he'll wake up."

Rick did as instructed. "Evan?" he said softly. No response. He shook him harder and raised his voice. "Evan, it's Rick and Cameron. How you doing?"

His head moved back and forth, then his eyelids struggled to raise. It took him a moment, but soon he focused in and a look of recognition flashed across his face.

"Hey guys."

They smiled back, delighted that he seemed to be all right. "You picked one hell of a way to skip class," said Cameron.

Evan gave a faint smile. "I've still made it to more classes than you have this year, Cameron."

He laughed. "All right, no fair taking shots when I can't hit you back."

Rick finally jumped back into the conversation. "So tell us what you've been up to all this time. Just hanging out and goofing off?"

"I wish I could remember everything so I could tell you."

"Tell us what you do remember," said Rick.

Evan had to think for a moment. His mind was still not his own. Every thought, every action, took a conscious effort to enact. As if his mind were moving in slow motion. He had been told about the drugs in his system, and odd combination of barbiturates and benzodiazepines, and they had certainly done their job. The doctors said they would clear within the next twenty four hours, but they hadn't left yet.

"There was this room," he said. "A small room with a cot and a toilet. I think I've been there for several days, but time was hard to keep up with."

"You were missing for four days," said Rick. "You think you were in there that whole time?"

"I think so. I don't really remember being anywhere else."

"How'd you get there in the first place?" asked Cameron.

"I think somebody hit me from behind and knocked me out."

"Did you see who it was?"

"No, I never saw it coming. I just remember this awful pain in my left shoulder and neck, and then waking up in that room."

Cameron had taken over the interrogation. "Were you at Harper's when this happened?"

Evan looked over at the detective. "If I tell them something illegal I might have done, is that gonna get me in trouble?"

"I can't promise you anything," he answered truthfully. "But if we're ever gonna get to the bottom of this, then we'll need to know everything you've got."

He seemed satisfied with that response. "I'm remembering more now than the last time we talked," he said to the detective. "I remember going to Harper's that night. Friday night." He looked to Rick. "I was supposed to get you, but decided to go alone. I guess I didn't want to get anyone else in trouble."

"Why were you so eager to risk your neck for this?" asked Rick.

"I kind of wondered that myself, really," he answered. "I never really came up with a good answer. It's a little embarrassing, but I think I was just having fun playing detective."

"So what happened after you got to Harper's?" asked Cameron.

They could all tell that Evan was growing tired, but he wanted to continue. "The place looked empty when I got there. No cars or anything. I found a window that was unlocked and slipped inside to get a look around."

"Did you find anything?" Cameron asked what they were all thinking.

"That's where it starts getting kind of blurry. I remember looking around a little, but it wasn't long before I got hit. Next thing I know I'm waking up in that little prison or whatever it was."

"Did you see who hit you?"

"No, I never saw him. They must have snuck up on me from behind."

"They?" asked Rick.

Evan shrugged. "I didn't really mean they, I guess. I never saw who it was. Him, her, or them, I don't know."

Detective Sparks finally spoke up from his chair at the foot of the bed. "Did you see anyone at all while you were there?"

Evan closed his eyes. For a moment it looked like he had fallen asleep, but then they opened and he spoke. "I may need to rest for a little bit, guys. I'm feeling kind of nauseous all of a sudden."

Rick could tell he was starting to fade. There would be plenty of time for questions, and Evan needed his rest. "How 'bout we check back in the morning?" he asked.

Evan nodded but didn't speak. His eyes were closed again. Rick felt awful about what had happened, still blaming himself for not reporting everything sooner. His motive for silence had purely been self preservation, and he wasn't proud of it. He made a personal vow to uncover every loose end that remained. Harper appeared to be the central figure, and he was now dead. But there were still a stack of questions yet to be explained.

Rick looked over at the detective. "Can we come back in the morning?"

"Sure, I don't see why not. Someone's relieving me shortly, but I should be around most of the day tomorrow."

"Do you know what room he's going to?"

"Six thirteen is what they told us. Said they were cleaning it a little while ago, but it's supposed to be ready anytime."

All three men began walking towards the door. "Thanks for letting us in to see him," said Cameron.

"No problem. I'll see you guys in the morning."

Rick looked up at the clock as they left the room. It was nearly five o'clock. "Look how late it's getting."

"Some kind of day, wasn't it."

They started walking back through the hospital, heading towards the dorm at the other end of campus. "What are you gonna do for supper?" asked Rick.

"I'll probably just whip up something in the room."

"I think I'm gonna get a bite here in the cafeteria before I head back, if you want to join me?"

"No thanks, I'm too damn broke."

"All right, suit yourself." They arrived just as they were opening the doors, and stopped at the front entrance.

"I don't know how you can eat that crap every day," said Cameron.

"It's not so bad once you get used to it."

"Well you just have at it, chief. I'll catch you tomorrow."

"You going to class?" asked Rick, already knowing the answer.

"Yeah, look for me on the front row. I like to get there early so I can get a good seat."

"Well, I'll give you a yell sometime tomorrow then."

"All right," he said, starting to back away. "Let me know if you hear anything from that lieutenant buddy of yours." He turned and headed back to the dorm without waiting for a response.

Rick walked into the cafeteria in search of something to eat. He first went straight back to the registers, but Jessie was nowhere to be found. He then walked a little further, into the dining area, looking for a familiar face, but finding none. There were mostly people from the hospital, the part of campus he still knew little about. It was barely five o'clock, and would be closer to six before any kind of crowd would gather.

Realizing he would be eating alone, he got his food in one of the Styrofoam containers with a flip lid to eat back at the dorm. At least there he would have the television to keep him company. He paid full price for his meal, then headed out the side door, down a long hallway, outside across the drive, and into the dorm building. He nodded at a few familiar faces from class on the way up to his room.

Inside, he turned on the local news and sat down to eat. If they had run anymore about Harper's death, he probably missed it. They had already moved on to the weather. Ninety five and humid for the next five days, according to the exclusive Doppler weather forecast. Whatever that was.

He managed to eat while largely ignoring the food. The same could also be said for the television. Rick's thoughts were elsewhere tonight. Too many questions running through his wandering mind. Who killed Lloyd Harper and why? How did Charlie Ellis' body get to the anatomy lab? Why was Evan Sanders kidnapped and held captive for days? Questions were plenty, but answers few. He was so deep in thought that he didn't hear the phone until the third ring.

"Hello."

"Rick. It's your father." He always sounded a little uncomfortable on the phone.

"Hey dad. I just got in a few minutes ago."

"I know. I've been trying to call. Are you all right?"

"Yeah, I'm ok. I guess Lt. Mulholland's filled you in on our conversation today."

"He did. Did you go see that Sanders kid yet?"

"Cameron and I just came from there. He's pretty whacked out on some kind of drug, but it looks like he's gonna be ok."

"Was he able to tell you anything more?"

"Not too much. Apparently he broke into the funeral home and was looking around when somebody cold cocked him from behind. They kept him drugged up in some little room since Friday."

"Did he find anything?"

"He said he couldn't remember much of what happened inside there."

"Well, I just got off the phone with Roger. Apparently they found something to implicate that professor of yours."

"Dr. Shires?" asked Rick.

"Yeah, Dr. Shires. They're picking him up right now."

"What did they find?"

"He wouldn't tell me what it was, but it sure sounds like he's your man."

"I'd love to know what it was they found out there," said Rick.

"I tried to get it out of him, but he wasn't talking. I can't blame him really. I'd be doing the same thing if it were me."

"I thought I'd visit Evan again in the morning and see if he might remember anything else. It sounds like Shires is going down."

"So you think he's been getting his bodies from Harper to fill up the lab?" his dad asked. "That's pretty reprehensible, if you think about it."

"It sure looks like that's what happened."

"Well, I'm sure it will all come out eventually. I just wanted you to know about it."

"I'm glad you called."

His dad cleared his throat, a sure sign of an impending lecture. "Listen Rick. I hope all this hasn't become such a distraction that you've forgotten about school. You've still got your classes to worry about. This will most likely blow over and leave you out of it, and then you'll just be a freshman medical student again. I don't want you to get so involved that you lose sight of that."

Rick realized all this of course, but it probably did him good to hear it from someone besides his conscience. "I know dad. I'm planning to stay right here and study tonight, and should be back in class in the morning."

"That's good to hear. Your mom and I are here if you need us. Keep me posted if anything comes up."

"I will. Thanks for all your help."

"Good night."

Rick picked at his supper for a few more minutes, but his appetite had left him. He finally gave up and tossed it into the hallway trash can half-eaten. He would probably be starving by seven or eight, but it had no appeal to him at present.

The next three hours were spent pretending to study. He tried different subjects and different positions, but nothing seemed to help. The first few lines of a page went fine, but by the time he was halfway down his mind had strayed. What had been the most important thing in his life last week was now taking second stage to the murder mystery as it slowly unraveled. After two trips to the snack machine, three to the bathroom, and one to his car for something he just had to have, Rick finally threw in the towel. Tomorrow would be another day, one that would hopefully start by attending his eight o'clock lecture.

The phone rang just after nine, and Rick was thankful for the interruption. He reached to pick it up, then thought about Monika. She had said she might call tonight, or did he say he would call her? Either way, he had little interest in striking up a conversation, knowing where it would soon lead. By the fourth ring, he could stand it no longer.

"Hello."

"Rick?" He could barely make out the whisper on the other end of the line, but recognized the voice nonetheless.

"Evan? Is that you?"

"I've just got a second. The policeman in here fell asleep and I wanted to talk with you about something without them listening in."

Rick pressed the phone harder into his ear to pick up the words. "Sure Evan. What's going on?"

"What I said this afternoon about not remembering everything wasn't exactly true. I did find some stuff while I was in there. Inside one of the desk drawers." He paused, prompting Rick to speak.

"What did you find?"

"I probably should be telling the police about this too, but I wanted to see what you thought about it first." Another pause.

"Well, are you gonna tell me or not?"

"I'm telling. Just let me finish. I found some other things that Harper was involved in. Illegal things. And I'm talking about more than just selling bodies to the medical school, which he was doing, by the way."

"Selling them to Shires?"

"Yeah. He sold those three to him last week, including your friend Charlie, for five thousand dollars apiece. It wasn't the first time they had done business, either."

"So it's true," said Rick.

"You were right. But there's plenty more. And not just with Shires, either."

"What kind of stuff are you talking about?"

Evan didn't answer right away. "I'll be fine in a few days Mom, I promise."

"What are you talking about?" asked Rick.

"Ok, I'll see you soon. I love you too."

With that the line went dead. Rick realized his companion must have awakened, and Evan was quick to cover the call. Rick was left with one hell of a cliff hanger to mull over for the night. What was Evan about to reveal? What had he found deep inside Harper's House of Horror? He would be forced to wait until morning to find his answers. It would be a very long night.

CHAPTER 21

Rick awoke to his alarm at seven AM with the same questions running through his mind. Unfortunately, eight hours of asleep had not yielded any answers. The puzzle seemed to be growing with every turn.

There were many things on his agenda today, but he decided to make attending class one of them. At least for part of the day. He also had an ulterior motive, for he decided that would probably be the best way to find out what had happened with Dr. Shires. Word of his arrest would most certainly spread quickly, and Rick wanted to find out all he could.

He would also make time to visit Evan this morning. He didn't know if he could catch him alone, but he had to find out what else he knew. Something he had seen Friday night that he was now remembering. Something he didn't want to tell the police.

It took only thirty minutes to shower, dress, and eat a quick breakfast. A couple of classmates in the showers ragged him about skipping class yesterday, but nobody mentioned Shires' arrest. He called down to Cameron's room before he left, but there was no answer. Either he was sleeping hard, or had already left for class. Somehow he favored the former.

He had allowed enough time for a detour through the cafeteria. He wanted to grab a cup of coffee, but more importantly he hoped to run into Jessie and pick her brain. If there were any rumors out about Shires, she would be right on top of them.

He filled his cup and headed for the line. Much to his dismay, she was not at her usual post working one of the cash registers. He paid for his coffee and was walking out the door when he saw her in the back of the dining area wiping off tables. Glancing at his watch, he turned and walked over to her. He would make time to find out what she knew.

"Good morning Miss Jessie."

She turned and smiled. "Good morning Dr. Stanley. How are you this fine morning?"

Always the same uplifting spirit. "I'm surviving I guess. It's been quite a week."

"It's only Wednesday, Dr. Stanley."

"That's what I'm afraid of." They both laughed for a second and then he continued. "I was actually hoping I might run into you this morning, Miss Jessie. I was wondering if you've heard anything about Dr. Shires at all?"

She resumed wiping, and at first he wasn't sure that she had heard him. Finally she spoke. "I heard he finally got put where he belongs."

"So you know about his arrest then."

"I've heard some things," she said without elaborating. It was like pulling teeth, but he had a feeling she had more to say.

"What have you heard about it?" he finally asked.

"I just heard they found something around that man's body that told 'em that doctor did it."

Rick had heard the same story from his father the night before, but wondered how Jessie would have heard such a thing. "Not that I don't believe you, but how would you know something like that?"

She didn't seem offended by the comment. "I told you about my son Daryl who works upstairs, right?"

Rick nodded.

"Well he's not my only boy. My oldest is a sergeant in the precinct where they took that doctor last night. He didn't know just exactly what happened, but he heard they found something out there that belong to that doctor."

"You don't know what it was?" asked Rick.

"He didn't know. But whatever they found, it made them go arrest him." Jessie smiled. "Couldn't have happened to a nicer white man."

"How many boys you got, Miss Jessie?"

"Just them two. Course I got five girls too."

"It sounds like you've made spies out of all of them," said Rick.

"That's how I keep up with things."

Rick looked up at the clock and saw he was already five minutes late for class. He thanked Jessie for her help, made an apology for his hasty exit, and headed off to the lecture hall. They had an anatomy lecture scheduled for eight o'clock, one that Dr. Shires was supposed to give, and Rick was curious how things would be handled. He walked in from the back of the room just as Dr. Williams was approaching the podium. He quickly took a seat in the back to listen.

"Good morning ladies and gentlemen," he began. "We've had a slight change of plans for this morning. Dr. Shires will not be in attendance today. I will be giving my lecture early while they line up a substitute to present the anatomy lecture."

Rick watched the class for their response. The few that were really interested and paying attention seemed mostly confused. It was apparent that nobody knew of the arrest last night, or if they did, they were keeping quiet. He looked for Monika, who would most certainly know what had happened, but she was not there. He did not expect to see her the rest of the day, certain she would be trying to help her father in any way she could. Cameron was not in sight either, but that was certainly no surprise. If fact his presence there would have shocked most in the class. At least those that knew who he was.

It took Dr. Williams a few moments to settle in and get prepared. He was probably told at the last minute that he would go on early, and did not look eager or ready to begin. It was fifteen after before he showed his first slide, and Rick had a feeling that rather than leave anything out, he would run over into their break. Ninety minutes later, he was right.

"We seem to have run over a bit due to the confusion this morning. Dr. Greenfield will be presenting the Gross Anatomy lecture in Dr. Shires' absence. We'll give everyone a few moments to stand and stretch, but then we need to move ahead in order to get back on schedule."

The class was already restless from running over, and Dr. Williams's announcement elicited more than a few moans. Everyone stood slowly and began milling around, and Rick took that opportunity to make his break without being seen. He gathered up his notebooks and slipped out the back door, the same door through which he had snuck in late.

Rick had spent all the time he could afford in class this morning. He had other more pressing matters at hand. First and foremost was Evan Sanders. Whatever he was about to say last night sounded important, and he had to find out what Evan had uncovered at the funeral home. Something he didn't want the police to know about just yet.

He stopped by the front desk of the emergency room and confirmed Evan's room number with the receptionists. She offered him directions, which he politely declined. He met a couple of classmates in the hallway upstairs heading the opposite direction.

"You going to see Evan?" one of them asked.

"Yeah. He's down this way, isn't he?"

"He is, but you're wasting your time. The big gorilla at the door won't let anyone in to see him. He's not like under arrest or something, is he?"

"I think they're just trying to protect him," said Rick. "I'll see if I can sweet talk him a little bit."

"Maybe you'll have better luck than we did, but you're probably wasting your time."

Rick walked down to Evan's room and saw what they were describing. The uniformed cop at the door was huge. Not fat huge, but muscle huge. He looked like one of those male strippers who dressed up like a policeman, but this guy was legit. If anything he was bigger than Andre the Giant from last night. The academy must be doing their recruiting down at Gold's Gym, he thought. Rick tried to show no fear.

"Good morning," said Rick.

The man stood and crossed his arms. "Can I help you?"

"Yes sir. I'm Rick Stanley. I'm here to see Evan."

"I'm sorry, but only immediate family is allowed inside."

"Is Detective Sparks here this morning?"

The man looked puzzled, but recovered quickly. "How do you know the detective?" he asked.

About that time Evan's door swung open and Detective Sparks stepped outside. "It's ok Jason, he can come in." He motioned Rick inside with his right arm. "Back for another visit, Rick?"

"Yes sir, I thought I'd see how he was doing." It took a moment for his eyes to adjust to the room. The blinds were turned shut and the curtains drawn. The only light came from the bathroom, and the door was mostly closed. Rick still hadn't gotten used to all the hospital smells, and a stale medicinal aroma filled the room. He glanced down at Evan lying on the bed. He was wearing some type of hospital gown and was half covered with a sheet. His eyes were closed. "Has his head cleared up anymore from last night?"

Evan spoke. "I wish everyone would quit talking about me like I'm dead or something."

"Your eyes were closed," said Rick. "I thought you were asleep."

"Well you could have lowered your voice if you thought I was sleeping."

"Damn, you must be feeling better, snapping like that."

"I'm ready to get out of this place and get back to school," he said. "All they want to do around here is take x-rays and draw blood."

"So when are they gonna let you go?"

"Who knows. These doctors won't tell me a thing. I'm starting to think it's the police that want me kept here for a while." He smiled over at Sparks.

"We just want you to get better, son," he replied. Rick thought he detected a touch of sarcasm.

"So how's your head coming along?" asked Rick. "Any new revelations come to you in your sleep last night?"

"Nothing much, I guess. I feel like I'm remembering most of it. There's just not that much to remember." He glanced at Sparks once again.

"What are you gonna do about your class work?"

"They're supposed to bring some stuff to me this afternoon. Assignments and lecture notes and that sort of thing. I feel like I'm home sick in junior high school or something."

"Well, hopefully you'll be back by the end of the week." Rick was stalling, trying to think of a way he could speak with Evan in private. He obviously had something to tell him that he didn't want to say in front of Sparks, but Rick couldn't figure out how to get him out of the room, and Evan didn't seem to be trying.

"Is there anything I can get for you while you're here?" asked Rick.

"Actually, I was hoping you could get some of my books for me this afternoon."

"Sure," said Rick. "Do you know what you need."

Evan opened the top drawer of his nightstand and pulled out a folded sheet of paper. I've written them down for you," he said, sitting up to hand it to Rick. "They should all be on my desk in my room. The ladies in the front office can get you the key to get in."

Rick took the paper and stuck it into his pocket without reading. He realized what Evan was doing, and was ready to get out of there before Sparks got interested in what kind of books he wanted. "I'll bring them by later this afternoon, if that's ok?"

"Sure, that'll be fine. Just whenever you get time. Hopefully they'll let me out of here soon and things will get back to normal."

"I'm sure it won't be long," said Rick. "I better get back to class before I need somebody bringing me my assignments."

"Thanks, Rick. I appreciate it."

"Don't worry about it. I'll see you later this afternoon." He looked over at Sparks. "You gonna be around all day?"

"I'm leaving at five, but I'll leave word to let you through if I'm not here."

"I'd appreciate it. I thought your boy out front was about to bench press me through the wall a minute ago."

"He's pretty harmless as long as you don't piss him off."

"I'll try to remember that." Rick walked through the door, smiling at The Terminator on his way out. He resisted the urge to say 'I'll be back'. The paper from Evan was burning a hole in his pocket, but he waited until he was down the hall and in the stairwell before pulling it out to read. What he saw came as quite a surprise. At the top of the page was indeed a list of books that Evan would need to catch up in school. But it was followed by something much more interesting. Rick read it twice, then once more to be sure it still said the same thing. He then walked slowly back towards the dorm to begin formulating a new plan.

*   *   *   *

Rick sat in his room for over an hour trying to decide what his next move would be. His first thought was to take everything to the police and let the chips fall. Then he started having second thoughts. Started thinking about ways that he could look into the matter on his own. Finally he came full circle and was back at the police. He didn't regret going to them yesterday in the first place, and decided that withholding information now made little sense.

He called up Lt. Mulholland, and after ten minutes of negotiating, fast talking, and a little pleading, was actually able to get him on the line. He arranged another lunch meeting, this time at the Burger King across the street from where they met yesterday. Rick was a little surprised that he was so generous with his time, and knew his father's influence must have played a role. At times like this it was good to have a few strings to pull.

On his way out, he tried Cameron's number once again, but there was still no answer. The man's schedule was certainly his own, and Rick had already given up trying to fight it. He pulled into the restaurant right behind Mulholland, and they parked side by side towards the rear of the building. It was almost noon and bustling inside. They got out of their cars into the screaming heat and talked for a moment in the parking lot.

"You're sure making my lunches interesting this week, you know that Mr. Stanley?"

"Don't take this the wrong way, sir, but I really wish I never had to meet you."

He laughed heartily. "I'll try not to take that personally."

"I'm glad you understand."

"Let's get out of this damn heat," said Mulholland. "I've already sweated through one shirt today."

They walked into the cool air conditioning and took their place in line. The maze of people wound back and forth, ultimately leading to the cash register and food at the front. Rick always felt like a rat looking for the cheese when he was in one of these lines.

They made small talk as they walked, and Rick picked up a few interesting stories about his dad. Mulholland seemed very interested in medical school, and Rick enjoyed talking about it. It took a full fifteen minutes before they got their food. Rick offered to pay and Mulholland thanked him without objecting.

The table they found had just been vacated, and they had to clean it off themselves before they sat down. With the chit chat out of the way, Rick started asking questions.

"I heard that you found some things out at Harper's that implicated Shires?" Not exactly a question, but he phrased it as one.

Roger finished chewing and took a drink before he answered. "We've come across a couple of things." Another drink. "I s'pose you heard we arrested him last night?"

"Yes sir, I did. I don't guess you can tell me what he's saying."

"I can't really go into too many details. He is denying he had anything to do with Harper's death, but that's no big surprise. We're gonna get it out of him before too long."

"What did you find out there?" he asked again, hoping to get more of an answer this time. He didn't.

"Now you know I can't go tellin' you about the investigation, Rick. Your father tried to hit me up for the same thing, and I wouldn't tell him neither." He smiled widely. "I know y'all are dyin'to know something, but it'll all come out in time."

"Do you feel certain he's your man?"

He had to think about that one for a second. "If you want my gut feeling, I'll tell you there's no doubt in my mind that he's involved and probably directly responsible for the death. Now proving that is a whole different story."

Rick was suddenly having second thoughts about telling Mulholland the reason he wanted to meet. He didn't know why, really, other than wanting to look into it a little more himself before he screwed up someone else's life. He wouldn't hold back the information long, he rationalized to himself, but needed a little time to put everything into place. No more than twenty-four hours, he promised himself. Just one more day.

They finished their lunch quickly, talking around and about the case, but never in much detail. It was clear to Rick that Shires had been arrested because of something they had found at the funeral home. Whatever that was, it was enough to convince them to move on Shires. Mulholland would tell him little else.

"I've got to be running along, Rick." He stood and headed towards the door, leaving their trash on the table. "I'll try to be in touch, but I can't promise I can tell you much just yet."

"I understand sir."

"I'm glad to hear your friend's gettin' better. Hopefully his memory will come around and help us out even more."

"I expect it will soon, sir." Rick was following him out to the car now. "Lieutenant Mulholland, I've got one more thing I'd like to show you, if I could?"

"Sure son, what is it?"

Rick stepped over to his car and opened the trunk. "I'd like for you to have a look at this, sir."

* * * *

Gross anatomy lab was about the only class that was strictly forbidden to miss. The lectures were not a problem. Nobody took attendance, and Cameron was not the only student who chose to sleep in late. Even the microanatomy lab could be missed and made up on one's own time. But the gross anatomy lab was different. It involved three to fours hours of dissection, three times a week. To miss just one lab meant endless hours working alone late at night, surrounded by twenty-five dead bodies, trying to follow along in the manual. Nearly impossible without the help of one of the many graduate students who spent their afternoons going from table to table to give directions and advice. Despite his predicament, Rick forced himself up to the lab.

He arrived early, going straight there after lunch. A few of his classmates had begun to arrive, and Rick joined them in getting an early start to the day. By the time Cameron arrived, he was already on the third page in the manual.

"Look at Stanley, runnin' and gunnin' up here with the top dogs."

Rick looked up from his crouched position. "I figured we'd be a little short handed this afternoon and thought I'd get a jump on things."

"Is your girlfriend coming in?"

Rick shot him a look and didn't answer right away. Finally, "I told you, she's not my girlfriend. We had one date. That's it." He spoke softly and looked around to be sure he was not overheard.

"So is she coming?" he asked again.

"I haven't talked to her, so I couldn't tell you. I figured with her dad in jail, she might be a little tied up today."

"How's Evan?"

"Better. I tried to call you this morning before I went over to see him."

"I turned the ringer off and crashed," said Cameron. "I didn't wake up until almost noon."

"How the hell can you sleep so much?" asked Rick.

"It's a gift," he replied. "So any new revelations from the little man?"

"Nothing new," said Rick. He wanted to hold back until he had all his ducks in a row. "Hopefully he'll be getting out of the hospital in a day or two."

"He's gonna be further behind than I am, and that's saying a lot."

"You're actually admitting you're behind. I don't believe it."

"Oh I'll be fine when exams roll around. I'm just not much into studying until crunch time."

"Well, anyway, I'm bringing him some books and stuff this afternoon. He's gonna try to keep up with what he can while he's just lying around up there."

"So it's just you and me, huh? Think we can handle it?"

"If you don't slow me down, we'll do just fine. I'm about halfway through already." Not quite the truth, but close.

They spent the next two hours working diligently. Their conversation was mostly limited to shop talk as they opened the chest cavity and exposed the heart and great vessels. The lungs were not until next week, but they couldn't resist taking a quick look at the pink puffy air sacks. This part of the human body was fascinating, and they both became lost in their work. Time flew, as it usually did there, and soon it was three o'clock. They had worked well together, and were the second table to finish their assignment.

"Pretty good work there, don't you think, Stanley?"

"Not too shabby," Rick replied. "I always knew those other two were holding us back." They joked on the surface, but Rick's mind was focused on other things. He was ready to clean up and head back to the room. He was expecting an important call.

They closed the lid on their body. They had talked about finding a name for him last week, but it never really came up again. Rick resisted the urge to look over at Charlie, preferring to remember him as he was before his heart was lying between his legs. They scrubbed their hands for five minutes in a futile attempt to remove the formaldehyde. A quick change of clothes and they were down the elevator and outside once again.

"I guess we just wait to hear something from Mulholland then?" asked Cameron.

"I suppose so. What are you gonna do?"

"I don't know. I need to run to the bank and get a few groceries. I guess I'll be back in the room after that."

"I'm gonna round up that stuff for Evan and then try to catch up on some studying."

"You need any help?"

"No, I think I got it. It won't take but a few minutes."

"Let me know if anything comes up then," said Cameron.

"You'll be the first."

Rick stopped at the dorm office as Cameron split off towards the parking lot. He had no trouble getting the key from the desk, and walked down the hall to Evan's room. This time the door was locked. Inside, Rick found the books that he had requested and stacked them into Evan's backpack which was lying on the desk. He felt strange being in the room alone, and made a quick exit.

Arnold was still guarding Evan's door, but this time recognized Rick and let him pass without incident. Rick walked inside without knocking and saw that Evan was asleep. A new man was at the bedside, someone he didn't recognize. He set the books down on the floor and whispered to the officer.

"These are the books he had asked for. I'll check back with him later."

"Are you Rick Stanley?" he whispered back.

"Yeah," he smiled. "Heard of me?"

"Sparks said you might be coming by. I'll tell him you were here."

"Tell Evan or Sparks?"

"Both."

Rick smiled at the sentry on his way out of the room. He walked back to the dorm, opened his door, and heard a familiar voice leaving a message on the machine.

"...me a call this afternoon as soon as you get in. I'll be here until six or seven tonight, and after..."

Rick ran over to the phone. "Lt. Mulholland?"

"Is that you, Rick?"

"Yes sir. Just walking in the door."

"I'm glad I caught you. We need to talk."

"Sure. Did you get anything back on that stuff yet?"

"That's what I'm calling about. We just got a match back. You need to tell me where that's from, son."

CHAPTER 22

Rick arrived at Monika's house just after seven o'clock that night. Sunset was still almost two hours away, and the stifling heat showed no signs of dissipating. The air conditioner in his car had little time to work during the short drive from campus. Rick was sweating profusely, but maybe more from nerves than heat.

He had called her first, asking if he could drop by later this evening for a few minutes. She had just gotten home from visiting her father, and sounded anxious about Rick's visit. Not as anxious as he was.

She had apparently been watching out her window, as she opened the front door just as Rick was walking up the steps.

"Spying at me through the window?" he asked.

"Just happened to see you pull in a second ago. Come on in out of this oven."

He followed her into the old house, enjoying the cool air as it struck his body. He followed her into the living room and took a seat on the couch at her direction. If she were nervous, she hid it well.

"What can I get you to drink?" she asked.

"You got any tea?"

"Sure. Sugar?"

"Artificial if you've got it. Otherwise sugar's fine."

"Be right back."

He watched her walk into the kitchen and out of sight. Rick was thinking about what he had to say. He wanted to word it just right, but he knew it probably would not come out as he intended. It took some work, but he finally convinced Lt. Mulholland to let him do this. It wasn't long before she returned with two tall glasses of iced tea.

"I couldn't find any of the pink or blue stuff, so you're stuck with real sugar."

Rick took a drink. "It's great, thanks."

She sat in the chair to his left and crossed her legs. Rick tried not to stare. "So tell me, Rick Stanley. What's so damn important that you just had to rush over and see me tonight? Couldn't resist my girlish charm?" She smiled as she flirted and he realized he was still not immune to her spell.

"I know about your dad," he blurted out. No warm-up. No preamble. Short and sweet and straight to the point. He decided that would be best.

"I'm not sure what you mean." She played the role on an innocent with great credibility.

"Why didn't you ever tell me that Shires was your father?"

She leaned over to pick up her glass and took a long drink. Rick knew she was stalling, trying to decide what next to say. He waited patiently.

"You think he killed that man, don't you?"

Rick had been expecting her usual evasiveness, and was quite shocked by her response. He recovered quickly, however, and took it all in stride. "Do you?"

"Of course not." This answer was quick and from the gut.

Rick decided to take advantage of her talkative nature tonight. "You know more about the cadavers than you've let on, don't you?"

She switched over to the defensive. "I know that he does whatever it takes to provide a proper education for his students. Now whether or not he breaks a few rules is really none of our business."

"When it involves somebody I knew, it damn sure becomes my business." He was trying to keep his cool, but his voice was rising, along with his blood pressure.

"That was unfortunate."

"Unfortunate? Is that what you call it?"

"You heard me." She wouldn't look up from her tea. "But whatever he did to obtain those cadavers doesn't make him a killer. I don't know how Mr. Harper died, but I promise you my father had nothing to do with it."

"So who do you think killed him then?" She asked this question slowly, finally making eye contact with Rick as she spoke. Now he was the one to study the ice in his tea.

"Maybe somebody who was trying to protect a personal interest."

"What the hell are you implying?" she asked.

"For the last couple of days, I wasn't sure what to think. But we've found out some information earlier today that shed some light on the whole matter." He looked up at her. "I don't think you're involved with the murder, Monika."

She answered with a touch of sarcasm. "Well that's certainly good to know."

"I'll be honest with you," he continued. "Up until this afternoon, you were my prime suspect."

"How could you think I would be involved in something like that?" She seemed truly upset.

"Pretty easily, if you think about it. Once I found out that Shires was your father, it all kind of made sense. I never really thought he was capable of murder."

"And you thought I was!"

"For a while. But like I said, I don't believe you were involved now. I just wish you would have told me who you were."

"It's not like it was a huge secret or anything," she said. "It's just not something I really wanted to talk about, that's all. I didn't want any preferential treatment here, and I didn't think that would be possible if everyone knew who my dad was."

"Well, your dad's in deep shit right now. Even without the murder charge, he still may lose his job over the whole cadaver thing."

"So who do you think killed Harper?" she asked.

Rick stood to pace. "That's why I'm here tonight. I'm gonna need your help."

"My help? What could I do?"

"I found out this afternoon who killed Harper, but I can't prove it yet."

"I still don't see how that concerns me."

"It concerns you because if we can prove who really killed Harper, it clears your father. At least clears him of the murder."

She softened a little. "So what would I have to do?"

"We've got to get him to confess."

* * * *

After making the call, they sat together in the house, waiting for him to arrive. Rick told Monika everything, deciding now that she could be trusted. He was relieved that she wasn't really involved, but the man that did the crime was every bit as shocking. Monika was skeptical at first, but once she heard all the evidence, there was little doubt in her mind. Evidence that was very damaging, but perhaps not enough so to guarantee a conviction. They needed a confession to lock up the case. That was their mission tonight.

They rehearsed the confrontation several times, changing it significantly with each run through. Rick was nervous, and could tell that Monika was as well. They alternated pacing the floor, drinking tea, and running to the bathroom. Rick's palms were sweating profusely, something he hadn't experienced since the high school prom. His head was spinning and his stomach ached. His blood pressure was certainly through the roof.

It was getting dark outside, the last rays of sun peaking through the slats in the wooden shudders. On his twelfth trip to the window he saw the headlights. The car was three blocks away, but he knew it was him. The time was now.

"Here he comes," he said to Monika, motioning her to the window. She stood beside him and peered out the glass as the car pulled into the driveway and stopped. They watched as he put some things from the backseat into his bag and headed to the front porch. They backed away from the window to avoid being seen.

The door bell made them both jump, even though they knew it was coming. They answered the door together.

"Come on in," said Monika.

He pulled open the rusty screen door and stepped inside. "How is everybody tonight?" he asked.

"Great, Cameron. Glad you could come."

He walked inside and set his backpack down next to the piano by the front door. "I don't know about this study group crap," he said. "You know I'm not much into studying, especially when the test isn't for another two weeks." He noticed the half-empty glasses in their hands. "You got any of that tea left, Monika?"

"Sure, I'll go get you some." She disappeared into the kitchen.

"Have a seat," said Rick, motioning to the couch. He sat back down in the chair across from him.

"You checked in on Evan lately?" asked Cameron.

"Earlier today. He looked pretty good. Said he might get to go home in a day or two." He looked nervously over his shoulder, waiting for Monika to return so they could begin their interrogation. "I brought him his books and the reading assignments so he won't be too lost next week."

"Knowing Evan he'll be ahead of us all by Monday."

"You're probably right," replied Rick.

Monika finally returned, carrying Cameron's glass in one hand and a pitcher of tea in the other. "You ready for a refill, Rick?" she asked, handing Cameron his glass.

"Sure, I'll take some more." She filled it to the top, then picked up her own glass from the table and filled it as well. "Let me stick this back in the fridge and I'll be right back."

Cameron leaned over to Rick and smiled. "So what's the deal with you two, anyway?" he whispered.

"There's no deal. We just had a date, that's all. I'm not talking about it."

"Sounds like I might have hit a nerve there?"

Monika returned just as Rick was about to stand. He wasn't in the mood. She looked to Rick for guidance as she sat. They had talked about how they would approach this, but it was all together different with Cameron in the room.

"So what are you two so spooked about tonight?" asked Cameron. "Everyone's walking around on pins and needles."

Rick took the lead. "We need to talk about some things, Cameron."

"So talk," he replied, sipping casually on his tea.

Rick looked over at Monika for a little moral support. He was extremely nervous and ill-at-ease, and could feel the tension coursing throughout his body. She looked into his eyes, but did not speak. This was his interrogation.

"I'm not really sure where to start with this, so I'm gonna just jump right in." His voice cracked uncontrollably and he could feel a flush in his cheeks. "We know that you're involved in Lloyd Harper's death."

Rick paused and waited for a response. Cameron sat passively and stone-faced, almost as if he hadn't heard the accusation. After several seconds, he leaned forward, took another drink of tea, and spoke.

"So what's the joke?" he asked.

"There's no joke," replied Rick in eerie monotone. "We know you either killed him or had him killed, and then got Shires to take the fall."

Cameron looked from Rick to Monika and back again. "You two aren't serious?"

"I've never been more serious in my life," said Rick.

Cameron looked to Monika for help. "Are you buying this crap?"

She seemed frightened and looked as if she were afraid to talk. "I didn't believe it at first, but then I heard the evidence from Rick and I knew it had to be true."

Cameron laughed, apparently not taking any of this seriously. "So when do I get to hear all this damning evidence?"

"It started with something Evan saw Friday night when he broke into the funeral home," said Rick. "An entry that Harper had made on his desk calendar."

"Which said what?" asked Cameron.

"It mentioned a KKK meeting on August 5th, then out to the side said 'bring Cam'."

"You think Harper and I went to a KKK meeting last week?"

"Kind of looks that way, doesn't it?" replied Rick smartly.

"I don't know how it looks, but that's bullshit. I've never been to a KKK meeting in my life."

"So how do you explain the calendar?"

"How the hell should I know? I can't control what some crazy son of a bitch writes on his little date book. If that's what you're basing this whole thing on, then you've lost it, Stanley."

"There's more," he said.

"Like what?" Cameron was becoming exasperated.

"Like the glass," said Rick.

"What glass?"

"The glass that we used to lift the prints off the dead guy in the back of that hearse. The one's you gave to my father's deputy."

"I remember. What about it?"

"They matched to a middle aged black man who had been in a car wreck the day before. His body was taken to Harper's that afternoon."

"Yeah, so what?" His mood was changing from exasperation to anger.

"That was no middle-aged man we found in the hearse that night. He was thirty at best and looked like he had been beaten to death."

When Cameron didn't respond, Rick continued. "I still had that old piece of plastic, the one that we tried before we used the glass. I gave that to Mulholland earlier today and found a whole different set of prints on there. They belonged to a gentleman down in Corman County, Calloway Washington. It seems that Mr. Washington was running for state senate and mysteriously disappeared last week. Somehow his body found its way to Harper's, which means that the prints on the glass had to be switched." He stood and looked down at his friend. "And you were the last one to handle that glass."

There it was. Rick had dropped the bombshell. The evidence could not be disputed. There was no way that he could deny his involvement any longer.

"So that's it, huh," said Cameron. "You've got it all figured out, nice and neat." Now it was his turn to stand. "Are you ready to slap the cuffs on me now?" He held his hands out in front of him as he walked over to the front of the room and sat at the piano bench. Rick and Monika were watching his every move. "You two are really something, you know that?"

"I haven't heard you deny any of it," said Monika.

"Where's your police buddies, Stanley? They gonna bust out of the closet in a second and take me downtown?"

"I haven't told the police everything yet," he said. "I thought I'd give you a chance to talk first."

"So what now, is it time for my big confession?"

"If you'd like."

"I'm afraid I can't help you there, chief. I can't really confess to something I didn't have anything to do with?"

"You son of a bitch," said Rick.

"You're not the least bit interested in hearing what I've got to say, are you? You just want to wrap up your neat little case. Big Rick Stanley, mild-mannered medical student by day, double nought spy by night. Nails the bad guy, and still manages to get the girl." He motioned to Monika. "Well I hate to screw up your perfect little scenario, chief, but you've got the wrong man."

"You're gonna make this hard, aren't you?"

"If easy means I get the gas chamber, then you're damn right I'm gonna make this hard." He stood and looked out the front window. "Let me get this straight in my mind for just a second. You're willing to call me a murderer because Lloyd Harper writes 'bring Cam' in his little notebook, and some no-neck deputy from Bumfuck County says the prints don't match."

"Something like that," said Rick.

He paused as if thinking. "Let's take the little note first," he said. "Did you ever think that maybe he was reminding himself to bring his camera, or maybe his camcorder. Or even if it is a name, I don't think I'm the only person in town whose name starts with C-A-M."

"That's weak," said Rick, "but even so it still doesn't explain the prints."

"All right, let's look at the prints," he said. "You said that I was the last person to touch the glass that day, which is not entirely true, if you really think about it." Another pause. "I gave it over to the deputy, like you said, but I handed him the same glass and the same prints that you handed me that morning."

"There's not really any way to prove that, is there?" said Rick.

"No, I don't suppose there is. But I'm telling you, that's how it happened. I didn't switch that glass, and I certainly didn't attend some KKK meeting with that crazy bastard."

Rick was feeling very unsettled. Five minutes ago, he had the entire story neatly wrapped and ready to turn over to the police. All he lacked was the final chapter, which would have been complete tonight with Cameron's confession. But now he had thrown a wrench into the whole works. Could there be any truth to his story? He supposed the note could have meant something else. But what about the prints? Believing Cameron's story meant that someone in the Corman County sheriff's office, his dad's office, had switched the glass or lied about the prints. Rick didn't buy into most conspiracy theories, but if Cameron were telling the truth then something had to give further up the ladder. The pounding in Rick's head crescendoed.

"Kind of reached an impasse, haven't we?" said Rick, rubbing his temples.

"It seems that way," said Cameron.

"So what do we do now?"

"I'd like to think that you believe me, Rick. I'm a little taken aback that you would accuse me of such a crime."

Rick grimaced. "I want to believe you, Cameron, I really do. I'm just not sure I'm ready to quite yet."

"Have you told all this to the police?"

"A good bit of it. I've sort of been working with Mulholland on it."

"I guess that means I'm coming downtown for questioning in the near future."

"I don't know what he's gonna do. I don't know what I'm gonna do, for that matter." Rick's shoulders slumped. "I just wanted to find out what happened to Charlie."

Cameron stood in the middle of the room, his hands crossed over his chest. "So what do we do now?"

"*We* don't do anything," said Lt. Mulholland, as he walked through the front door. "I want you to go back to the dorm and wait to hear from us."

"Where the hell did you come from?" asked Cameron.

He pointed towards the door. "Right out there on the porch, weren't you watching?"

Cameron either missed or ignored Mulholland's attempt at humor. He looked inquisitively over at his classmates. "Rick?"

"We had to get some answers," he said without hesitation or apology. "We had to hear what you had to say for yourself."

He looked back at Mulholland. "So what's the verdict?"

"Jury's still out," he answered. "And while they are, I expect you to be extremely easy to locate over the next few days."

"Am I under arrest?"

"Do you see my handcuffs anywhere? Am I putting you in the back of my car?" Cameron didn't answer. "Now get the hell out of here and wait by the phone for my call."

Cameron gathered up his backpack and headed toward the door, remarkably calm considering how his evening had gone. He looked up at Rick, started to speak, then apparently changed his mind and walked out to his car. No one in the room spoke until they had all watched him drive away.

Rick was the first to break the silence. "So what do we do now?"

"Like I told your buddy, *we* don't do shit. You let the department worry about things from here."

Rick wasn't satisfied. "When are you gonna talk with that deputy?"

"We'll talk with him soon, and I'll let you know if anything develops."

"Come on, lieutenant, you can't shut me out now. We even helped with your little sting here tonight."

He softened a little. "Listen Rick, I know you want to help, but you've got to let us do our jobs. We'll take care of things from here, and I promise I'll let you know something when I can. I'd also appreciate it if you wouldn't speak with your father about any of this until we get things sorted out."

"Dammit, Mulholland, you can't tell me I can't speak with my own father."

He kept his patience. "Just give us a day or two to make some sense out of all this, that's all I'm asking. I know you don't want to jeopardize the investigation."

Rick suddenly picked up on the insinuation, and was shocked. "If you're thinking that my father may be involved in this in any way, then you're chasing a dead lead."

"Don't worry Rick, I wouldn't suspect your dad for a second. But we do have to look at the possibility that someone in his department may have a hand in this. I'm trying to believe your friend tonight. I thought you'd be pleased about that."

"I don't know what to believe anymore," he replied honestly. "I just want to be a medical student again."

"My sentiments exactly." Monika finally broke her silence.

"Well for now, that's all you two need to do. Let us handle this, and I'll let you know what develops."

Rick wanted to do more, but he knew Mulholland was right. He had lost his objectivity anyway, and was no longer able to think clearly about anything involving this case. In his mind, the list of suspects had included his girlfriend, one of his best friends, and now maybe somebody in his father's office. He realized it was best to sit back and let the police finish out their investigation.

Rick hung around for a few minutes after Mulholland left. He and Monika discussed the case briefly, but came up with no new revelations. Neither felt like studying, or anything else for that matter, and Rick made a quick exit. He took a roundabout way home, and the two minute drive took about thirty. He desperately wanted to talk with his father, but finally decided to wait as Mulholland had asked. It wasn't easy.

There was nothing left to do but follow the lieutenant's advice and become a med student again. He spent about an hour halfheartedly thumbing through tomorrow's assignments, then changed out of his clothes and crawled into bed. He was emotionally exhausted, and fell into a fitful sleep in minutes.

CHAPTER 23

By noon the next day, most of Rick's questions had been answered. He had made it to the first two lectures of the morning, although got little out of them. Neither Cameron nor Monika were anywhere to be seen. Evan was to be released from the hospital later in the day, but Rick halfway expected to see him this morning in his usual seat. He had just set his books down when the phone rang.

"Hello."

"Rick? It's Roger Mulholland."

Rick tensed at the sound of his voice. "Yes sir, good morning."

"I thought you might like to hear who killed Mr. Harper." Always straight to the point.

"I'm almost afraid to ask," he said truthfully.

"Relax, it's probably nobody you know. And your father's not involved."

"Was that ever in doubt?"

"Not in my mind," said Roger.

"Can you tell me what happened?"

"I probably shouldn't, but I'm sure you're gonna hear it from your daddy anyway. Besides, you've kinda earned the right to know." He paused, then continued when Rick didn't respond. "There's a fella by the name of Jimmy Wilkins, lives down in your daddy's county. Real piece of work. Heads up the KKK in that region."

"I think I've met him once or twice when I used to live down there. He's the one who killed Harper?"

"That's how it's starting to play out," he replied. "It looks like your buddy's story last night has some truth to it."

"You mean about the deputy?"

"We picked him up early this morning and took him in for questioning. J.P. Tanner. Real cocky son of a bitch. He's not some hometown buddy of yours or nothing, is he?"

"I know him a little bit, but I haven't talked with him in years. We actually did go to school together. I think he was a year or two ahead of me."

"Well he came in with a pretty good attitude first off, but changed his tune when we started talkin' about electric chairs and things like that." Rick could see him smiling through the phone.

"I don't get what these two had to do with Lloyd Harper," said Rick.

"Neither did I at first, but then Mr. Tanner helped educate us. Cameron was right about the glass with the prints. Tanner ran the glass he was given, and when Calloway Washington's name printed out, he knew something was up. He didn't actually admit to it, but I bet he was involved in whatever lynch mob kidnapped and killed that man. Anyway, he says he called Jimmy Wilkins, who then called him back with the name that he gave to you."

"So why did Harper have the body at his place?" asked Rick.

"Apparently they had quite a little system worked out. Whenever the KKK needed somebody to disappear, they would get the body to Harper who would take care of it for them."

"And he'd just bury it somewhere?"

"Probably so. Either doubled them up with another, or switched them out."

"So what about Charlie?" asked Rick. "How did he get caught up in all of this?"

"We've still got to talk with Shires again, but I think he was buying bodies from Harper to keep the anatomy lab full. I doubt he had anything to do with the KKK or any of these murders."

"Has he confessed to anything yet?"

"Not yet, but I bet he and his lawyer will jump at the chance to confess to buying a body if it means getting out of a murder accusation."

Rick couldn't help but laugh at the whole situation. It was almost a giddy feeling, one of relief brought on by closure. Everything now made sense.

"So what happens to everyone?" asked Rick.

"Hard to say just yet. Shires is still in some trouble for buying bodies, but at least it's not murder. Wilkins is going down for at least two murders, and probably more. I don't know about Deputy Tanner yet, but he's in pretty deep as well. He swears that no one else in the office had any involvement."

Rick knew he was referring to his father, but left the comment alone. "What about Cameron and Monika?"

"Neither of them really did anything wrong, so I guess they're sentenced to four years of hard labor in medical school. And you'll be smashing up big rocks right alongside them."

Rick thought about the illegal investigating that he and Cameron and Evan had done throughout the past week. He wanted to ask where they stood on that, but decided it best not to remind him. "I can hardly wait," said Rick. "I don't know what to say, Lt. Mulholland. I sure appreciate everything you've done."

"Don't thank me. You're the one who did most of the work. Even if your conclusions were a little off," he laughed.

"I'm just glad they were."

"I am too, son. I've talked with your father already this morning. I told him you'd probably be calling him soon, which is fine with me, by the way."

"I plan to do just that," he said. "Right after I find Cameron."

"Good luck with that," said Mulholland. "I haven't talked to him since last night. Thought I'd let you break the good news."

"Thanks again, sir." Rick hung up the phone and took his first deep breath in almost a week.

*   *   *   *

TWO WEEKS LATER

Rick thought he had arrived early, but nearly half the class was already seated. The room was remarkably quiet as each of the obsessive-compulsives went through their own private pre-test rituals. He scanned the room and was surprised to find Cameron already in a seat and ready to go. He had a cup of coffee in one hand, and several number two pencils in the other. He looked like a real student.

"Mind if I join you?" asked Rick.

"Sure, have a seat." He was tapping the pencils nervously.

"You ready for this thing?" asked Rick.

"Ready to blow the top off the curve. You?"

"I suppose. I don't think I could study for it another minute, I'll tell you that."

"Ditto. I am glad we all got together last night to go over everything one last time," said Cameron. "I feel like it really helped."

Rick looked around at the other tables. "You seen Evan or Monika yet?"

"Haven't seen 'em. I figured Evan would have camped out last night to get the perfect seat."

"You think we ought to give him a quick call?" asked Rick.

Cameron looked up at the clock. "It's only ten till. Let's give 'em a few more minutes. I'm sure they'll show."

Rick abruptly changed the subject. "Mulholland called me last night."

"Any news?"

"Jimmy Wilkins confessed."

"You're kidding," said Cameron. "I figured he'd have half a dozen high profile Klan lawyers working to get him off."

"Apparently they dropped the capital murder charges in exchange for the plea. I guess he decided to save his skin."

Cameron smiled. "He's gonna have lots of fun new boyfriends when he gets to the state pen."

"Couldn't happen to a nicer guy."

"So you wanna get a beer tonight after we finish our little quiz?"

"Actually I've kind of got plans already."

"Monika?"

"Yes, and shut up about it," said Rick. "We're gonna give this thing another try. Hopefully get off to a little better start this time."

"I think it's great. I always thought you two looked pretty good together. You think she'll be happy with you since I turned her down?" he said smiling.

"You're so full of shit, Cameron."

"That's why you love me so."

Evan suddenly appeared with a backpack full of books. He looked half dead, and had no doubt been up most of the night cramming. He was probably the one person in the class who didn't need to.

"Hey guys. Did I miss anything?"

"You think you got enough books there, Sanders?" said Cameron. "What'd you bring all those up here for anyway?"

He set the heavy load down on the table with a loud thump. "I don't know, habit I guess."

Monika walked up as Evan was settling in to his seat.

"Y'all better have saved me a place," she said.

"Right there next to your boyfriend," said Cameron.

Rick shot him a look, which was largely ignored. Monika pretended not to hear. She quickly took a seat, then looked up as her father stepped to the microphone.

"Ladies and gentlemen, let's all quickly find our places so we can begin. I trust everyone is well prepared for the first exam of your medical career. We will begin passing out the tests now. Please leave them face down in front of you until I give the word to proceed."

The four friends looked up at each other and smiled.

Printed in the United States
3304

9 781893 162211